Presented to
Clare

on June 25th, 2000
our
40th Wedding Anniversary
from your fellow
reader Love Mary
For you to enjoy before
Sunday July 9th when
we speak at Celebration
Writing

SUMMER
GONE

David Macfarlane

SUMMER
GONE

a novel

ALFRED A. KNOPF CANADA

PUBLISHED BY ALFRED A. KNOPF CANADA

Copyright © 1999 by David Macfarlane

All rights reserved under International and Pan-American
Copyright Conventions. Published in Canada by Alfred A. Knopf
Canada, a division of Random House of Canada Ltd., Toronto,
and simultaneously in the United States by Crown Publishing
Group, a division of Random House Inc., New York, in 1999.
Distributed by Random House of Canada Limited, Toronto.

Canadian Cataloguing in Publication Data

Macfarlane, David, 1952–
Summer gone

ISBN 0-676-97190-3

I. Title.
PS8575.F294S96 1999   C813'.54   C98-932414-1
PR9199.3.M333S96   1999

Printed and bound in the United States of America

For Sandra Gwyn

*This is ecstasy, and behind the ecstasy is something else,
which is hard to explain. It is like a momentary vacuum
into which rushes all that I love.*

— VLADIMIR NABOKOV, *Speak, Memory*

SUMMER
GONE

THE PULL

Pull the blade directly back with the lower hand,
while the upper, curled over the paddle's butt, punches
forward on a plane level with your nose. Then, with
a roll of the wrists, pry the blade outward through the
water, away from the canoe's hull, against your forward
propulsion. The median of these opposing forces will
become your chosen course. With practice, the two
components of your stroke will become a single motion.

fig. 1

– The Outdoorsman's Guide

H E TURNED from the window in his office when I knocked softly at the open door. "Well, well," he said. He told me he'd been surprised I'd found him. I said it hadn't been so difficult.

It was a bad day, in a bad summer. The smoke from the grass and brush fires to the north had drifted down over the city. Beyond the glass, the reaches of highway concrete and industrial parks were the colour of the brittle leaves that clung to the citybound trees. Even the traffic had lost its shine in the August heat. On my way through the parking lot, the wind had been a dusty rattle. Now I was glad for the rush of the air-conditioning in the building. It smoothed itself up the wall of glass and then fell over us where we stood in his neat, spartan office.

I had wondered if we would embrace. But we shook hands. It was all more ordinary than I had expected: the single blueprint on his desk; his pale, veinless hands; the slight turning of his belt; the faint pleasantry of his deodorant. "So," he said, "what do you want to know?"

"Everything," I said, and smiled.

He smiled back. "You know, I didn't really know him very well. In a way."

"It was a while ago."

"It was. But I could tell you about when we dumped. You don't forget something like that. He thought it was a miracle, of sorts. That's what he told me. So I suppose I could tell you about that. About the canoe trip and about his summers. I think I know something about his summers. But they run together in my head. They overlap. Because we stayed up and talked just the once. He told me about them that night."

"Summers will do." I smiled again.

"It was almost the only conversation we had. At least, as I recall. We stayed up late. But over the years I've thought about that night so many times I'm no longer sure what he really told me and what I've added myself. We change things so gradually. And now I suppose I don't really know where he ends and I begin. But maybe that's the way it always is, with fathers."

"I wouldn't know."

He motioned me toward a chair. He looked out the window, over the outskirts of the city. "You know," he said, "he went out in the canoe by himself that night. Quite late. We'd been talking. Or, rather, he had been. I was watching him from the shore, and I remember him calling back to me from the water. He wanted so much to teach me about canoes. He said it was important to leave me something. Not that he was exactly an expert. I remember him wobbling a bit out there, in the dark, and saying 'There's an odd moment when you're just starting to paddle, when it doesn't feel like you're going to go anywhere. The canoe seems stuck between the back and forth of your stroke.'"

Caz turned from the window, and looked at me. "So, I could tell you about that. About that night. Or, I could tell you about how we dumped the canoe earlier that same day. That was something. I mean, there are all kinds of things. It's hard to know where to begin. Look, I could even tell you about the summer he went to camp."

"That would be fine," I said.

Caz sat down. I watched him carefully, trying to see whatever I could as he spoke. He had a lean face, with the soft beginnings of a double-chin. He had thinning straw-coloured hair. He wore a white short-sleeved shirt and no tie. He said that he could remember Bay saying that at the camp the boys always waited on the dock for their canoe lesson after dinner. I can see them, I think. I believe I can. I can say: the boys stood on the dock, as if I know for certain that they did. I can say that, thirty-six summers after that, Bay Newling leaned waist-deep into the push of the water, as if I had been there. But everything has changed, and these words seem to come from very long ago. We all run together. We all overlap. And now, I can't be sure what are the memories and inventions of a father, or of a son, and what, of all this, is what I have heard, or misunderstood, or simply made up in order to add something of myself to stories that were, for the longest time, not mine to tell.

fig. 2

ONE

T HE BOYS stood on the dock. It reached about twenty feet from a lip of sand and grass into a pond at the back of the camp island. It was calm here. The rise of surrounding rock, the boughs of pine protected the glass-green water. This was where canoeing lessons were given. Evenings were best. This was the summer of 1964.

They had come down after dinner. They trailed over the red-brown path, around outcrops of granite and the sheltered clusters of wooden cabins, through the maze of juniper, and over the spine of the northern island to the little bay. Alone, well behind them, their counsellor followed.

Most of them would not remember this. They would forget names and faces and voices. Things would go.

But this was also true: every now and then, in one city or another, in high-rises, or townhouses, in unsatisfactory rented rooms, in expensive hotels, in deep suburban silences, alone, or with their unconsoling wives or lovers turning away from their empty arms, they would each dream of the path across the island.

They would know every rock and root and turn and drop. They would feel the weightless air, see the particular skein of a summer evening, smell the pine-needled turf of their racing footfall.

They always made a hollow sound as they ran, as if passing over a roof of rock and shallow loam. Racing up, around, and over, along to here, then across, just so, past and down, and through the grass to the sneaker-rattled wooden dock on the shore of the calm little bay. The dreams would be as vivid as light. In their sleep, they would know the path as well as they knew anything—an unaccountably familiar way through their own bewildering darknesses. In the morning, it would be gone.

———————

Bay Newling leaned waist-deep into the push of the water. He was turning. He was turning wildly, and turning. He was losing his footing and splashing upright again. He was saying something, over and over.

He was a heavy man, of forty-eight years. He had thick grey hair and a broad red face. His polo shirt clung to his expansive stomach and chest. He held his paddle above his shoulder. He held it a little ridiculously. Like a torch. Like a blade.

The summer sun dazzled the surface of the river's mouth. It hit the tumbling blue current with a blizzard of light.

He'd grabbed the paddle just before the rush of water took it away. Somehow his deck shoes were still on his sockless feet. He stood. He couldn't see a thing, it was so bright.

So bright. And what had happened was this. There had been just the two of them: father and son. The canoe had gone over. They had dumped, and he was the only one who came up.

———————

Hey, come on.

Hey, wait up.

The boys had brought their paddles, as their counsellor had asked. They had also brought, in their pockets, in the moist secrets of their warm palms, the useless and distracting things that boys always bring: jackknives, sweetly foiled wafers of gum, impossible tangles of fishing line, perfect skipping stones, deadly whittled sticks, crayfish claws, serenely swiped sugar cubes. They stood on the wooden dock, listening to what he was teaching.

Their counsellor was a boy of eighteen with a thick fall of dark hair and a long, bony face. His name was Peter Larkin. The boys were listening to him. Sometimes, because they felt it was important to have a counsellor with a nickname, they called him Lark. But the name didn't really stick. It came and went, like his changeable moods. He was kneeling in a canoe a few feet away from the little wooden dock.

All afternoon he had been mostly silent. At dinner, at the head of the table, he had ladled out stew without comment. He had offered no smile to the pretty waitress who leaned with upswept hair, with sun-browned throat, with freckled face over the table beside him, putting down the yellow Melmac serving bowl of stew.

This happened sometimes. The boys had come to know this. Something settled over him. The waitresses called him moody. It had an appeal.

In the canoe, his feet were bare. He was wearing baggy old shorts. He was paddling on the left side. He had no folded towel, no spread life jacket between his knees and the syrup-coloured cedar ribs.

He grinned up at the boys. "I've just thought of something," he said.

They felt the sudden change. They had seen this before, too. Something passed through him, and the silences ended abruptly. It was like sunlight advancing through woods after the rain.

Peter Larkin sometimes looked handsome, sometimes homely. Sometimes he looked lit from within. Sometimes he looked almost asleep. His lean, horse-like features shifted suddenly, without warning. His voice sometimes dropped. His eyes sometimes went flat and dark.

And then, without warning, his enthusiasm—for the sky, for the summer, for the pretty waitress with upswept hair and freckles, for a new way to teach boys about canoes— would return.

He laughed at secret things. He sang songs that no one else knew. He told ghost stories at campfires and played his guitar. He did little jigs while the campers waited out- side the dining hall for the screen doors to be opened, as if he were unable to contain his bursting energy. Whoop- ing, crouching, he sometimes outran his group across the island.

In these moods, his happiness took over things. He could catch boys up in its excitement.

"Look," he said. "Maybe you can picture it this way." He swung farther away from the dock, pointing his canoe into the little bay.

———————

Bay tried to squint the light away. He tried to blink past it, to see.

Then he realized he could hold the paddle up, using its shadow like the beam of a flashlight over the surface of the water. This all took an instant. He was aware of no sequence to things. He thought he saw.

There.

Like a foot. Like a hand.

No. Only a pale rock.

He turned.

There.

Like a leg. Like an arm.

Only a water-worn log, caught between two stones.

He was turning wildly, and turning. He was saying something. He did not hear himself. He was calling for help. He was calling a name, over and over.

Bay slipped, splashed. He stood again. He turned back, upstream. He lifted the paddle. He held it there, searching the water beneath it. His heart was racing. The rush of his panic, already beyond any fear he had known before, was still rising.

The current pushed against him. He turned, and then— so he told Caz that night—he knew. He turned again. He said: Don't ask me how. He just knew. A miracle, he told his son. Of sorts: the descent of certainty. And after that calm, inexplicable moment—like the sea parting, he said; like the dead rising—he began to make his way upstream. He had to go, he knew, about twenty feet, exactly to a spot where the current formed a tumbled vee not far from the shore. He knew absolutely where—so he told Caz later that night. Don't ask how. He just knew. He had no doubt. It was, he said, very odd.

The force of the water felt like tightly wrapped silk. It clung to his legs. As he picked his deliberate way over the rocks, the water wrapped round his waist and trailed behind him, toward the river's mouth, into the widening blue train of summer.

Peter Larkin pointed his canoe away from the dock. He spoke back, over his left shoulder. "Hey guys," he said. "You could think of it like the present. It's here, and then it's gone. Here, gone. Here, gone. Am I right, Bay?"

The boy looked up from the smooth black stone he held in his hand. He was quiet and pale and soft. He was aware that the counsellor was always trying to include him in things. He stood slightly apart from the group. This was his first year at the camp.

He said, "What?"

Peter Larkin said, "Time goes from the past. To the future. Past, future. Past, future." He waited for the boy's reply. "Well, doesn't it?"

"I guess," the boy said. He had no idea what the counsellor was talking about. He often didn't. Starboard, port. Windward, lee. West is best, east the beast. All these were new to him.

All the other boys in his group had been to camp before; he feared they knew everything; he feared they would laugh. They sometimes laughed. His name was Bailey Newling, because his mother's family name was Bailey, and she had said that was what she wanted her son to be called. His father went along. But he called him Bay, because it was more ordinary. More like Jack, or Tom, or Bob, or Jim. The boys at the camp called him Baby.

They would know what the counsellor was talking about. Like moss on one side of the white pines, not on the other. Like red sun at night, and red sun in morning. Like the card games, and the dirty jokes, and the snake going around the tree before it goes down the hole.

The other boys nudged and elbowed and laughed on the dock. They had no idea what Larkin was talking about either.

"So the question is . . . how do we hold onto what's in between? How do we make them overlap? Because if we don't hold onto it somehow, everything's over as soon as it begins."

On the dock, one hand passed half a stick of gum to another.

Lark paddled hard, away from the dock. The canoe surged forward. "If you only use a forward stroke, if you just pull through the water, you can go fast, but you'll end up suddenly way over here." The canoe veered off sharply to the right. "As if you've shot way, way off into some strange place in the future. Like Tom Swift."

A boy fingered a jackknife.

Lark pulled his paddle back hard through the water. The bow of the canoe swung back around until it pointed directly out to the mouth of the little bay. "But if you only back-paddle," Lark said, "if you only use the pry of the stroke, you get stuck back here, back in the past, and you can't get anywhere." The canoe turned around, facing the wooden dock.

A boy poked a finger through a brittle crayfish claw in his pocket. It gave a little snap.

"So that's the question." Lark paddled toward them. "How do you hold onto the line in the middle? How do you find a balance so you don't go crazy?"

He came toward them. He said, "I'll show you."

The canoe was poised on an unwavering angle, its low gunwale only a couple of inches above the water, the high side giving the impression, somehow, of a rakishly worn hat. His stroke, combining the thrust of the pull with the correction of the pry, was a single graceful motion. The canoe held its course.

A boy scrunched a fistful of snarled fishing line.

A boy tumbled pocket-fuzzed sugar cubes in his shorts like dice.

Two boys coughed. Politely, they covered their mouths.

A boy stifled a fart and smiled shyly.

"See?" Lark said. He stopped paddling. The canoe glided toward the dock.

His laughter spread over the calm water. It echoed briefly on the surrounding rock. It sounded beyond itself for an instant. It disappeared into the sad dimming of the evening.

TWO

H E DIDN'T start to talk about the deaths until after they had stopped laughing. And that took a while. It was one word that did it.

Bay had said, "There's something I should . . . There's something I should tell you about. . . ." He had not intended his pause to be portentous, but it had seemed that way to Caz.

The boy was already apprehensive about what he took to be a gathering solemnity to the evening. He could feel something coming. He had felt it closing in on the flickering little circle of the stone ledges of their campfire, their unwashed frying pan and Melmac dinner plates, their blackened pot of leftover pasta, their opened food pack, and the bristling twigs and snapped branches of their scrappy little woodpile. The boy, like most boys, did not much like the idea of confessions, especially when they came from his father.

They were sitting on rocks in front of the fire, on the third night of their canoe trip. They were on the north shore of the Waubano Reaches, at the mouth of the Skin River, on a stretch of mainland just beyond Moriah Island. The stars were emerging as the glow of late-summer dusk faded above the blackness of pine trees; the moon had not yet risen. The wind had dropped. The column of faint grey smoke

wreathed straight upward into the dark, and everything—
their clothes, their hair, their hands—smelled of three days
of burning branches of oak and pine.

There were still loons then. There were crickets in the
grass at the edge of the woods. Bay took a final drag on his
third cigarette since dinner—the unsurprising menu: a pan-
ful of onion, garlic, and tomato sauce, slopped abundantly
over enough buckwheat noodles to feed a family of four—
and flicked the butt into the coals.

"There's something I should tell you . . ." Bay took a sip
of his cognac from a pale yellow plastic teacup. He grimaced
a little. His wide, round face looked flushed in the light of
the flames. He passed a hand through his thick, dishevelled
grey hair. Caz waited.

". . . about canoes," Bay said.

Whatever the embarrassing words Caz had imagined
might conclude his father's pendant sentence, "canoes" was
not among them. And it may have been simply the surprise,
or the relief of surprise, that started him off. What do twelve-
year-old boys fear their fathers are going to feel obligated
to say to them on auspicious occasions? There's something
I should tell you . . . about life. About death. About sex.
About God. About your mother. About myself.

"Canoes" seemed like the punchline of a joke to Caz,
under the circumstances—circumstances that Bay, in miraculously dry khaki pants and checked flannel shirt, was obvi-
ously not considering.

Bay's thoughts, pulling and prying their way through the
choppy waves of his own time, were far removed. Throughout the meal he had been marshalling a collection of notions
and memories that he had not quite marshalled before. He
had begun to see a direction emerging from within them,

and he felt that tonight, as this course took a single, pronounceable shape, it would be important to pass the story on to his son. He had not passed on much to his son.

He had almost said "my summer stuff." He had almost said to slender, lank-haired Caz, whose left foot was bare to the late summer's surviving mosquitoes, and whose right foot was wrapped with a bulge of gauze and adhesive and tensor; he had almost said to Caz, whose face seemed longer and more angular than it had even a few months before, and whose underarms, Bay had noticed during their two nights in the tent, had a sour smell that a child's body never has; he had almost said to Caz, his son whom he loved: There's something I should tell you about my summer stuff—about camp; about a cottage; about the divorce, about homesickness and a Beatles song and my own parents; about summer itself, and about what I recall of being poised, like you are now, between the past of childhood and the future of whatever it is that comes next.

But that was where Bay had paused—had shifted his bulky beige haunches on the rock, had sucked down the last drag of his Marlboro Light and had sipped some of the Rémy Martin he had wisely packed for the canoe trip, and had given things a second thought. He was inclined to second thoughts. He was a corrector. He was, by profession, an editor—*the* editor, actually, of a once highly regarded, now reasonably successful but, in Bay's opinion, generally awful national magazine called *The Weekender*—and he, better than most people, knew the dangers of a cryptic introduction. What sense would anyone make of "summer stuff"? He wasn't entirely sure what sense he made of it himself. And so, remembering what he had been taught one summer long ago by a teenaged counsellor named Peter Larkin—

about how a canoe's chosen course was, like a rest in music, a balanced stillness; about how a canvas-and-cedar hull's single direction was poised between the two countervailing forces of a paddler's stroke—he had settled on an image very much at hand. "There's something," said Bay Newling to his son, "that I should tell you about canoes." Caz's eyes widened. His head gave a little jerk of astonishment. And then, after a stifled moment of attempted respect, his cheeks bulging, like someone trying to hold his breath, his son laughed out loud.

Burst with it, as a matter of fact—for the laughter started at full volume. It was unbridled and irretrievable from the start.

For a moment or two, Bay was hurt. He was about to broach something serious and complicated and heartfelt. This was, so it seemed to him, the time and the place to do so. After all, the canoe had gone over in the river mouth that afternoon. It had been a close call.

He looked with some surprise to where his son was sitting—rocking, actually, back and forth on a flat stone, his arms clutched round the middle of his dark-blue hooded sweatshirt, his narrow shoulders quaking, his eyes squeezed shut. Caz was already almost helpless. "A little late for that, Dad," he just managed to say. And Bay's inquisitive, but forced smile began to loosen and then to crumble as he watched his son laugh. He gave a parental chuckle, but that fell apart pretty quickly, too. The day came back to him—the bright, sun-dazzled current; the rocks underfoot; the fear in his chest; the terrible curtain of pine—and a kind of giddy relief welled up in his throat. Soon enough the laughter swamped them completely.

It was some time—the happiest they ever shared—before it let them go. Then, finally, after the few last coughs and gasps and sputters, when their silence, stretching on into the crickets and into the occasional crackle of sparks, seemed to be solid, Bay started talking about the deaths. And Caz giggled. And Bay paused—there was a cry of a loon; there was a splash of a small fish jumping—and then, after a minute or two, he started again.

He knew that his son knew the outline of the history, but not its details, and certainly not what Bay made of them. On one hand, it seemed strange to Bay, but they had never really talked about all this. On the other, he decided, it wasn't so very strange: his son had only recently been a small child. And Caz, wiping away tears with the back of his hand, took a few deep, calming breaths, let his wide grin relax to a contemplative smile and then to polite attention, and settled in to listen.

Bay reached to his breast pocket for his crumpled pack of Marlboro Lights and his matches, and lit a cigarette, and pushed his hair away from his forehead, and tossed the match into the fire, and, half expecting to be interrupted again by laughter, ventured to say that what he had been trying to get at, or at least part of it anyway, was that the sudden and simultaneous deaths of both his parents occurred two years after he and Sarah were married. After they bought a modest house in downtown Toronto. After Caz was born. Bay had just been appointed editor of *The Weekender* ("Canada's informed monthly commentary on politics and the arts" was its commercially doomed self-description in those days), and Bay, who was thirty-five, had just stepped out of the shower when the phone rang.

He padded down the bare-wood hall. He was pale, soft, large. He stood towel-wrapped, dripping, in the bedroom of their three-storey, charming, steps-from-subway, Victorian handyman special—the house, now tastefully refurbished

by an army of handymen, none of whom had been irre-
deemably unhandy Bay—that Sarah had continued to live in
after the divorce. The same house, now without a mortgage,
and now with a tiny but beautiful garden that Sarah tended
constantly, and now, so Bay had noticed on his regular visits
to pick up Caz, with a toilet seat that would not stay up during a pee—that Sarah and Caz lived in still.

But at that time Sarah and Bay were in the middle of
the interminable archeology of stripping the bedroom wallpaper. Such youthful domestic enthusiasms. Such peaceably
modest ambitions: a house, a child, a bedroom that would
someday no longer have layers of grim florals on its un-
square, uninsulated walls.

Bay had managed to get down the hall without tripping,
stepped over the paper-steamer and the scrapers, and eyed
the torturously slow progress they had made on the wallpaper as he snaked his hand over and through the maze of
water glass, Kleenex box, baby's bottle, gripe water, child-care
manuals, nasal suction tube, and clock radio that guarded the
telephone on the bedside table on Sarah's side.

Sarah, who was usually up early, with dark circles under
her eyes but with her cropped blond hair as tousled and
youthful as a teenager's; with her comfortable sweatshirts
and her trim, efficient-looking blue jeans and her plain loops
of earrings that the baby loved to tug; with her attractive,
if slightly comic, intentionally ironic horn-rimmed glasses
pushed up on her head away from Caz's smudgy little fingers; Sarah, who had not yet returned full-time to her job
in production at Children's Press, and who maintained, cheer-
fully, when the baby started to cry, again, that she loved
the city best in the brief, gritty freshness of its summer early
mornings, Sarah had taken Caz in the stroller to get some

groceries before the day became too hot. Bay, who had been up late extricating flashbacks from within the flashbacks of a convoluted cover story that he would happily have killed had he anything to use in its place for the September issue, had slept in. He was almost an hour behind his usual schedule for showering and dressing and fuelling himself with caffeine before heading in to the *Weekender* office. It was only by chance that anyone was at home.

Constable Warburton of the highways detachment of the Ontario Provincial Police spoke as if he were delivering a traffic summons. He tonelessly pronounced the names. Bay could actually hear the flipped pages of a notebook over the telephone.

"Margaret and Alexander Nelling."

"That's Marjorie. Marjorie and Alexander Newling."

"That's correct, sir." Variance of sound was, apparently, as lost on Constable Warburton's ears as it was on his tongue. "That is the information we have at this time."

It had been strange, but from the first ring of the telephone, from the moment Bay was out the bathroom door, the slice of time—the passage down the hallway; the close, rumpled, unpopulated bedroom; his not quite secure towel, his bare white feet—had the whack of authenticity to it, the wallop of reality. It may have been simply that it was an unusual time for anyone to call, but the house—all the unfinished emptiness of it; all the paint-smelling, tool-scattered potential of it; all the promising little zones of loving, organized comfort of it; all the enclosing debt of it—seemed to echo very loudly with the ringing telephone that morning. The noise had startled him. His thoughts, in an unusual moment of clairvoyance, had leapt from the bathroom, from the hallway, from the bedroom doorway he was approaching, to his parents. He knew they were driving, that morning, up north—to Guaranty Life's annual retreat at Timberside Lodge. This was a series of meetings, and strategy sessions, and dinner-dances, and bridge games, and "outings for the wives" that the Newlings had attended every June for as long as Bay could remember. No children were ever allowed—which meant that Timberside had always loomed in Bay's imagination. When he was very young, he had often pestered his mother to describe the lake, and the old rowboats, and the wooded lanes, and the cocktail cruises, and the swimming raft, and the white-painted boulders that lined the pathways, and the antlers above the great stone mantel, and the raftered dining room that smelled always of saltine crackers and cream of celery soup. Bay's father was now well past retirement age, but his parents went to Timberside every June, because his father was still working. He continued on six-month contracts because—so he explained with a perfectly indecipherable balance of bitter weariness and bureaucratic pride—now, after all these years, Personnel had discovered that he was irreplaceable.

"They've been what?" Bay had asked, dripping, still unbelieving, into the receiver.

P.C. Warburton said it again, slowly, as if it were a difficult word: "Identified."

The funeral was held in Cathcart, Ontario. Cathcart had once been a town—almost, in fact, a city—a fair ways from Toronto. "A fair ways" being a typical, now-forgotten Cathcart idiom.

Cathcart was where Bay grew up. Cathcart was where Bay's father, Sandy Newling, had worked as an actuary in the grand stone office of Guaranty Life Assurance. Cathcart was where Bay's mother, Marj Newling, usually wished she wasn't—wished for all her married life, and, after the death of her second child, a newborn daughter, wished mostly from inside the drifting daytime dreams of a low-ceilinged, flounce-curtained bedroom of a bungalow in a postwar subdivision called New Cathcart.

In those days, in that new suburb, in the early 1950s, in the bustling town of Cathcart, Ontario, people were just starting out: with young families, with tentative friendships, with new plastic highball glasses and cheap patio furniture. The women were pregnant, mostly. The men were establishing practices or taking their first steps up the corporate ladder. People were cheerful about their modest possessions. They expected to be moving quickly on.

Marj had been born and raised in Toronto, and had always expected that someday her husband would be promoted to Guaranty Life's even grander, even stonier Toronto head office, and that then the Newlings would move triumphantly to the centre of the universe, taking their rightful place in her fabled city of streetcars and lakeshore parks, and newspapers with such a thing as a social page, and decent coffee shops, and restaurants where ice-cream came in pewter bowls with long spoons and arrowroot ladyfingers, and shops where salesgirls actually knew something for a change about dresses or shoes or lambswool coats. But the years had passed, and Sandy's promotions were unspectacular. Somehow things didn't change. He remained stubbornly dark, and handsome, and slight. He stayed in the same little office at Guaranty Life. He was always overly conservative about money, and so they stayed in the same little house on Ardell Crescent in New Cathcart. Marj stayed in bed and dreamed.

The Newlings only visited Marj's flat, grey home town now and then—to see the Simpson's Christmas windows, to obtain some appliance unobtainable in Cathcart, to visit Marj's fading, ageing, peppermint-wafer-smelling, antimacassared and armchaired relatives—and when Bay was growing up, Toronto was an hour's drive from downtown Cathcart, mostly through countryside. His father drove with his pipe jutting from his mouth; his mother sat, motionless, beside him, as if held in place by the same spray that held the waves of her hair. From the window of a 1952 Buick, Bay learned to say "cow" as they passed a field which, by the time he was twenty-five, had become acres of pipes and tanks and the blazing chimneys of a high-fenced, brightly lit petroleum refinery. By the time he was thirty, there wasn't a cow between Cathcart and Toronto.

By the time he was thirty-five, sitting beside his wife at his parents' funeral, Cathcart was a withering municipality few commuters even recognized as they passed through unchanging tracts of suburb and industrial park and shopping mall on their way to and from their work. The name might still ring a bell with some. Cathcart was an old-fashioned terminal on a bus route seldom taken anymore unless a car was in the garage or somebody missed the express. Cathcart was a grandly cavernous and usually empty station for a train that now ran only twice a day. It was, for most people, two exits and about a six-minute stretch of six lanes of highway. They never suspected the existence of the clock at the corner of Main and King, a city hall, the churches, the Cubs' apple day, the Brownies' cookie drive, the breaded veal cutlets and mashed potatoes at the Estaminet restaurant, the shaded ravines, the alleys (which, in Cathcart, were always called alleyways), the honour rolls in the polished hallways of the red brick schools, the air pumps of the bell-ringing gas stations. They never guessed at Sally's Smoke and Gift on Locket

Street, or the Keystone Grill, or the venerable green drinking fountains on the sidewalks, or the dusty red maples, or the summer thunderstorms, or the asphalt playgrounds, or the fountain in King William Park, or the green-tiled public washrooms, or the tomb-like stone solemnity of the Guaranty Life offices. They whisked by—going to Toronto, coming from Toronto—and probably never thought that once, not so long ago, the mileage they were passing through had been a place.

The funeral was at Greystone United, the church that Marj and Sandy had faithfully—or as Bay sometimes felt, desperately—attended. He had gone to Greystone himself, as a boy. He hadn't much choice. His father insisted. When, the weekend after the funeral, Bay and Sarah had sorted through his parents' things, he found his own multi-barred, perfect-Sunday-school-attendance lapel pin in his father's drawer—which, after a moment or two of sad contemplation, he dropped into the green garbage bag at his feet.

The funeral reception had been in the memorial room, across the hall that ran behind the choir stalls of the Greystone sanctuary, and as Bay and Sarah stood there, greeting his parents' friends, and colleagues, and fellow church members, Bay wondered how they had all got so old, so suddenly. For the longest time, these faces, and voices, and hairdos ("hairdo" being another lost Cathcartism), familiar to him as a boy (they sang in the choir; they took up the collection), familiar to him during his increasingly infrequent Sunday visits to his parents as an adult (they still sang in the choir; still took up the collection), had seemed frozen in time. Not in youth, certainly. Not even in middle age. But for ever and ever these leathery faces, and gravelly voices, and razor-sharp parts and starched white cuffs, and pinned scarves, and elaborately curled mounds of sprayed, immobile perms had remained unchanged. And now, as Bay bent forward and shook the small, feeble hands, as he raised his voice and thanked Mrs. Perry again for her condolences, as Sarah passed the sandwiches she had made in their unfinished kitchen in Toronto the night before and said to Mr. Morton that, yes, it had been a terrible shock, and as Bay tried to remember how long it had been since he had last visited Greystone, he found himself surprised by the rheumy eyes, the limps and canes, and the loose puckers of pale skin at collars that, ten years before, would never have been allowed to get so frayed.

There was a new young minister. Like the steady stream of new young ministers who had stepped in and out of the Greystone pulpit over the past dozen years, he was busy working on a doctoral thesis while he went about the business of attending to the placid, middle-class concerns of Greystone's diminishing congregation. This had been a regular complaint of Bay's father: unlike ministers in the old days—unlike, as a case in point, old Dr. James, who, so it always seemed to Bay, was as permanent a fixture of Greystone as the stained-glass windows he had stared at so often as a boy during the interminable services—the new ministers never stuck around. Their wives didn't bake cookies for the church circle. Their children didn't attend Canadian Girls in Training or the boys' Bible study group. The new young ministers were never at a church long enough to know anything or anyone. "I doubt he has any inkling that we have a son who went to Sunday school for so long," Sandy Newling said more than once to Bay—"any inkling" being a Cathcartism; "he" being any one of a half-dozen callow, preoccupied, fleeting new ministers. Like the commuters on the highway, they were just passing through, focused much

more on where they were going than where they were. Cathcart, Bay's father admitted in moments of candour, might
not be the most exciting place in the world. But still.

And this new minister, whose first name was all Bay could
ever remember, was even more preoccupied than most. Not
only did Brad have a doctoral thesis to worry about, he had
arrived at Greystone after the axe, long predicted by Sandy
Newling, the church's treasurer, had fallen. "Demographics
have worked against us," Brad had said at the board meeting.
It was clear: Greystone could no longer sustain itself finan-
cially, and Brad, whose thin, flaxen hair was a little on the
long side, who wore boots with zippers at their sides instead
of shoes, who had a penchant for appearing tieless and open-
necked at Church board meetings, was in charge of the
complex amalgamation of what was left of Greystone's congregation with a newer, younger, more conveniently located
church, across from a busy mall where, on a Sunday, there
would be no shortage of parking.

Bay had heard hardly a word of the funeral service. He sat
beside Sarah in the front pew, surrounded by the solemn
little cluster of his parents' friends and colleagues, bathed in
the vast coolness of the place. He looked up to the great
wooden beams and the slowly turning fans of the vaulted
ceiling—its height alone a memorial to the distant affluence
of another generation—and remembered. He remembered
he used to get dizzy looking up. And he remembered the
smell of his mother's fur coat. And he remembered how,
partway through the service, "the young people" were called
forward, and a door mysteriously opened at the side of the
sanctuary, and, as if following the Pied Piper, the children all
poured out into the narrow, carpeted hallway that led to the
classrooms. He remembered that as a boy he had always been

one of the few constants in the constantly fluctuating membership of the Greystone Sunday School. His father had always been adamant about attendance.

Unlike real school, Sunday Bible classes had no mechanism by which to enforce attendance. This seemed to Bay an inexplicable liberalism on the part of a God capable of slaying all of Egypt's firstborn. As a result, those few who attended Sunday school regularly—none more regularly than Bay—became accustomed to a constantly changing roster of classmates. Most parents were not as steadfast in the religious education of their children as Sandy Newling. Faces came and went. Hastily scrubbed, buttoned into infrequently worn white shirts, unfamiliar boys appeared for a Sunday or two in Bay's class. They sat there, a little bewildered, as the regulars flaunted their knowledge of sycamore trees, and wine gourds, and pallets. Of Sanhedrin, and Deuteronomy, and Genesis. Of Nebuchadnezzar. Then, with their parents' guilt assuaged or forgotten, or with their parents' need to sleep in or make love on a Sunday morning satisfied, these mysterious classmates disappeared.

Liturgical confusion was the result. The church calendar never seemed very orderly to Bay. Grade school, he well knew, had a relentlessly linear progression: numbers began the fall in a cheery, simple way; by the spring they were nightmares of integers and long division. Brave, happy explorers set out for the New World in September; by June their good and adventurous intentions had turned into twenty-five-mark questions of treaties and proclamations and dates of battles. But in Sunday school, things did not move forward so clearly. His teacher, Miss Rathnaby, was often called upon to talk about the miracle of Easter to students who, having missed the previous Sunday and most Sundays of their lives before that, were not perfectly clear on where Jesus had spent Good Friday.

Bay suffered no such confusion. He wore an impressively elaborate attendance pin on the lapel of his jacket and was always called upon to take part in the twice-yearly pageants that the Sunday-school classes performed for the adult congregation. One at Easter. One at Christmas. No other festivals warranted such Catholic extravagance at Greystone United, or so annoyed Dr. James.

Dr. James was squat, bald, and mushroom-coloured. His constant complaint—conveyed mostly by a jowled, monochromatic grimness—was that the quotidian demands of the church calendar (the announcements, the junior choir's occasional performances, the treasurer's annual report, the Sunday-school pageants) left precious little time for the unravelling, multisyllabic, erudite eloquence of his sermons. During the Sunday-school performances, he always sat beside the pulpit and bowed his forehead into the point of his thumb and index fingers: never once looking at the little children; suffering them as best he could. Dr. James wore a strained approximation of a smile whenever the congregation laughed at a little lamb going the wrong way, a halo slipping, Pontius Pilate forgetting his lines.

In these seasonal performances, Bay's role varied. He met angels in fields. He presented frankincense in stables. He waved palms at the gates of Jerusalem. Once, he slunk off into the shadows of the choir stall with a bag of thirty bottle caps. His bare feet and bathrobe were always a memorable departure from the Sunday uniform of white shirt, grey flannels, black shoes, grey sports jacket, grey-striped tie.

And, because these pageants were so memorable—or perhaps, because the rest of the Sunday-school liturgy was so forgettable—Bay was left with a weirdly static notion of the life of Christ. He thought of Jesus the same way he had always pictured ghosts before the summer he went to camp: not as terrifying Indian paddlers, not as mad hunters, but as pathetic, vaporously domestic figures caught in an eternal hiccup of time.

Every spring, it seemed to Bay, Jesus got through the difficulties of the Easter weekend. Year after year, he was denied, doubted, not recognized (How? Bay always wondered; were they idiots, those people?). He ascended unto heaven, and spring finally warmed up, and the storm windows came off, and Bay got his bicycle out of the basement. Then, after a long and poorly attended string of Sundays throughout the humid, heat-buzzing summer, throughout the chill, leaf-kicking fall, the church returned, like summer stock to Neil Simon, to the annual festival of Christ's birth. There was always a packed house, ruffling with babies and winter colds. There were always white gifts and candles. And there was Bay, in his bathrobe, spotting a star in the east. Bay, trembling before the heavenly host. Bay, suggesting to his fellow wise men that, improbable as the whole business seemed, it might be best to push on to Bethlehem.

It occurred to Bay, when at Brad's nod he stood in the pew and moved up the marble steps to the pulpit to say a few words about his parents, that this was probably the only time in his life that he had addressed a Greystone congregation when he was not wearing a bathrobe. He spoke briefly, and remained dry-eyed, and afterward, in the memorial room, Sarah whispered that she had been proud of him. He was proud himself—but mostly because he had worked into his remarks a secret allusion to the sense of humour he could remember his mother having when he was still a boy. This was lost history—he could scarcely remember her smiling during his teenage years. But when he had been quite young—sitting between his parents at church—he had felt the quivers of a giggle through the sleeve of her Persian lamb coat when, apropos of nothing other than a break in the composition of his own sermon, Dr. James said something like: "As, during those dark days last week, while the ever-reliable Mr. Cronkite imparted to us the gravity of the Cuban situation, I could not help but recall Paul Tillich's seminal work." These artless segues to books that no one in the congregation had ever heard of, much less read, amused Marj Newling. And so Bay, looking out over the thirty or forty politely blank faces gathered at his parents' funeral, had said, in private remembrance of his mother's long-gone laughter: "When I received the shocking news about my parents, I could not help but think of the brutal economy of Humbert Humbert's parenthetical acknowledgment of his mother's death in *Lolita*"—parentheses that Bay drew a little awkwardly in the air above the pulpit as he slowly quoted Nabokov. "(Picnic, lightning)." Bay was pleased, on behalf of his dead mother, to see the gathered faces in front of him go blanker still. And, as a kind of descant, he could hear in his imagination the harridan's voice of his current publisher telling him that no reader could be expected to understand the literary allusions of which he, the editor of *The Weekender*, was so inordinately fond. You're wrong, he could hear Bunty Brownlea hissing through thousands of dollars' worth of orthodontic endeavour, if you think our average reader knows who Nabokov is. Tough, thought Bay for once.

"They were there," Bay said in closing from the pulpit. "Then they weren't there any more."

It was an odd way to end a eulogy. Brad waited a little
uncertainly for Bay to start down the steps before uncrossing
his zippered boots beneath his robe and rising to conclude
the service. There was a hymn. There was a prayer. There
was the blessing. And then everyone was invited back to the
memorial room, where the crustless egg sandwiches would
circulate in grief. Where toothpicks and napkins would col-
lect sadly in men's jacket pockets. And where, at the bar—
"a bar that took a little doing," said Bay to Caz—Bay would
meet Ewen Eccles, a retired colleague of his father's.

"The thing is," said Bay to Caz, as he leaned forward and
carefully placed a thick piece of oak on the glowing chamber
of the campfire's coals. A little blossoming of sparks shot upward into the night. The boy's head rested across his arms
and upraised knees, and with his face turned away from Bay
and toward the fire, Caz could almost have been a young
girl—so narrow was his neck, so slender were his legs, so
peacefully attentive his posture. "The thing is, and it's something you'll probably discover when you're a little older . . ."
It was strange, he said, but Bay had to admit that he didn't
mind funerals. He hated weddings. He told his son that weddings unnerved him completely. He attended them, terrified
always that something would go terribly wrong. He knew
that everyone was looking for auguries of happiness—in the
weather, in the notes achieved by the tremulous soloist,
in stumble-free readings, in gaffeless speeches. And so, Bay
always expected the worst: the ring would be dropped down
a cold-air return, the bride would start to giggle, the minister
would get the names wrong, the groom would tearfully
announce that he was homosexual, a grandmother would
keel over.

"Or they'd get divorced," said Caz.

"Or they'd get divorced."

Funerals, by comparison, were a relief. After all, what more could go more wrong?

Bay also noticed that, at weddings, alcohol always had a syrupy effect on him. It depressed him. It descended on him in glass after glass of insufficiently chilled chardonnay, insufficiently dry champagne, leaving him coated with a numb sugary thickness that evolved through the evening and through the fitful Saturday night into a Sunday hangover that neither black coffee nor cigarettes could do very much about. God, Bay said to Caz on the third night of their canoe trip, which happened to be a Saturday, how he hated Sundays.

Funerals, on the other hand, seemed to bring out the best in a good stiff drink. He tended toward Scotch, himself. It seemed appropriately peaty and elegiac. And the first sharp, serious swallow always went directly to the part of his brain that he wanted a drink to go to: his vision cleared, his spirit calmed, his edge honed. And this was why, in contravention of provincial liquor laws and Church policy, Bay had guessed, correctly, that Brad's liberal instincts could be relied upon to raise no objections to the bar, set up by Bay in the memorial room. The bar, over the linen tablecloth of which he was passing Ewen Eccles a rum and Coke.

"If I can ever be of any assistance," Mr. Eccles was saying. This kindness of these people touched Bay.

Bay gave a slight toast with his own glass and took a sip. The Scotch tasted like freshly turned earth, like burning leaves—and suddenly, surprisingly, for the first time in three days, he felt tears. He looked away with some embarrassment. He swallowed. Suddenly he remembered in unsettling detail the blur of light of the picture window behind his parents' hi-fi in their living room, and he saw there, in the sheered rectangle of white curtains, the fading suburb, the reflected Scandinavian and tartan interior, the sliding glass doors, the Ray Conniff records, the sleeping pills, the blue toilet water.

Eccles—Bay remembered the name. He had heard his father mention Ewen Eccles a hundred times. A senior actuary. A twenty-five-year man. A silver-haired gentleman of forgettable good looks who favoured pale colours, and vests. He used to come over to the Newlings' house for drinks now and then.

Bay said to Mr. Eccles—

"Ewen, please."

Yes, it had been a shock. And well, he and Sarah were fine, under the circumstances. Yes, one—a baby boy, back in Toronto with Sarah's mother and stepfather. And yes, thank you, it was kind of him to say; yes, his parents were, had been, good people. Yes, it was true. They didn't make them like that. Not any more. Yes.

And then, emboldened by the snapping warmth of the Scotch, Bay posed a question. He realized that he would never, likely, be able to ask anyone again. And so he said, "Ewen, I hope you won't mind me asking, but you know, I've always wondered."

As Bay was growing up in Cathcart, Ontario, many of the Newlings' original neighbours moved—away from Ardell Crescent, away from the postwar suburb of New Cathcart. All around the Newlings, their friends and neighbours seemed to outgrow their starter homes. They left the slapdash crescents and courts. They abandoned the immature trees, the sun-browned lawns, the youthful cheapness of their optimistic beginnings. In moving vans the size of great ships, they headed across town, to older, deeply shaded streets

of gabled, red brick houses. To the country club Sandy Newling could not afford to join. To the private schools he
couldn't consider. To condominiums in Florida and summer
cottages up north.

The men had got their promotions, had taken over their
firms, had established their practices, had come into their in-
heritances. They had their maturing investments, and their
dividends. They had children who knew how to slalom ski,
who won ribbons at regattas, who wore blazers and ties and
who, in their glorious summers, sat, shirttails flying, on the
stern gunwales of outboards. These men had wives who
grew thinner and more blond and more rapaciously sexy
with each passing year of tennis games and manicures and
lip-glossed summer tans.

Sandy's peers grew heavier. They became more dignified,
and confident, richer and more important. The decades—
those particular decades—bestowed abundance upon them.

Sandy had never been tall; he remained slight and girth-
less and small. As he grew older, his good looks took on a
weightlessness that he seemed unable to overcome. His
dark, thick hair seemed trivial and cosmetic beside balding
wisdom, beside patrician silver, beside patriarchal domes.
His pipe—a straight-stemmed Brigham Sportsman—never
quite suited him; he smoked it often, but always seemed
somehow too young for it. His face, unaged by furrow of
brow or wisdom of spectacles, was more pert than handsome. He did not understand why he was being left behind
by such easy affluence, and although he remained stoic, although he remained as dignified as he could, envy churned
in his small, effortlessly trim stomach.

Bay said to Ewen Eccles that he had always imagined
his mother had something to do with his father's lack of

advancement at Guaranty Life. He said that he wondered if Sandy had been held back because of Marj—because of her gin, and her Seconal, and her days in bed watching television. He wondered if his father had been overlooked because, at office parties, Marj wore the glassy, vaguely terrified smile of a stranger at a gathering of old friends.

"Not so," Ewen Eccles had said. He dipped his head of white hair down to his glass. His lilac-coloured tie matched his pocket handkerchief. "Your father didn't do so badly, really. Just not as well as he might have hoped. The sad thing, though, was that your father's problems were only accidental. They were only bad luck. Bad timing. There was no good reason for them at all.

"People don't think this can happen. But believe me, it can. Your father was living proof."

He told Bay that, while Sandy Newling had shuffled slowly upward, he had not made the leaps that he probably should have, because he had been the victim of unforeseeable shifts in the corporate structure of Guaranty Life. By sheer bad luck he had entered a professional channel that didn't lead upward very far. No one could have predicted this.

It wasn't that Sandy Newling's superiors regarded him as incompetent. If anything, his work was overly rigorous. It was just that, by unhappy chance, executive attention was always diverted by something else at moments when he should have been promoted. Again and again, his time came: but always it came at the same moment as a hostile takeover bid, a catastrophic tornado in the Midwest, oil embargoes, dizzying market corrections. Again and again, Sandy Newling felt the spotlight of head office inch toward him. Again and again, he felt it yanked away.

As well, there were several occasions when, on the very brink of a big upward step, Sandy Newling was left where he was. Temporarily, it was always implied—temporarily left in his cubicle because there was nobody who could, at that precise moment, fill the position he would leave. Promotions were postponed. Then postponed again. And eventually, it was assumed, vaguely, that there must be a reason that Sandy Newling had been passed over so often.

So the Newlings stayed put. They might have moved at one or two points in their lives, but Sandy liked to be prudent about money. He didn't like uncertainty, he didn't like risk. And so, the hedge grew around their property on Ardell Crescent. The window caulking cracked. The crabgrass spread. The skeletons of poisoned mice turned brittle and white beneath the floorboards. An aluminium trailer— a Northbound Caravan—sat on its blocks in the garden, its fridge kept ajar with a paint-stick.

Greystone was Sandy's link with his former neighbours. It was the only United church in Cathcart then, and so their old friends continued to come back on Sundays. This was something. They came back, across town, from the old part of Cathcart, once a week. And in their attendance, Sandy Newling saw a chance to claim the position in the community he felt he deserved. He insisted that once a week the family go to church. He became treasurer. And he hailed his fellow elders with greetings and waves in the church parking lot, with firm handshakes in the vestibule. At church, at least, he was one of them: greeting parishioners, delivering flowers, compiling his budgets, standing in the convivial huddle of grey and blue suits outside the back door of the narthex for a smoke before taking up the collection.

Suddenly. North of Toronto. This was the announcement—

rushed, as it turned out, in order to get the information into the Greystone calendar, and because of the hurry, by some hasty inadvertence, it read: *Nerling. Marj and Sandy.*

"So you didn't get to say goodbye," Caz said, looking sideways at his father, his head resting on his knees. A new moon had appeared just above the dark shape of the opposite shoreline. And his son's voice—just beginning to waver flatly—surprised Bay. Bay had been looking straight into the flames of the campfire as he had talked, and if his attention had wandered at all from what he was saying, it had wandered no further than to the glowing chambers of coals in front of him, and to three names he remembered from Sunday school and from some song that had been sung at campfires, the one summer he had attended camp: Shadrach, Meshach, and Abednego. He had almost forgotten that anyone was listening, and he turned his face to look at Caz. He thought: my son. Bay couldn't tell if Caz was listening really, or if his comment was the kind that students learn to make in school in order to give teachers the impression that they are interested in what is being said.

"I suppose that's right," said Bay. "And I suppose that's why when Laird died . . ."

"I don't really remember him."

"Not the cigars?"

"Not really."

"The music?"

"Not very well."

"Well," said Bay, "you were only six. It's funny what you remember. And what you don't. But you were a great favourite of his. . . . You're right. I didn't get to say goodbye to my parents. And I suppose that's why when Laird was dying I involved myself. With things."

"Things?"

"Well," said Bay. "Funeral things."

When Dr. Alistair Laird fell suddenly ill early one spring, not long after his seventy-first birthday, his wishes were that no ceremony attend his death. He was a handsome, crag-faced man. He was known as Laird to everyone, including his wife, Nora, and his three stepdaughters, Julia, Pru, and Sarah. He was kindly, in his way. He was also bombastic, in his way. And for someone who was dying, and dying rather quickly, Laird made his exit plans known with some force.

"Perhaps," said the hospital chaplain, who ventured once and only once into Laird's room, "a memorial service, a gathering of family and friends . . ."

Laird moved his dry lips.

"I beg your pardon." The chaplain leaned forward.

A gasp of stale breath. "Get out."

It was Bay who witnessed this. During those unsettled and sad days, it was Bay who was often there, in the hospital room.

Of course, it was Laird's wife who bore the brunt. Nora, whose round, open face had taken on a strained expression no one had seen before. Nora, who always wore the perfume Laird liked, and who always had a kind word for the nurses, and whose substantial weight was beginning to bear down on her tired legs, as she paced the corridor in her comfortable old cardigan when the doctors came into Laird's room. It was Nora, of course, who was in the hospital for long bedside shifts, but when, finally, she was exhausted, when finally she went home, to a bath, to some food, to the blankness of the sleeping pills she was using for the first and only time in her life, she wanted someone to be there. Julia and Pru, and their husbands and young families, lived far from downtown. It was the busiest time of the publishing year for Sarah—three children's novels, two nursery rhyme anthologies, and the usual raft of Learning to Read paperbacks were coming out of Children's Press. And so it was Bay who was sitting in the hospital room, across from the end of Laird's bed, beside the window, when Laird made his wishes so clear to the chaplain.

Bay was a little taken aback—not nearly as taken aback as the chaplain—but not particularly surprised. The views that Laird held on the subject of religion and its attendant ceremony were well known to his family and his friends. And his views on these matters—and on the subject of funerals—had not softened in the least now that he was face to face with the green walls, plasma drips, fish sticks, and plastic pill tumblers of his own mortality.

"Nothing," Laird had said. "I'd like. Nothing."

This was when the subject first came up. Or rather, when it came up for the first unwhispered time. For although Laird, by then, had known for a week what was quickly to come, his family had been floundering from doctor to doctor, hope to hope. As families will.

The family meeting took place in Laird's hospital room. Sarah was sitting at the foot of the narrow bed. Her mother was in a chair at the head. She was holding Laird's hand. Sarah's two younger sisters, and their husbands, were standing by the large, unadorned window. Bay was at the closed door.

Beside Laird's bed were piled a few of the history books he had always enjoyed reading. They were now too heavy for him to hold. Beside the books was the Walkman the family had bought for him in the hospital, and which he said he hated. Tapes of his favourite Schubert, his favourite

Beethoven sat there, ignored. "Music," he had said, "must echo around things. To be alive. Can't be injected."

Laird's feet were pale. He complained of how cold they were. Sarah was massaging them. She said, "We can't do . . . nothing."

There was a faint echo of Laird's old, gruff growl. It was a very characteristic growl. The growl his family had heard so often when they were growing up—when they came back from school to report that they were memorizing Psalm 23 for an assembly, or that their teacher liked to start the day with the Lord's Prayer. From his pillows, Laird looked at Sarah fiercely. "Why not?" he asked. "Why not do nothing?" His eyes gleamed for a second with the old fire of the debates he had so often waged at the dinner table. "'Nothing' seems fitting. Under the circumstances."

"Well," she said. "There's Mom."

Nora's eyes were wide and attentive. Her fine skin, her abundant white hair, her long, pretty lashes, her unbearable concern were all poised there. She was on the edge of something. She was unable to speak.

Laird said, "Nora is a big girl." He gave a feeble pat to the back of his wife's hand.

"And there's your friends. And there's us . . ."

"Look." Laird wheezed. He coughed. "I'm the one. Who's bloody well dying."

It was the first time the word had been spoken openly. So matter-of-factly. It hung there, amid the leafy cloy of the delivered flowers, the odour of untouched dinner, the scent of moisturizer cream and soap and disinfectant, the dim smell of bedsheets.

"So what I want," Laird said. "Is. After the cremation. Throw out my ashes. With the garbage."

He had forbidden a funeral, forbidden a memorial service, forbidden his family the expense of anything beyond the most rudimentary disposal. He was a doctor. A stubborn pragmatist. A faithful atheist. A Scot.

Laird frowned. He said, "And I mean. Regular pickup. No goddamn recycling."

He had become ill very quickly and very uncharacteristically. Bay could not remember him ever having so much as a cold. Only a few weeks before, Laird had gone with Nora for a tennis holiday to Florida. They had been doing this for some years. At their age, they said, they were impatient with the cold, with the slush, with the reluctance of a northern spring. They had not been born in this godforsaken country, after all—as Laird always took pains to point out. The older they got, they said, the less willing they were to tolerate something as ridiculous as a Canadian winter.

They wanted to sit with gin-and-tonics and to read their books. They wanted to listen to the warm, bright *pok-pok* of the tennis courts from the balcony of their time-shared condominium. They wanted to stroll the cooling beach and stop to watch the sun sink red into the nightly calm of the Gulf of Mexico.

At first, on the tennis court in Florida that spring, Laird had played as keenly and as sneakily as ever. His exasperating spin serve seemed to bounce up from the edge of the service court at right angles to the baseline. But he noticed, as he played, as he marched triumphantly from service court to service court, that he could not easily regain his breath.

Eventually he had to stop. This was unheard of. He sat, glumly, for the rest of the holiday, reading. He knew something was very wrong.

He told Nora it was nothing. A strain. A pull. A bruised rib. It was unfortunate about the holiday, about the tennis. But it was just bad luck. Bad timing.

He went to see his doctor when they got home. He was admitted to hospital a week after that.

So there, as Laird put it, they were.

Bewildered and unprepared, with the shifts of gentle nurses coming and going. Never-seen-before doctors appeared, left, were never seen again, in the incomprehensible maze Laird was now entering: a puzzle of polished hallways; of medical bureaucracy; of echoing, fluorescent-lit health care.

Laird's strength evaporated. The family organized itself. Time ran out.

For Bay, on the last of his bedside watches in the hospital room, what was most disconcerting was not the rasping breath, not the slackened face. What he found most unsettling was the suntan. The Florida tan was still apparent on Laird's arm. It was a healthy-looking arm, a strong-looking arm, a tennis player's arm. An arm draped loosely over the stiff white sheets. An arm attached to the IV unit beside his bed.

Bay sat in the orange chair in Laird's room, waiting. He was thinking that he'd felt like this before. He was remembering camp. His summer at camp had been the first time he had ever been away.

He did not believe that homesickness was an insignificant thing. He did not think you grew out of it. He did not know a sadness that compared. It was there, always; it would come back.

He remembered the sensation. A hollow in his stomach that held him tight, that kept him almost from breathing. Late

at night—wide awake in his sleeping bag, curled into the flannelette of casting fishermen and leaping pike, staring up into
the darkness of the cabin's rafters—he usually started to cry.

It was there. It would stay there: the curled trembling;
the swallowed, held-back sobs. Thirty years later, when he
sat in Laird's hospital room, looking out the window at the
bleak view of pebbled rooftops and air vents, listening to the
rasp of Laird's irregular breath, he thought of it again.

The room was on the fifteenth floor, and looked over the
city. The day was overcast. Out of an old habit, Bay searched
the sky for a bit of blue.

"Enough blue to patch a pair of Dutchman's breeches,"
his counsellor, Peter Larkin, used to say when it rained—
when the boys were stuck in the cabin, tired of *Superman*
comics, and giving up on crazy eights. When they were
bored with their half-hearted letters home, Lark invented
a game.

He made them sit on the porch of the wooden cabin,
surrounded by the soggy moat of pine needles left by a
storm. He told them to search through the trees to the sky.
He told them that if they caught sight of a patch of blue and
cheered it on, it would grow. The blue would wedge itself
between the banks of grey. It would elbow its way to the
fore. If they shouted, and clapped, and stamped their feet,
it would banish the clouds. It would take dominion over the
slippery swimming docks, and the puddled paths, and the
canvas hulls of the upturned canoes. Peter Larkin said if they
believed hard enough, the camp would come back to life.

Shutters would bang open. Light would sweep the alder
and the sumach. Shadows in the woods would turn sharp
and deep. Everything would shine. Boys would shout.
Junipers would brush cold against bare, running legs. There

would be a splash of a body hitting the water. Then another, and another. The rocks always dried quickly in the hot out-bursts of sun.

In the hospital, there was a row of pay telephones out-side Laird's room. It was a disturbance. Nora had objected. But no other room was available. And now, everyone was accustomed to them. Now, Laird no longer heard them.

The people who used the phones spoke with a kind of anxious incredulity—as if they had memorized the lines long ago but couldn't quite believe that they were being called upon to deliver them now. No one expects this, Bay realized. Not ever. No matter how inevitable it is. He heard a man saying, "They're not sure. The fact is, at this point in time, they just don't know."

Laird's breathing rose and fell. Bay stared out the win-dow. The dull sky was a relief from the white light of the interior. Bay watched the scudding clouds.

Lark had told them that the Indians believed the souls of the dead travelled in poised, beautiful canoes. He said they passed through the eddies and swirls of the Milky Way. Bay liked that. From the time he had gone to camp, he had al-ways imagined souls flying.

At low altitudes at first. They escaped the city. They dove from windowsills like Superman. Then: winging over roof-tops and streets, they headed by angelic instinct for the north. God's country. In the instant before anyone sitting in a hospital room sees the transformation that has taken place, they swoop beyond farms and highway hamburger stands and souvenir trading posts. They head toward the woods and the blue lacework of lakes. They bank from the path of the highways. They follow the narrow, gravel roads like low-flying bombers evading radar. They break out from the shore and skim over the water. They leave gusts across the surface as if trailing baby blankets, graduation robes, wedding dresses, hospital sheets. They weave over the islands and inlets. They fly over long, smooth points of granite and pines. And on the ground, beneath a narrow opening in the tall trees, those among the living who are attentive enough might hear a slow ruffling of overhead wings.

They are going—out past the reefs to the open water. Uncertain of their resolution, they are just going. Over the brown shoals and over the depths of the blue waves, rising higher, climbing toward the piled dusk of clouds.

Bay turned away from the window. And there it was.

He wasn't surprised. Whatever it is that happens, had happened. One of Laird's eyes was cocked, unblinking as a bird's.

And so—so Bay explained to Caz, as he rose stiffly to his feet and burrowed through the food pack for the brandy flask—he involved himself with things. Funeral things. And, by strange coincidence, that was how their summer plans had fallen into place. Because it was two days after Laird's death that Bay was sitting beside a stranger, a woman he did not recognize, in the vestibule of the Caldicott and Son Funeral Home.

Laird had been perfectly serious in his last request. But his last request had been too much. Nobody could see themselves dumping his remains into the groaning maw of a garbage truck. Nobody could imagine gathering on the sidewalk, snuffling into handkerchiefs, dabbing eyes, shaking hands with mournful, overalled municipal sanitation workers.

And so it was decided that, by way of a memorial, his remains would simply be present, on the mantel, at a family dinner on the first Thursday after his death. It had been Nora and Laird's custom to leave Thursday evening open for a family dinner—which usually, since Sarah's two sisters lived in the distant, suburban outskirts of the city, meant Thursday dinners were for Bay, for Sarah, and for young Caz.

The memorial dinner seemed an admirable compromise. There would be no hymns. No prayers. No collects for the dead. But there would be roast lamb—Laird's favourite. There would be lots of Laird's best wine. And there would be music, played loudly, echoing over the furniture, from the stereo—as Laird had always played it: Casals, unaccompanied Bach; Pollini, the Schumann Fantasie; Jessye Norman, the Four Last Songs.

But these ad hoc arrangements had an unpredictable effect on Nora. The absence of custom, ceremony, and ordered procedure left her adrift. With no ritual to follow, no tradition to uphold, she felt it necessary to create her own. She did not want to fly in the face of Laird's wishes, and so the process of her mourning was private and mostly invisible. The only outward sign was that she became obsessed with the timing of things. When would this happen? And this? And this? That was what she wanted to know.

She wanted to be with him, to follow him in her imagination, in her closely held prayers. She wanted to know at precisely what hour the body would be removed from the room in the hospital and taken to the hospital's morgue. She insisted on knowing exactly when delivery would be made from the morgue to the crematorium. She needed to know the hour of the cremation and how long it would take, and when the ashes would arrive, from the city necropolis, at the Caldicott and Son Funeral Home. When would they be picked up? At what time? Precisely? And, precisely, at what time would they arrive, from the funeral home, at the apartment?

But there was more. This, the marking of Laird's passage through hospital corridors, city streets, mortuary hallways, and sheets of flame, overlapped with another minutely turning realm of Nora's ritual: When would somebody pick up the gin for the martinis? The new potatoes? The Stilton?

"Don't worry, Nora," replied a chorus of helpful sons-in-law. "We'll pick up them up."

But that wasn't what she wanted to know. She wanted to know *when*.

On the first Thursday after her husband's death, she was going to set the table when she got back from the bakery and the butcher at exactly two o'clock. She was going to walk up the street to the flower shop at exactly two-thirty. She would arrange the flowers by three. She was going to put the rosemary and garlic and white wine and mustard–basted lamb in the oven at four. She would start the slow, buttery simmer of the creamed spinach at four-thirty. She would open the wine to breathe at five. Select the music just before everyone arrived, and serve the drinks and hors d'oeuvres at five-thirty. For Laird, she said, never took a lunch at the office. He never liked eating dinner late.

She stated and restated the schedule. These quotidian arrangements, entwined with the precise chronology of the funerary procedures, had become her ritual. And so, when she told everyone, and told them again, that it was important that they all be on time on Thursday, they had, by then, come to understand what was going on. She had invested the hours of that day with the stately measure of a requiem. And she insisted, therefore, that the passage of that ordinary time be exactly observed.

In the allotment of family tasks that attended Laird's death, it had fallen to Bay to pick up the ashes at the funeral home. Having vetoed Laird's most extreme request—the Glad Bag casket, the curbside eulogy, the waved goodbyes to the closing compactor—the family felt compelled to follow the rest of his wishes scrupulously. Laird had wanted everything to be done as inexpensively as possible, and so to Mr. Caldicott's professional chagrin the family had not only forgone the chapel, the organ, the ushers, and the printed order of service, they had dispensed with the option of home delivery of the remains by hearse and driver.

"I shall be picking up the ashes at four-forty-five," Bay told Mr. Caldicott on the telephone.

"That will be satisfactory," Mr. Caldicott said, managing to imply that it was anything but.

When Bay called Sarah at Children's Press to tell her that he was leaving the *Weekender* office and was on his way to the funeral home, Sarah said, "For God's sake don't be late, Bay. I think Mom will have a nervous breakdown if this doesn't go like clockwork." An admonition, as things turned out, that only increased Bay's anxiety when Mr. Eugene Caldicott, Jr., of the Caldicott and Son Funeral Home, came into the vestibule and announced a delay.

He was a large man, Mr. Caldicott. Junior only by association with his no doubt resplendently buried father. He had padded forward on little funeral-director feet. His hair, once blond, was thinned to a few strands and darkened only by the stuff that kept it flattened, like wood grain, against the pale lumber of his skull. His face was square, as were his spectacles. He directed his solicitous and magnified gaze toward the two clients who were seated before him. His voice was unexpectedly high for so gravity-bound and Rotarian a presence. "A brief delay," he assured the two strangers, who were sitting across from each other. "Very brief."

The vestibule of the Caldicott and Son Funeral Home, in its attempts to appear not at all like a vestibule in a funeral home, was an unsettling place. Its walls were dark, intensely knotty wood panelling. Its drapery and upholstery were a murky tartan. The room was lit with several small, oddly shaded lamps—lamps that seemed somehow to be casting the shadows rather than the splotches of washed-out light. An ornately framed portrait of a rimlessly spectacled elderly gentleman—presumably Mr. Caldicott, Sr.—presided.

The woman who was sitting across from Bay coughed nervously. She looked quickly at her watch. They were both, apparently, there for the same reason. Both, it seemed, were eager to be on their way.

Mr. Caldicott's apology acted as a kind of introduction. He disappeared on hushed rubber soles into his office, and the two occupants of the subdued little room managed the slight grimace of politeness that Canadians reserve for moments when they cannot, realistically, go on pretending they are not in the company of another human being.

She was remarkably thin, but was possessed of a kind of wiry durability. She wore an unbuttoned beige Burberry and a white Shetland sweater. She had thick, silver hair. She had a leather shoulder bag at her feet.

She told Bay that she was eager to beat the traffic. She had to drive up north, to an old family cottage. "Mother always said she wanted to be disposed of without delay. She didn't like the idea of being stuck in some vase. She wanted her ashes spread on the water. From the point where she always had her morning swim."

Bay was now curious about these things—these funeral things. He wondered, "Will you do anything else?"

"Pardon?"

"For your mother. A prayer? Or something?"

"Good God, no." The woman looked startled by the suggestion. "There was a poem Mother liked. She clipped it from *The New Yorker* years ago and kept it pinned up in the outhouse. She said it could have been written about our summers. Perhaps I'll recite it by way of a ceremony."

Bay asked what poem.

"Octavio Paz," she said. "'The wind sings in its turnings, The water murmurs as it goes, The motionless stone is quiet, Wind and water and stone.'"

He said, "That's very beautiful."

She said, "Yes."

A pause.

She asked about him.

Bay explained his situation. He explained his mother-in-law's anxiety. "Timing," he said, "is crucial." He glanced at his watch.

She said, "I see."

Another pause.

A pause into which entered Mr. Caldicott. He stepped mournfully, and with a certain soft, professional aplomb, into the plaid-stricken vestibule.

He seemed to be steeling himself for something. He had an announcement. He said, "Yes. Well. Both of your loved ones passed away on Tuesday afternoon. Both, coincidentally, in the same hospital. And both families, choosing cremation, requested possession of the remains . . ." He peered downward at them with some slight, barely perceptible trace of disapproval. "Requested to pick up the remains by Thursday. Which is to say, this afternoon."

Bay watched the woman's keen, brown eyes widen with alarm. "Is there a problem?" she asked.

But Mr. Caldicott was not to be steered from the chosen course of his explanation. He raised what he intended to be a calming, all-in-due-time hand.

From under the cuff of her raincoat, the woman shook her wristwatch again. It hung loosely, leather-strapped, underside. She looked at it pointedly.

Mr. Caldicott continued. "While this is by no means an impossible constraint of time, it is, as you might imagine, a slight acceleration of customary procedure. As a result, the releases were filed from the crematorium at only three-forty-five today. The remains, of course, are here." He glanced down again at his forms. "But. They are. So I have discovered. They are. Unfortunately. They are, it appears, still . . ."

Mr. Caldicott, whose professional life was largely based on euphemism, found himself, unfamiliarly, at a loss for one. He hesitated, and for one of the most extremely peculiar moments of Bay's life he felt certain that the funeral director was going to say that the remains were, unfortunately, it appears, still . . .

Alive.

Bay pictured terrified grandchildren hoisted mantelward to a gloomy urn in order to hear its faint but persistent heartbeat.

"Still . . . ," said Mr. Caldicott.

"God's teeth," the woman said under her breath.

"They are still . . . warm."

Bay and the woman looked across the vestibule's coffee table at each other. An expression of relief and of what they both recognized as level-headedness passed between them. There was a glimmer, in the woman's eyes, of something dangerously close to laughter.

They told Mr. Caldicott not to worry. They said the

issue of temperature didn't matter in the least. They said that it was entirely their fault the procedures had been hurried. They were grateful for his concern.

"For your sensitivity," the woman said. Her voice had a swooping confidence to it. "Most grateful."

"But . . . ," Bay said.

"All the same. . . ."

"Still. . . ."

"I think we would both rather. . . ." The woman glanced at Bay. He nodded enthusiastically. "We would both rather take possession of the remains now. There is some pressure of time involved, you see. For both of us, actually."

But Mr. Caldicott, cognizant of professional standards that his clients could not begin to appreciate, would not hear of it. The ashes would have to remain, he told them, for twenty more minutes. In the "refrigerator." A word he pronounced with a kind of sophisticated unfolding of syllables that conveyed to them that this was no ordinary refrigerator.

"So. Miss Larkin. Mr. Newling, if you will excuse me. . . ."

And that—so Bay said to Caz, seating himself again, lowering himself carefully to the rock so as not to spill the little plastic teacup of cognac that he had poured from the flask—that was when it came to him.

"When what came to you?"

"That I knew who she was."

Bay said that as soon as Mr. Caldicott had said her name, he knew. It came to him so vividly—for the family resemblance was very strong—he could not believe he had not recognized her at once. It was plain as day. The memory—in her eyes; her voice; her narrow, equine face—was absolutely clear.

"Do you know," Bay said to Miss Larkin. "It's the most amazing thing. But I think I must have gone to summer camp with . . ." Here, Bay paused for a moment, adding up the years, assessing her silver hair, the lines of her face, the sparkle of her keen eyes, the suppleness of her thin wrists. How had he not seen it? "With your brother," he said quickly. "He was my counsellor."

Elizabeth Larkin was astonished at this, for Bay's identification was quite correct.

"Great heavens."

It was Peter Larkin who had told Bay about the perfect campsite—the one on the north shore of the Waubano Reaches, at the mouth of the Skin River, on a stretch of mainland just past Moriah Island. He had said that, when Bay came back to camp, the next summer, or perhaps the summer after that, he would be old enough to go, and that what Lark liked to do when he led a trip to the Skin was to get his group to paddle at night, through the dark shapes of the islands, under the impossibility of stars, across the slither of moonlight, so that if their timing was right they would approach the mouth of the river just as the sun was rising. The sun came up behind the easy little tumble of rapids, and if you were lucky, Lark had said, the mist would be rising from the water, and light would be cutting through the red shadows, marking the opening past Moriah. And as you paddled into the little bay where the river emptied, it would look as if your canoe was entering the rising smoke and the uncontainable flames of a great furnace.

"But," said Bay to Caz, "unfortunately, it never happened. I only went to camp the one summer. But here we are. The famous campsite."

The grey smoke wreathed up into the dark. The moon was higher now.

"What happened to him?" Caz asked. "To Lark."

Bay was staring into the red coals. Three figures were walking there. In the company of a mysterious fourth they were walking in the furnace, untouched by the terrible flames, and when Miss Rathnaby asked their names Bay had whispered Curly, Larry, Moe, but Miss Rathnaby hadn't heard, and she said, "Yes, but who was the fourth? That is the key." And everyone in the Sunday-school class had laughed, and Miss Rathnaby looked confused. And the memory made Bay smile as he pushed another piece of wood into the coals.

"Well, I never got to say goodbye to him. To Peter Larkin. I had to leave a few days before the end of camp. He was in the infirmary, and I never said goodbye."

The crickets. The crackle of sparks. The splash of a fish rising to the lure of the moon.

"Like with your parents," Caz said. "No goodbyes."

"Like with my parents."

Bay had always thought that he would get to know his parents better as they got older. He had imagined that they would sort things out. They might even have become friends. He had imagined, as all children imagine, that he would find the right moment to talk.

He had thought the time would arise. Things would proceed, with a certain ritual, a certain pace, a certain steady progress toward a resolution. It would, perhaps, be the last possible moment, but because he had been allowed to see it coming, he would not let it slip away. He would steel himself. He would know when to act, and he would bend and kiss his father's old, stubbly cheek; he would embrace his mother's shrunken frame. He would not let the moment slip away with all the other moments that make up the inadvertence of a life, and he would say that he was their son and that he loved them—all before they went winging from the windows of hospital rooms, from the balconies of old folks' homes, from the stale peace of their nurse-tended beds at home.

He said he felt robbed. "But then maybe everybody always does."

Over and over he saw them, in his mind's eye, on their way to the annual conference at the Timberside Lodge. This is what must have happened, so the police said. They had stopped for gas. And he could see them, plain as day. His father had just lit his straight-stemmed pipe while standing beside the Premium pump at the Key to the North Highway Gas Bar. Bay pictured it. (That moment.) His father thought he'd waved out the match. He tossed it, and his mother had just turned in the passenger seat to look, without realizing what was happening, at her husband.

fig. 1

MANY YEARS LATER, long after everything had changed, Caz tried to capture his father's voice. In his office, when we met, he remembered him, in a canoe, late at night, calling back from the black water to the shore. He tried to bring the voice to mind. He told me that as a child he had had a gift for mimicry; he could often get voices, often with surprising accuracy. But as an adult, when he reached for his father's, it was sometimes like a word he couldn't quite recall or a face he couldn't quite picture.

There was not much to remind him. Summer by that time was a glare of light through brittle leaves, a swirling of hot, grey dust, sunset after sunset of the same bloody red. The changes had been predicted, but that did not mean they had been expected. What his father had thought was merely the flat, lamentable emptiness that lay between cities turned out to be the sprawling city itself. The malls and the industrial parks and the warehouses and the subdivisions and the convenience stores and the fast-food chains, and the gas stations, and the multiplexes, and the drive-thrus, and the muffler shops, and the hydro towers, and the bus shelters where no one ever waited for a bus at the gritty, weed-poisoned corners of twelve-lane intersections, proved not to be the suburban confusion that cities faded into; they were, in fact, what cities became. Bay had never imagined this. Nor did he ever imagine that what he and Sarah had taken to be Caz's difficulties at school—what they had worried about; what they had met with teachers about; what they had paid psychologists about—would prove to be not a disability in the least. Spelling, reading, grammar, composition—the old-fashioned mainstays of Sarah's and Bay's lives—never existed in Caz's. "A bright boy but . . . ," his teachers always said: *but* he had probably never actually finished a book; *but* he seemed never to understand paragraphs, or capital letters, or periods; *but* he ran his thoughts, and stories, and memories together, as if they occurred in no discernible sequence; *but*, even as a teenager, he seemed not to notice that he sometimes misspelled his own name.

As it happened, this inexplicable gap—this "mental hiccup," as Sarah put it—scarcely mattered. The world he grew into didn't care if Caz could spell, or read novels, or write a complete sentence—any more than it cared whether the old downtowns lived or died. Caz was fine. He did well enough, and from the place where he ended up—in an office, at a point where the heat wavered from concrete; where the white streets were as barren as furnaces at noon hour; where the pall of smoke from the fires to the north hung constantly over the city's highways and back-lit billboards and black, air-conditioned towers—he said that sometimes, now and then, he could capture his father's voice.

Occasionally, a turn of phrase that Caz used would do it:

an inkling of something, a fair ways back. This is what sons do. We guess, as best we can, about our fathers. As we grow older, we listen for similarities in our voices. In order to imagine our future, we watch ourselves for gestures that we recognize. We look for new expressions that we have not invented; we seem to remember them—they seem to come from long ago.

There were undammed lakes then; there were loons at night; there were places, still, where you could land a canoe, and pitch a tent, and build a campfire by a river up north. It was long, long ago—but Caz stopped at the window of the office where he worked and looked at the sun glinting on the sea of parked cars below. He turned. He said that sometimes he got it, that voice, the way it sounded the summer his father died.

fig. 2

THREE

IT WAS NECESSARY to get at the sadness that was in it. That was the key, but it was by no means obvious. It wasn't the first, or the second, or even the third thing that anyone would notice about Bay's voice. It was an undertone. It was a finish, perhaps—if you imagine the complexities of a voice being like the complexities of an interesting wine.

The first note was its articulation—a kind of extravagant unwinding of phrase and apposition that, while slowed by the routinely abundant details of his description, found its way, always, to a grammatically satisfactory conclusion. One of the few recurring disagreements Caz could actually remember his parents having when they were still together was that his mother—a woman of short, direct, sensible sentences—would sometimes grow impatient with his father's artful meanders. Before the year Caz was six; before the spring when Bay, by coincidence, found himself sitting in the vestibule of a funeral home with Elizabeth Larkin; before the summer when Caz and Bay and Sarah went away for their rental holiday at the Larkin cottage in the Waubano Reaches; and before Sarah and Bay's marriage struck the uncharted rock that so abruptly sank it, Sarah would sometimes, at the dinner table of their downtown Toronto home, with a prodding, circular wave of her hand, encourage Bay to speed up, to get more quickly to his point, to cut the asides and the elaborations. This directing of conversational traffic irritated Bay—but in those days his irritation subsided quickly. It was usually calmed quickly enough by another glass of wine, by a second helping of dinner, by Sarah's laughter, by a frowned-upon cigarette with his coffee. They were, they believed, happy.

His voice also had, above the gruff smoker's rumble, a hint of a high, mischievous tremble. This was not so much an expression of humour as it was an indication that irony was never very far beneath the surface of his restrained daily activity. It was the place in his voice where humour would have presented itself more prominently, had humour been a more prominent part of his character. Had he known a quality that we might as well call gaiety, had he been able to break out of the confines of his own background, this is the part of his voice that he would have inhabited more constantly. He might sometimes have been helpless with laughter. He would have taken more obvious delight in things. He would have been better with children.

Had you noticed the sadness, you might have imagined it as a kind of resignation. You might have thought it an expression of professional disappointment—for this was the regret Bay kept closest to the surface, not far, in fact, from the helpless shrug and thin, ironic smile. He would push his grey hair off his forehead; he would lean forward, cupping his hands together over his considerable waist; and he would say, "Ah, the good magazines. Yes, there was a time. A heyday I missed by a generation."

He had been plucked from what he had regarded as the ignominy of freelance journalism, of speech-writing, of producing corporate annual reports, by one of the three middle-aged heirs of the Westell family fortune (cotton mills that switched, with impeccable timing, to dental equipment). Billy Westell wanted to make Bay editor—Bay had done some copy-writing for several of Billy's rarely successful enterprises; Bay had enthused about Nabokov, had lent Billy *Speak, Memory*—and at the meeting where the appointment was concluded, Billy told him that his job was simply to produce an excellent magazine. Which quite suited Bay.

But Billy wasn't the level-headed, hard-nosed capitalist his grandfather had been. In fact, Bay came to discover that Billy wasn't all that bright. Billy seemed to think that losing a million and a half dollars a year on *The Weekender* was a reasonable price to pay for the influence and prestige that would accrue to the proprietor of a magazine that, so its disgruntled advertisers came to believe, no one read. Neither Billy's older brother nor his younger sister was particularly sympathetic, and as the magazine's losses accumulated, their disagreements with Billy became more strident. Finally—with deep regret—the Westells sold the magazine. Sold it, as it transpired, to a series of owners who, with Bay at the ever-adjustable helm, tried to find ways to cut costs, increase ads, expand circulation. Tried and failed, until *The Weekender*, on the very brink of extinction, was saved by the brilliant smile, steely eyes, perfectly manicured nails, and steamroller charm of Bunty Brownlea.

She was a friend of the Westells'. Her husband, whose family money had come from the insurance business but who had made a fortune himself developing shopping malls, had gone to school with Billy. Apparently, there had been a conversation one night at a dinner party at the Westell house—though conversation was not always a feature of the Westells' lavish entertaining—and two and a half bottles into the Côtes de Beaune, Jack Brownlea, while acknowledging that his wife knew "fuck-all about magazines," pointed out to his admiring friends that she had come in on budget with the extensive renovation of their country house, and that she had also "known fuck-all about contracting and interior design and landscaping." So he had told Bunty, across the dinner table, to the scattered applause of the bleary guests of the Westells', that he would come up with the required capital. Because she said *she* knew how to save *The Weekender*, said she knew how to make it successful. "Because," as Jack put it, "running a magazine couldn't be any more expensive than another goddamn renovation." And so, in the first meeting between old editor and new publisher, Bunty Brownlea, glinting with whitened teeth and fine jewellery, told Bay that she could explain her intentions for the magazine with a single word: "Lifestyle."

"Is it?" Bay had asked. "A single word, I mean."

Bay thought of himself, after all, as a literary man—a strike against him, from Bunty's point of view. But Jack was right. She knew fuck-all about magazines, and about the magazine world, and Bay had practical skills she couldn't do without. He happened to know how to commission, improve, cut, and rewrite stories. He knew about heads and about introductions. He knew about drop caps, and knock-outs, and widows. He could deal with art directors, meet printers' deadlines, accommodate advertisers. Unlike Bunty, he could spell.

Bay, for his part, was always proud of the fact that he could make a living doing what he did, and so, dim as he felt his magazine's once-promising light was becoming, he stuck with it. He adapted—largely because there was no place else for him to go. His skills were becoming a more valuable commodity than his notion, outdated and fast becoming antique, of the importance of good writing and precise grammar and graceful turns of phrase. His problem was that he never saw the real centre of commerce: the value of overpasses, the profit of malls, the dividends of industrial parks, the wealth of apartment towers, the bonanza of subdivisions, the riches of hamburgers and pizzas and tacos. He had always imagined a more genteel downtown of beautiful words and interesting, smart, unabridged ideas. "More fool I," he said.

When Caz remembered his parents actually laughing together, he saw them sitting in their little patch of a downtown garden, on a flagstone patio, underneath the lilac tree. His father was telling his mother of the heads and decks—"the bloody, god-awful, ridiculous treatments"—he composed for his well-bred, tastefully put-together staff. "The Ladies' Auxiliary," he called them. "The Junior League."

"Much Ado About Sponging: the new creativity of wall treatments. Brideshead Redecorated: achieving grand English style without a grand English home. Eaves of Class: modern attic makeovers."

Caz remembered Sarah taking off her glasses, putting her thumb and index finger to the bridge of her nose, her tousled blond hair tumbling over her face, her shoulders shaking helplessly. "Oh, Bay. Stop. Please, no more."

"Remembrance of Sinks Past: spouting off about antique faucets. Great Expectations: spare-room-to-nursery conversions made easy. Sofa's Choice: new options for old chintz."

"Bay, you're not serious."

He found it amusing, at times. More usually, he felt defeated by what he thought of as the century's abysmal conclusion. "Things," he said. "Everything is about things." But it was clear to him: if he wanted to keep working, if he wanted to keep earning a salary, he could no more withstand

the trends that Bunty Brownlea kept seeing advancing toward *The Weekender*'s steadily growing readership than turn
back the clock. Much as he would have liked to spend his
working days fine-tuning exquisite essays and commission-
ing daring forays of investigative journalism, he took some
pride in the fact that he earned a living in a segment of the
economy where many believed no real economy existed.
"The magazine business," he said, whenever anyone asked—
well aware of how this surprised some people. Rich people,
usually. There he was: a good suit; an oxford-cloth, button-
down shirt; a clubby-looking tie; a substantial girth; a solid
pair of shoes; a blustery red face; broad shoulders; a firm grip;
an untroubled, confident voice. And, as far as many people
were concerned, he might as well have said, "The string
quartet business."

But the sadness that could be heard in Bay's voice was
not his unrealized hopes for his career, only. Nor was it the
end of his marriage, only. The faint hint of desolation in the
rising and falling of his voice—heard by Caz as Bay poked
the campfire with a stick; noted by Caz as Bay patted his
breast pocket for his Marlboros and matches—had been part
of him long before either of these two failures.

"Summer stuff," he said to Caz. They had been talking
for over an hour on the third night of their canoe trip when
Bay explained this to his son. "Somehow," he said, "as a kid,
even before the one time I went away to camp, I picked up
this notion of summers. Don't ask me how. Rather the way
a boy who can't skate worth a damn develops a fantasy about
hockey. Or a kid who can't run dreams of being a sprinter.
Crazy, really. But somehow, from things my mother told me
about the lodge she went to every June with my father, or
from kids at school who had cottages or who went to camp,

or stuff I'd read. . . . Somehow, I don't know, I put together this whole elaborate creation. There was a kid in my class who never went away for summer either, and I used to tell him all these lies. Enormous, magnificently detailed lies. About cottages. And boats. And lakes. Summer stuff. I invented a whole childhood of northern summers."

This was Bay's sadness. Walking home from school when he was nine, or ten, or eleven; sitting at the edge of the playground in Cathcart with a gimpy-legged kid named Rigby O'Connel, Bay talked and talked and talked. He lied compulsively: about the time his father's old outboard caught fire in the rock-cut near their white-frame, boathoused, cottage; about how his father used to make little boats from peanut shells when they went out to a nearby island for a picnic; about what the sound of his father pumping up the Coleman stove was like; about how his mother used to drape the towels in front of the fire when, on cool August days, Bay and his father went bravely into the grey churning waves for their morning swim. In the playground, he could describe to Rig the boathouse; he could explain to him why he preferred a Mercury to a Johnson; he could rattle off the names of his father's summer friends—Foreman, McCallum, Simpson, Ward, Wilson—in the same order that their nameplates were posted in the boat slips at the old marina.

This was all invention. Everything was made up. These were all stories of holidays he never had.

He said, "It was quite weird. Summer was a talisman to me. I'm not sure why. It was as if I were a Jew and summer was an old-money country club that wouldn't let me in."

And this was what you could hear in him, if you had the ear. The sadness of never having received those things he had wanted only so that he could pass them on.

It was very subtle—a whisper-like hush that softened everything he said, that tugged everything downward, ever so slightly. It was hardly there, and yet if you missed it, you missed the one quality that made his voice entirely unique. As a child, Caz had known it as well as he had known his father's rumbling cough in the mornings, the creak of his slippers on the floorboards of the Toronto house at night, and the smell of his skin and tobacco and shaving cream when Bay reached down and scooped him up.

"Summer stuff," Bay said. "Odd really. Apt, in fact. When you consider what happened."

Bay had some photographs. He kept them at his place—in a drawer in the rigorously undesigned, entirely un–colour-coordinated high-rise apartment.

Sarah's theory about Bay's apartment was that there was nothing casual about its disarray. She believed that he was methodical in his aesthetic negligence. She never believed that it was a statement made to her, that it had anything to do with their divorce or with his loneliness. She believed it was his small, private, professionally harmless way of getting back at the ditzes (a favourite word of his) who sat with him at editorial meetings every week, and who thought that what the world needed was yet another feature on throw cushions, on kilim rugs, on rec-room makeovers.

His apartment was a not very neat, perfectly beige, dry-walled and Arborite blank. He refused to give his place any kind of "look." He Scotch-taped a few old Beatles posters behind his couch, but they fell down and he never put them back up. The little rectangles of tape went brown. The bicycle he never used, the flower pots he never planted, and the plastic bags of newspaper that he never seemed to get down to the recycling bin sat beyond the drapeless sliding glass door that opened to his bald, concrete, sixteenth-floor balcony. The view, Sarah said, gave her the willies: all off-ramps and overpasses and loading docks.

His place smelled of ashtrays that were either everywhere or nowhere to be found—depending on whether he was trying to give up smoking, and gaining weight, or dieting, and smoking like a fiend. Speaker wire ran across the middle of the living-room floor.

There, high on the sixteenth floor, Bay was free of spring trends and summer sensations and fall forecasts and winter home projects. Naturally, he ignored the advice of his magazine on the subject of family photographs—"Remembrance of Things Snapped: a pleasing variety of photo sizes and an eclectic collection of frames can be displayed on a mantel, a desktop, or even a piano. The effect is as Victorian as it is modern."

Bay's photographs were all taken during the same six weeks. They were all from the same summer. They were, in fact, the only photographs he had. An entire married life on six rolls of Kodachrome.

Sarah had given him—thrown at him, actually—the bulging envelopes of the pictures they had taken at the Larkin cottage during their stay there. "You take them. There it is— our perfect family summer."

And there she was, murkily lit at the woodstove, proudly holding her first two loaves of home-baked bread. There was Caz, aged six, perched dubiously in the outhouse— a poem clipped from *The New Yorker* just visible, tacked to the wall behind. There was Bay, in the Larkins' old canoe. Caz again, naked, running joyous on the flat rock of the Waubano Reaches, the remnants of a picnic in the lower left-hand corner. Sarah and Caz waving at the wooden rail of the Larkins' weather-bleached front veranda.

And there were a few shots—just to tell the unexpurgated story of how Bay spent his summer holiday—of Kathleen. Kathleen Hagan. Kathleen the au pair, the raven-haired, baby-oiled mother's helper from across the way.

What did she look like? That night at the campfire, Bay told Caz that he actually forgot sometimes. And sometimes, he wondered. He wondered enough to dig out the pictures from the kitchen drawer in his apartment—the drawer beneath the piles of magazines, pizza coupons, junk mail that announced that he, Bay Noting, had won a trip to the Bahamas, a cabin cruiser, a million dollars.

This was a sore point with Bay. He had a professional interest in correct spelling. And how variously, he often wondered, was it possible to misspell Newling? An ordinary name. Of ordinary Celtic-Scandinavian origins. Let him count the ways. Nawling. Nilling. Nerling. Nolling. His favourite was Nutting. Yes, you, Mr. Bailey Nutting. This is your chance to win a thousand dollars a month for the rest of your life.

He kept the photographs in the drawer with the expired passport, the ruler, the pointless pencils, and the masking tape. And there, amid all this, was Kathleen: dark-haired, slender, necklaced. She was perfectly tanned, as if her life had been all summer. She was smiling into the camera in her white, white shirt. Her blue, blue bathing suit. She was there, with all hell about to break loose—as Bay could see clearly from the vantage point of his bachelor apartment, but had not, somehow, glimpsed then; in her flawless skin, in her blue-grey-eyed smile. He had mistaken her good manners for goodness. He had mistaken her smile for concern and for warmth. Something terrible was about to happen in these pictures of Kathleen: a click of catastrophic timing, with innocent six-year-old Caz squinting at the camera, his hand held, happy, at his baby-sitter's side.

But how did she really look? She looked, Bay often thought, like the two syllables of her name. "Kathleen," he said. In the first: rounded and soft, as open as arms, as dark and downward as he could reach. In the second: smooth as take-off, like a gleam of silver light. She looked, in fact, as any man would expect her to look: any man who remembers how girls look when all the shuffles of a boy's growing up align themselves miraculously into the surprising sequence, the amazing hand, the unexpected flush. Girls—ignored, teased, hated. And then a still, calm moment between things. The world stopped its turning. And there, one summer, when the pause ends, girls suddenly are.

On the deck of a ski boat, on the side of an outboard, wet-haired and baby-oiled, in the beer-warming sunshine, reclining like Egyptian queens amid the towels and the magazines and the tumblers on a weathered dock. When all the brief light of summer shines on their skin, on their hair, on their impossible promise. When, for the present, everything else is lost in their brightness. The past, left in the green shadows of dock cribs, of boat slips. The future, in the shadows of boathouse eaves.

Bay remembered the heat well enough. He remembered the reckless surrender well enough. He remembered the perfect brilliance of that cunt-smooth present. That day. And even so, he often forgave himself. Often, so he told Caz, he thought: no wonder.

He had not planned it. He had never imagined it.

Bay and Sarah often sat on the Larkins' veranda on warm afternoons that summer. They drank gin-and-tonics. They read.

They would read, and sip their drinks, and look up occasionally from the sun-bright pages. They would peer out from the cottage they had rented from Elizabeth Larkin toward the open water. They would look through the wind-streamed openings between the islands. The wood beneath the old deck chairs was hot. They could smell the fading stain, the weathered lumber.

The day—that day—had fallen unusually still. There was a drowsiness to the hours. Bay had just remembered that he had dreamed the night before of his parents' church. He had dreamed of the women in the choir and of their black gowns. "Oh, come let us sing of a wonderful love." With their shiny hair. With their surpliced arms raised. Come. The dream had just come back to Bay at that moment, that afternoon. So he whispered to his wife. That afternoon, on the Larkins' veranda.

They had time. It was one of the afternoons they had the Hagan girl. She came over twice a week, from the cottage where she was working as an au pair. It was a convenient arrangement. That afternoon, Kathleen had taken Caz around to the other side of the island to look for frogs.

Bay leaned forward. He whispered, low, and close, as if someone might hear.

Sarah smiled. She shrugged, laughed him away. "Bad timing, I'm afraid. Wouldn't you know."

And when he smiled wistfully back, smiled back with all the good humour and understanding in the world, she sent him a little toast of her plastic tumbler. She took a sip of her drink, and returned to her book.

Bay wondered if Caz remembered some of the same things he did. He wondered if they had fragments of memory that matched. Or whether a child looking for frogs, a child walking with a sitter along a shoreline path, moved through a different world altogether: remembered only, remembered dimly, a little cove of rushes and lily pads and pebbles and raccooned clam shells, vast as the coastline of a continent, secret as the shade. High grass. Water-dark, sunlight, stepping stones.

What Bay remembered were light eyes, dark hair, bare feet, the drop of wind, the careless pizzazz the gin had left, his sunburned face. He remembered later that afternoon: when it was time for Kathleen Hagan to go back.

Sarah and Bay and Caz were on the dock. Caz was waving goodbye to Kathleen. The painter had been untied. The boat was adrift. The flywheel was sputtering. Kathleen was in her blue bathing suit, in her white shirt, bending over the cord of the outboard motor, a cheap, cut-glass pendant hanging from her throat. She was smoothing back a strand of her hair. She was saying, "I've probably flooded it now."

Bay caught the rope. He pulled the boat back to the dock. Then he tried for a while. Red-faced, sore-armed, panting, he said, "Forget it. Leave it here. We'll get someone from the lodge to come out and have a look at it tomorrow. I'll paddle you back."

"I don't want to be any trouble," said Kathleen.

"No trouble," said Bay.

"Is it far?" asked Sarah.

"A fair ways," said Bay. "But the wind's dropped. I won't be too long."

And there was actually a snapshot of the two of them. Kathleen waving. Bay raising his paddle, as if in salute.

It would later seem remarkable to Sarah that she had not noticed that everything had changed. And perhaps, if she had known what to look for, she would have seen: a slick of oil, the cheap gleam of a noisy speedboat, a reckless waste, a squandering, a lie—an ordinary, predictable imperfection that would, eventually, make that summer far less extraordinary than, for those few weeks, she had imagined it was.

But she didn't see it, somehow. Somehow, even after that, everything seemed as before. Sarah, to her very great surprise, had fallen in love with the place by their third day; almost at once she understood the rhythms and the importance of the cottage, the island, the Inlet, the great wildness of the Waubano Reaches. She loved being there—with her young son, with her slightly distracted but nonetheless present husband—and she watched intently as the time unfolded. They were at Larkins', for their holiday, and the wide, blue days were passing. The summer was passing in the Inlet as it always did, or so she imagined. The light fringe of green around the shoreline grew taller and darker and more abundant. The blackflies gave way to mosquitoes, which, in turn, gave way to the cool, clear August nights. By the end of July the water grew warmer. For a few hot and cloudless days that they would never forget, Caz was never out of the water. The wild irises wilted in the midsummer heat. The cardinal flowers bloomed in the chill, mist-drifting mornings. The dragonflies were everywhere, and then, before the monarchs appeared, the dragonflies were gone. The old cottages were open wide, the boats were tied at the dock. Throughout the Inlet, the splashing children were told in the warm, calm, echoing evenings: please, not quite so loud, please. Then, too soon, the season turned. Then, too soon, the weather shifted. The wind changed. The water cooled. Too soon, the boats were lugged back to their cradles. The Javex buoys and swim rafts were pulled up. The shutters banged back into their winter places. The taxi boat was called. The bags were heaved. The summer places went quiet. Animals came closer.

"I didn't have an inkling," Bay said to Caz. "Honestly. Not an inkling."

It was Sarah who realized the truth about Caz's ability to get people's voices. It was Sarah who first guessed that this talent was something more than just a knack for imitation, more than just an uncanny ear for mimicry. She was the one who worried. Who fretted. Who drove him constantly—to psychological tests, to special tutors, to the guitar lessons, at which he was hopeless.

Initially, Bay thought she was being silly. He thought the reading would come. He was sure the spelling would come. He felt confident that the jumble of confused tenses and unfinished thoughts and overlapping events that resulted whenever a teacher asked the boy to put words—his own words—on a page would subside, diminish, disappear. Bay wasn't worried. After all, Caz was his son.

When Caz was very young, he was a great and relentless storyteller. He was a blond, pale child who looked as if light would pass through him. He had a taut, unstoppable voice. He'd arrive on Sunday evenings from his father's. His father had no idea, really, what to do with a young boy, and so Caz would arrive back with two days of Nintendo and comic books and video rentals under his belt. And he'd begin acting out the parts of the movies he had watched, the comic books he'd looked at, the cartoons he'd seen.

"Uh, Captain. We've picked up something in Vector Eight. You better have a look. At its current speed it will intersect with the starship just outside the range of the force field."

He could hardly sit still. He was wide-eyed with excitement. When he told his stories, he was full of the exploits of heroes and superheroes.

"Reckless disregard for galactic protocol is not the kind of thing we normally reward, Ensign."

"But sir . . ."

"There are no buts in this convoy, flyboy. One more infraction like that, and you'll be pumping tanks at the most distant refuelling station in the solar system."

And it was in her car, in the vinyl- and apple-core-scented warmth of her interior, on their way to his guitar lessons, on their way to his tutor, on their way to his dad's, that Sarah gradually realized. Unlike Bay and his eternally faraway uh-huhs, she tended to listen, and she noticed that Caz never, ever told a story in his own voice. He never simply told her what happened—in a film, in a comic book, on television. He acted out the parts, just as he acted them out when he sat in his bedroom at his mother's, his bedroom at his father's, and played on the blank of the carpet with the army of his *Superman* figurines, his *Star Wars* figurines, his *Spiderman* figurines, his *Terminator* figurines.

"No, no, please."

"You're dead meat, Spidey old boy."

"Not so fast, Exacto."

There had been signs. "A reluctant reader," his report cards often said. "Caz has difficulty formulating his thoughts and expressing himself clearly." But it was Sarah who, one day, stepped out of the car in front of her house, and said, with unusual severity, "Caz, come with me. There's something I want to see." He was nine.

She sat him down at the dining-room table. She put a piece of paper in front of him, and she gave him a pencil.

She said, "Tell me about the movie you were just talking about. But in your own words. Don't use the voices of the characters to tell the story."

He fidgeted. He complained. He cried. But she was insistent. And as she feared, what came out in the cramped, irregular letters of his handwriting, in his confusion of time and place, in his god-awful spelling, and in his constant inability to find where stories began and where they ended, was the barest language possible. His voice scarcely existed.

"Then Batman jumped."

"Then Spiderman swung."

"Then Luke swerved."

They were stories without descriptive detail of any sort. They took place in a void, like a game played with figurines on an empty expanse of broadloom.

Then the police called. Three years later, when Caz was twelve, Bay took him up north for the canoe trip, and on that Labour Day weekend, the police called Sarah. She had actually taken the receiver from her ear, held it in front of her face, and stared at it—as if a stern, realistic expression would get it to say something different.

She drove north, against the southbound traffic. She met with police; she filled out forms; she stood in the basement of a small hospital on the outskirts of a town with a name she couldn't remember and, staring down at the empty face, she said that yes, this was her ex-husband, felt her imagination falter—simple as it was, it was still impossible to comprehend; she made the arrangements; she went to pick Caz up. He had paddled, alone, back to a cottage he and his father had passed. The police had been called. He had been taken back to Walt's Cabins and Fishing and Sundries. His toe had been seen to; he had sat with his mother in the waiting room of a clinic for almost an hour. And by then she was too tired to drive back to the city. They spent the night at Walt's. They hugged, and cried, but they hardly spoke. He would always remember the little, paper-wrapped wafers of soap on the glass shelf above the sink in the cabin they took; the rattle of the too-light, ill-fitting drawers; the smell of Pinesol. He remembered waking beneath the shadowy rafters, turning under the thin blankets, and finding that he had been crying in his sleep.

They returned to the city the next day. They had always talked in the car. She thought: This is his chance to tell me.

Caz said, "Things were going OK. Then on the third day we came to the mouth of the river. . . ."

She asked, "What did it look like?"

It seemed a difficult question.

"Where you were. With your father. Past the island. What did it look like?"

She glanced toward her son.

"It was just pretty. Like a postcard or a jigsaw puzzle or something."

He seemed to live in a world without adjectives.

"Come on," she said.

It was like the story she had made him write three years before.

Sky, blue. Day, hot. Water, calm. Trees, green. Rocks, grey. "Then we turned."

"Then we paddled."

"Then we dumped."

She focused on the traffic as he spoke. There is a point, not quite a quarter of the way back to the city, where the secondary road meets the highway. A souvenir trading post, restaurant, gas station, and fireworks store sits at the convergence: vinyl teepee, split-rail fence, wagon wheels, and a parking lot marked off by white-painted rocks.

Here, the southbound traffic begins to take on a rushing urban density. It thins out eventually, before building up again a couple of hours later on the hot, shadeless outskirts of the city. By then—by the time the highway widens through the industrial parks, the billboards, the approaches to the airport, the overpasses and the off-ramps, the ragtag curtained high-rises—drivers are usually prepared for the city. They are tense and attentive.

But to the north, at the point where the roads converge at the Key to the North Highway Gas Bar, things sometimes come too soon, and too suddenly. The roads still cut through ridges of granite. There are still pine trees and little lakes like mirrors. Not everyone has left summer behind. Not everyone is prepared. And here, always, at the end of every long weekend of every summer, the worst traffic accidents occur. Of course, it's the last thing anyone expects: crumpled hood, spray of glass, life jackets and fishing rods and paddles and plastic sand toys strewn across the pavement; headlines on a Tuesday morning, on the bottom of page six: Holiday Ends in Tragedy.

They drove south. Sarah was listening. He told her, "Then I saw a dark kind of shape through the water. He said something just told him where I was. Then he just scooped me out."

Caz's voice, that summer, was still high and childlike. There were, here and there, little off-key wobbles that marked what turned out to be the beginnings of its change. It was the last year he would feel free to slip back into words that had been with him almost since he had learned to talk. Ascared. Stucken. Drownded.

Sarah paid careful attention to the road.

There was a truck loaded with timber.

There was a van with a green canoe on the roof.

There was a motorcycle she almost didn't see when she pulled into the passing lane.

There was a sign that said: Toronto: 308.

She had asked, "What did the two of you talk about for three days?"

To which, Caz replied: "Nothing much."

But many years later, long after everything had changed, when, on occasion, Caz got his father's voice, when it came to him sadly in a half-forgotten turn of phrase, he could hear him. He could see him sitting in front of the campfire, and he could hear Bay saying that when he was eight, his parents bought a small trailer. It was called a Northbound Caravan—the word written in gliding chrome cursive to the right of the aluminium door. It had a little propane fridge, and a tiny, foldaway table. It could sleep two comfortably, three in a pinch. There was a fire extinguisher the size of a caulking tube on the wall. There was a window with dollhouse-like curtains. There was a tiny, framed picture of the wooded shore of a lake. It looked like a jigsaw puzzle. It had a title, printed beneath it: Wilderness Splendour. You almost never see trailers so small any more.

There was an irony to the trailer, even then. It was the same good-natured irony that had originally attached itself to the modest suburban bungalow home of Bay's parents. These things—the house, the trailer, the suburb—were understood to be temporary, and they had a light-hearted, modern optimism to them.

The trailer was a confident investment. Its purpose was to go up north for a summer or two, to spend some time looking for the right piece of land, on the right point, on the right lake. And then, with a little money in the bank, they would buy. And then, after camping in the trailer for maybe one more season, they would build.

The trailer might be used for tools for a while. Or for storing gas tanks and paddles during the winter. But eventually a boathouse would be built, and a proper tool shed. And over the years, the trailer would be left to fall apart—visited by raccoons and the occasional bear, disappearing into the thick, mosquito-infested sumach and wild raspberry.

But the trailer Bay's parents bought never left their yard. Somehow things never worked out; that was all. The irony of their house, their trailer, their suburb slipped away. The trailer sat on blocks, for years, just past the white concrete squares of the patio, past the rusted barbecue, across the parched lawn.

Bay's father went from student actuary, to associate actuary, to "actuary A.S.A." at Guaranty Life. But, somehow, for all that, Sandy Newling never advanced through the firm as he hoped he would. He was not, as Bay came to learn, as pressed for money as he maintained. He was a cautious spender. He never became an officer of the company. And he stayed in the same cubicle, in the same department, for years.

During the summer holidays, Bay sometimes ate his breakfast in the trailer. This is what he remembered. He woke early, before it got too hot. Because when it got too hot those summers, all he could do was lie splayed on the stubble of hard, parched lawn. He would listen to the swish of the aluminium door as his father went in and out. He could hear the sprinklers, the rise and fall of cicadas.

But early in the morning he went into the kitchen. He got out the Cheerios. He poured out the milk. He was still in his pyjamas. He carried the bowl and his spoon across the backyard to the trailer. He was by himself. The dew felt pleasant under his bare feet.

He ate at the little Arborite table. The unused fridge, its door propped open, gave off a faint, queer smell. He liked looking through the little window, at the dark shadows of the maples on the lawn. It was still cool in the trailer in the mornings, but he could feel the heat of the sun building on the aluminium.

"I loved how cold the milk was," he said to Caz.

That was all. He loved how cold the milk was. It made him feel he wasn't in a humid, barren suburb. He was trembling when he said it. "My summers," he said. Caz was afraid he was going to cry.

How cold the milk was.

"But what did you do?" Sarah asked. She was looking directly ahead, through the windshield, down the highway.

"We had dinner.

"We kept the fire going.

"There were lots of falling stars.

"We laughed a lot. We sat up and talked. He told me about stuff."

"Stuff?"

"A friend he used to have. Weird stories he used to make up. Stuff about summer. He talked a little about the Beatles."

There was a transport truck. There was a sports car with the top down and two teenage girls with their hair flying around their baseball caps. There was a sign that said: Fresh Blueberries. Sweet Corn. There was a pickup with an old washer and dryer roped into the back.

There was a station wagon: two children were waving from the back seat.

The children looked like twins, a boy and a girl. The station wagon was piled to the roof with paddles and beach toys and camping gear. Caz wriggled his fingers at them. They laughed, and prodded each other with their elbows. They waved again.

Sarah drove south, toward the city. She drove the way she had when Caz was younger, when she was always taking him somewhere, returning him. She stared straight ahead, and listened, the way she always used to when he was younger, and he was beside her, acting out stories about Darth Vader, or about the X-Men, or about the terrible decision that Superman's parents had to make, before their planet was destroyed.

FOUR

THE LINE that marked Bay's waking that night must have been sharp and bright. He may have turned in his sleep when he arrived there. It must have been like a rip in the fabric of the darkness.

It would have been as thin as a blade. It would have been as quick as a sudden gasp of breath. For Bay would most probably have gasped. He would likely have opened his eyes in astonishment, closed them again tightly. Let's say he even shook his head in bewilderment, just before it split him, just before the warmth of his time slipped into the unordered cold, and he felt himself going—rising through the fall of dew, the shadow of pines, the refrain of stars.

It might have been like that. No one could ever really know, but it was a possibility. It must have been just before the first hint of dawn. Only a few hours before, Bay had been sitting in front of the campfire. It was getting very late by then, but neither father nor son felt much like sleeping.

The canoe trip had been an unlikely proposition to come from Bay. Despite his attention to the details of summer, canoe trips were not exactly Bay's thing. Nor were they exactly Caz's—if the boy's orange Fender Stratocaster T-shirt;

his brownish, greyish, knee-length surfer shorts; his lank blond hair; his Walkman, sockless Converse high-tops, and white skinny forearms were anything to go by.

There was, however, an old edition of *The Outdoorsman's Guide* on the dash of Bay's car. Bay drew it to Caz's attention when he picked him up to leave for the canoe trip. Caz was not much interested.

The *Guide* had been a remarkable publishing success. The 1964 copy Bay owned was its twelfth reprinting. Its original 1923 publication had coincided with a certain prosperity, with a joyous embrace of the simple pleasures of peace, with a grateful and appreciative quest for beauty and spiritual renewal, and with the heyday of the canoe in North America. This was the period when city folk referred to the northlands, without irony, as God's country. There were paddling and rowing clubs throughout Canada and the northeastern United States; the great canoe companies were flourishing; the northern woods and lakes of both countries were being explored by summer campers and cottagers. From the 1920s until the early 1960s, the *Guide* sold steadily. There was probably not a cottage in Ontario in those days that didn't have the distinctive dark blue cover and embossed bent pine tree on a bookshelf, beside *Wayside Ferns and Wildflowers*, *Field Guide to the Stars*, and the summer-tattered copies of mysteries by Dorothy Sayers and Agatha Christie.

Bay picked Caz up at Sarah's house and they headed east, through the oldest part of the city core—a neighbourhood of narrow, row-housed, tree-lined streets. They passed gables and porches and slate roofs.

This was early on the Thursday morning, before the Labour Day weekend. The sunlight caught the maples in rich, gold-green slants; the sidewalks and the intersections had the moist, semi-deserted calm that they often do in summer.

Then south through what Bay always called the valley of the shadow of hospitals and insurance companies—down University Avenue. It is like going through a gorge—steep walls of corporate fortunes and the grim, green-walled floors of the hospitals that are the inevitable end of actuarial prediction. They passed the head office of the company for which Bay's father had worked. They passed the hospital where Caz was born.

Caz, by way of Charles, which Sarah and Bay had settled on, but which once put to use sounded too princely and formal; by way of Charlie, which brought constantly to mind Chaplin and Good-Time; by way of Chaz, which Bay dug from his memories of *Boy's Own Annuals* and which Sarah said she rather liked. But which, it eventually transpired, their son could not pronounce. Caz was the best he could do. And so, Caz it was.

The back seat was piled with a tent, with sleeping bags, with backpacks, and Bay and Caz sailed down the wide and sterile, impatiens-planted, war-memorialized thoroughfare in silence. This was Toronto at its most empty, clean, and appalling. It always looked to Bay exactly like the cityscape of an urban planner's optimistically lifeless drawing.

West on the expressway—the elevated barrier of commuter traffic that in 1958 had forever cut the city off from its waterfront. Its construction was like an ill-considered and catastrophic extramarital fling. It didn't have to, necessarily, one couldn't have been sure that it would, but it did: ruin everything. Toronto was transformed by the expressway's pylons and re-bar and concrete guardrails and grit. Before its construction people could walk, or ride their bicycles, or catch a streetcar from their homes to the beaches and reedy swoops of Toronto's little bays. That was when the water was clean, or, at least, cleaner than it is now—which probably isn't saying much. People swam, rowed boats, took out skiffs. Once, the water would have been flecked with the canvas Chestnuts, the cedar-strip Peterboroughs, the lapwork Towns of the avid paddlers of the city's half-dozen canoe clubs.

"I was born," Bay said as he drove, "at a moment in history when the balance was shifting. The outboard came along, and by the time I was sent to camp, canoe companies were already going out of business. *The Outdoorsman's Guide* was no longer the success it once had been. When people said 'God's country' they were conscious, suddenly, that the term sounded antique and silly. It was like this bloody expressway—the balance had shifted, away from the important things and toward the things that were purely utilitarian. We were swerving off wildly, without correction, and do you know what, Caz? My guess is that we'll continue to do so. I think it's your generation that is going to pay."

This was the sort of thing Bay said when he was trying to be instructive. Naturally, Caz, watching the billboards flit by, was trying his best to ignore him.

Then, heading up the west side, around off-ramps, across express lanes, into the collectors. Past the service centres, and the appliance stores, and the warehouses. They were moving well, as the traffic reports on the radio informed them. They were, finally, heading north: up the highway to the secondary, to the long dirt road that led to Walt's Cabins and Fishing and Sundries. From there they would head out by rented canoe, past the camp, past the Inlet, on their way up past Moriah Island. On their way, on their third night out, to the campsite on the Skin River.

The scrappy little pile of wood that Bay had collected so hastily was still holding out: oak, mostly, hard and seasoned and dry—the preferred long-burning choice of *The Outdoorsman's Guide*, so Bay pointed out to Caz, who rolled his eyes at this triumphant little dig of camperly information. The fire was hot and steady; the bed of coals well established. But the flames were low and the light was subdued. It barely caught their wide-awake faces. Had anyone stood on the other shore and looked across the black water of the river mouth to the campsite, only two shadowy figures and the softest globe of flickering red would have been visible against the darkness.

The cognac and the Marlboros were holding out, too, and Bay, wondering what it was that made fathers so reticent about certain things with their sons, decided to tell Caz about the bedroom he'd had when he was Caz's age. "It caused," so he said as, stretching out his right leg, he realigned a stone of the fireplace with his foot, "my poor father some embarrassment."

It was in the basement of the house on Ardell Crescent. It was in a small, windowless alcove in the furnace room, where, prior to his settling in, his mother had hung several garment bags of the dresses Marj Bailey had worn during her size-eight glory years in Toronto before she married Sandy Newling and moved to Cathcart. She'd been a secretary at the frost-windowed, cigar-clouded office of Consolidated Mining Investments on Church Street, where—because of her dark hair and the wide sashes of hairbands that she wore—she was always called Snow White by her boss.

This pleased her immensely. She told Bay she rode streetcars to work. She ate mint ice cream and wafer cookies from pewter bowls in the Arcadian Court. Once she saw Myrna Loy leaving the Park Plaza Hotel.

That was Toronto for you. She used to say that at least in Toronto she could buy shoes that actually fit her high arches, her triple-A width. In Toronto at least there was some kind of reasonable selection. There were salesgirls who actually had some manners. Who knew something about fashion. Something about feet. Something about shoes. Which was more than she could say about some places she knew.

Originally, Bay's bedroom had been on the ground floor, in the same hallway as his parents'. It was next to the bathroom and across from what would eventually be transformed from storeroom to nursery and then, as it transpired, back to storeroom.

It was during his mother's difficult pregnancy—a period when she wandered the house, back killing her; when she parked herself in the kitchen with a movie magazine and a tin of the shortbread cookies she always asked Sandy to bring home; when her habit of keeping the hall and bathroom lights on all night was first established—that Bay began to ask if he could move to the basement.

This was an annoying, quixotic campaign. There was nothing that resembled a bedroom in the cellar of the New-lings' modest suburban home. This was perfectly obvious. But Bay was insistent, and his father, having been pestered once too often at the dinner table, finally folded back his newspaper with an impatient flap one March evening, and said, "All right. All right. I give up. Live in the basement for all I care."

It was Sandy Newling's expectation that his son would not like it. But Bay did. He liked it a lot. He cleared out the garment bags, and his mother, happy for the excuse, loaded up the station wagon with her youth. It was one of the last times Bay remembered her driving herself anywhere, and she took her load of dresses to the Salvation Army. She was seven months pregnant. There, at a counter in the Thrift Shop, with her stomach bulging, with her varicose veins straining, with her hair limp and thin, with her hands on the backs of her hips, she said goodbye to her full-pleated, flat-tummied past. Goodbye, Consolidated Mining. Goodbye, mint ice cream. And a little more than one month later, his mother and the new baby—a girl—were each in different hospitals.

The twelve-year gap between Bay's birth and that of his sister was the result, not of a late accident—as many of the Newlings' friends and fellow church-members believed—but of an early one. The demands that are made on young and aspiring actuaries during the first five or six years of their employment in a company as large and as established as Guaranty Life—fierce competition, years of difficult examinations, impossible workloads—result frequently in the judicious postponement of family life. As one might expect of someone with the prudence and foresight of an actuary, Sandy Newling had been studiously prophylactic in this regard; babies, he felt, would best come later—after he'd passed the last exam, when he had some time and they had some money, after his footing was secure on the corporate ladder. All his life, Sandy resisted spending money that might have another purpose, and the other purpose was always the long and potentially catastrophic expanse of the future that he eyed every day from his desk. Bay had come as a surprise.

Alexander Newling was Sandy to most people, although, in all ways, he was at odds with the easygoing nature that the name Sandy implies. He had a stiffness that seemed—the longer you knew him, the longer you looked at him—to make him too good-looking. He had a face that was so concise and inconsequentially handsome it seemed at times to disappear. He was trim and compact. Even as a boy, Bay could stare right at his father as if he wasn't there. He could stand in the door of the study. His father would not look up from the sheets of figures he often laboured over in the evenings, his straight-stemmed pipe jutting from his clenched teeth, his fingers expertly clattering the adding machine that sat in the pool of light thrown by the goose-necked reading lamp.

He would not look up because Sandy Newling was very good at not looking at people. He had a knack for it. He did this always, without ever appearing to be evasive. There was something about the jut of his jaw, the set of his smooth, perfectly parted black hair, the narrowing of his eyes that gave the impression that he was intent on something else not because he lacked candour, but because it so happened, at that particular moment, there was something more deserving of his keen attention.

This is what happened when he told Bay that there was going to be a baby. He was working in his study. He was smoking his pipe. He knew his son was standing at the door. It seemed a good time to mention it.

"When?" Bay had asked. He was astonished.

"Oh, late next spring," his father said calmly. He was confident and assured of the order of things. He then did look up, and gave his son a flicker of a smile. "Things will change around here come June." Then he turned his attention back to his sheets. "You'll see."

This was his father's most notable characteristic. He believed in numbers. Things added up. Bay, who had some difficulty with arithmetic in school, was always impressed with this. The wood his father cut on his work bench was precisely the length required. If he bought something at the hardware store, he did the tax in his head, and plunked down the precise change before the cash register rang it up. If he said things would change in June, then there was no doubt. Mysterious events unfolded in unmysterious patterns for Sandy.

Bay marvelled at his father's talent, for Bay never quite trusted things to add up to what they were supposed to add up to. He thought that the progression of a sequence was something of a miracle. Even in Sunday school, under the tutelage of Miss Rathnaby, he could never understand how the prophets knew that the whistling slingshot, the burning furnace, the circling lions of the Old Testament would lead to the miraculous conclusion of the New. By what complex route? By what convoluted grammar? By what intricate equation? He could never take for granted—the way, every Advent, Miss Rathnaby seemed to take for granted—that Isaiah was able to peer from the darkness of the present to an incandescent point in the future. The distant point when a child would be born. When a son would be given.

Still, twelve years between children was quite a gap. As a matter of fact, it was rather longer than Sandy Newling, A.S.A., had expected. Certainly, it was far longer than Marj had ever imagined it would be. But sometimes these things take time.

Sandy's exams had long been over. And at first they had intentionally delayed adding to their family—thinking that it might be prudent to wait; that the expected promotions would provide a little more stability to their lives. For Sandy was patient; Sandy was conservative. There were rumours in the office of a shift of executive personnel—a shift that would likely create an entire ascent of job openings above Sandy in the company. After all, he had done well in his actuarial exams. He took his work very seriously, brought it home with him often. He attended company seminars, the pockets of his short-sleeved white shirts lined with spare ballpoints, his narrow, murkily brown paisley ties clipped out of the way so that he could bend forward to take his notes without impediment; he read the company's monthly news bulletin, *A Matter of Policy*, from front to back, including "Laugh Insurance"—the page of jokes, the only jokes he told at the dinner table. As an employee, he was without blemish. As an evaluation actuary, he was particularly skilled in cash-flow testing and formulae of probability.

But the promotion did not come as expected and when further postponement began to seem unreasonable to Marj, the vagaries of procreation had come into play; they couldn't quite get the timing of things, for some reason. It didn't click, as it had with such accidental ease with Bay. Marj's doctor felt, at first, that this was nothing to worry about. But when it did eventually click—five years after Bay's birth, seven years after Bay's birth, nine year's after Bay's birth—there were miscarriages.

And this one was not an easy pregnancy, nor was it an easy time in the Newling household. Someone else—a younger man from one of the regional offices, Sandy had glumly announced to his pale, wide-eyed, and nauseated wife—had been given the position in liability management. This left things very unclear.

A tense unhappiness settled over everything—over the hi-fi at the picture window; the beige-broadloomed and pine-panelled hallways; the flaccid, unattended spider plant on the Arborite counter of the kitchen; the newly established baby-blanket-smelling nursery; the aluminium storm door and its curlicued letter N.

Then came the birth, premature and disastrous. Bay's mother and the baby didn't come home. That May, words flew around the house. They seemed all wrong to Bay. He felt like a cage of crows had been released indoors. The strange black nouns flapped madly around the Scandinavian living-room furniture, cawed over the vinyl-covered kitchen stools, scratched their talons into the pale veneer of the bed-side tables: *bleeding, placenta, uterine wall, oxygen deprivation, brain damage.*

The doctors were uncertain. These things were extremely difficult to predict. Bay's father, a precise and regimented man whose professional life was based on the mathematics of reliable prediction, found this unbearable. He was shattered by the random calamity. He was tortured by the kind of variable that he worked so hard to overcome every day, at his grey metal desk in his office cubicle, on his carefully lined spreadsheets.

The doctors said the next few months would be critical. Assuming no further complications. Anything could happen. But if they got through the summer they might be out of the woods.

This did nothing to help anyone. "It's the waiting," Bay heard his father say to a neighbour, and Bay began to fear that the unhappiness of it might not lift from the house. They might wait, anxiously, for ever. And, in this, so he told Caz, he was right.

The first time Bay saw his mother in the hospital bed, he actually didn't recognize her for a moment. She was white, and her hands, holding the little cups of watery orange juice and paper dispensers of pills, were shaky. She looked puffy and, at the same time, as if the air had been let out of her. Her broad, quick, slightly gummy smile had been unplugged.

Her hair was different—flat, unfluffed, shineless. Bay stood awkwardly on one side of her bed; his father stood awkwardly on the other.

Bay always knew which of the silences would lead to his father saying: "Well, Marj, I guess we should be on our way." When Bay leaned forward to kiss his mother goodbye, her breath was sour and her old smell—a faint, warm combination of perfume, Persian lamb, hairspray, peppermint, and lipstick—was gone. Bay remembered this, always, because he said it was a funny thing: the smell never came back.

Bay was not allowed in at the Children's Hospital. He waited on a pew-like wooden bench, in a marble-floored foyer outside the wide, swinging oak and brass doors of the main entrance. There was a gloomy, old-fashioned stained-glass panel there—a triptych: on the left, Abraham and Isaac and the ram caught in the bushes; to the right, the ascent of a winged, Cupid-like flock of innocents to the cloud-banked citadel of Heaven; in the centre, Jesus, suffering the ragged little children. Bay stared at this and, from his Sunday-school lessons with Miss Rathnaby at Greystone Church, was able, out of boredom, to decode the panel's narrative intentions: the past of the Old Testament to the left, the future of Judgement Day on the right—both bracketing the centred and eternal present of the haloed, sandalled, hem-clutched Saviour. These seemed, to Bay—sitting miserably in the whiffs of rubbing alcohol, the shuddering of the doors, the dreary light of the awful foyer—a depressing range of options.

He passed the time. He wondered idly, as he had always idly wondered at Sunday school, what Abraham and Isaac could have talked about on their way home.

Through the doors, he had only glimpses of the gurneyed, clattering hallways; the darkened, curtained-off chapel; the high, telephone-ringing, bright-lamped nursing stations. He waited, sometimes for as little as ten minutes, sometimes for as much as an hour. In the car, on their way back, he asked questions. His father told him, reluctantly, of the ward with the six cribs; of the solicitous attendants; of the reassuringly calm, maddeningly equivocal doctors.

It was during this period that Bay relaunched his campaign to move to the basement. His father seemed hardly to notice. Bay dragged a folding cot into the little space he had chosen. He found a small bedside table and a lamp that had to be connected by five extension cords to the nearest outlet. He put most of his clothes in an old steamer trunk of his father's. He hung his Sunday jacket, his grey flannels, his ironed white shirts, on the slightly wobbly rack that had previously held the garment bags. He lined up his shoes and slippers on the unpainted concrete floor.

"Dad," he called upstairs. "Dad."

He was eager for his father to see the secret cleverness of the little nook he had created. He had swept and dusted. He had hung his tartan bathrobe where it would be warmed by the furnace. The lamp cast a warm circle of light over the bedspread. The alarm clock ticked on the bedside table. His Hardy Boy books were arranged on the top of the trunk—an impractical and short-lived display since he had to move them every time he required a clean pair of socks or underwear.

It was a hideaway. It was as concealed as the blade of a jackknife. But as his father stood there—in his white, short-sleeved shirt, with his pipe in his hand—Bay felt the same plummeting disappointment he had felt when he had tried to cheer his parents up by playing a record that he wanted them to hear.

It had been given to him by a friend. It had a black and white cover, with four half-shadowed faces: John's curiously larger than the other three. Bay had slowly lowered the stylus of the living room hi-fi set to the third song on the first side: "All My Loving," his favourite. The song had a break— a pause between verse and chorus—that Bay thought fantastic. But when he played it, his parents sat stiffly on the edge of the sofa. They missed it completely.

Now, in the basement, Sandy Newling saw only the rough stone walls, the low ceiling and the overhead ducts. He took in only the absence of a window, the shabbiness of his old college trunk, and, three feet away from the side of his son's cot, the rumbling, huffing furnace. In all this, he saw, not his son's enthusiasm. He saw something his twelve-year-old son could never have guessed.

The typewritten notices were posted on the office bulletin board. The chairman was pleased to announce. Effective immediately. Three names. None of them Newling.

Sandy thought: We live in a house so small, my son lives in the furnace room.

His deflation was obvious. It settled so heavily that Bay, standing beside his neatly made bed, felt sure he had caused it.

His father said, "People will think we have a live-in chimney sweep." He turned to start back up the stairs, but then stopped. He looked back at his son, then looked beyond him as if noticing a leak in one of the furnace ducts. He said, "Oh, by the way, some news. We've decided that it would be best if you went to summer camp this year."

This was the first Bay had heard of it. Sandy had made some phone calls; it was late in the spring, and at first there had been no openings; then, as it happened, one of the camps called back. It was a place in the Waubano Reaches. The director was a man named John Tobias. Sandy thought he was a minister, an American, but wasn't sure. His voice on the phone was deep and rough and short of breath. There had been a cancellation.

"Just for this one summer," his father said to Bay. "We can't afford it exactly, but I think it will be for the best. Until we're out of the woods on this one."

Such were the circumstances that sent Bay Newling to camp. And they may well have been what charged his notion of summer with such poignancy—why, even as a boy, he was unable to disconnect the beauty of a northern summer from its brevity. Bay told Caz that he had never seen anything as beautiful as his first glimpse of the water, the rock, the pines, and the windy blue sky of the Waubano Reaches. But at the same time he had never felt anything that compared with the intensity of the sadness that had visited him when he woke in the middle of the night during his time away. He was homesick; he was in the most beautiful place he knew. Sadness and beauty. He had never, in his life, separated the two.

The camp was on an island, in the Reaches. It was, in those days, far away from everywhere.

For many years the Waubano Reaches had a fabled quality. There were people who thought it a romantic invention: a poetic fiction of the north. Its blustery water, wind-rowed skies, glacier-smoothed granite shores, and starkly galed pines were well known as a result of a few adventurous artists who travelled and painted there. But there were many people who assumed—since these tumultuous scenes looked quite unlike northern lakes anywhere else—that the artists were making the landscapes up.

Waubano Reaches storms, coming across the open, could be a little unnerving, if you were lucky, downright dangerous; if you weren't. The water was often too rough and too chilly for swimmers accustomed to more tranquil bathing. The maze of hidden shoals had a long tradition of ripping the bottoms out of the holidays of the few boaters who attempted passage up its shore without knowing precisely the routes of its secret channels.

The Reaches had raccoons and minks and black bears. Bass, pike, and muskellunge. Loons, ducks, and ospreys. Unlike the other, more populated and civilized summer lakes, it also had rattlesnakes. As much as the weather, the cold water, the barren rocks, it was the reputation of rattlers that discouraged many visitors. While much impressed with the paintings they saw of the landscape, people who didn't care for poisonous snakes and wild storms tended to keep it at that. They stayed away. And the Waubano Reaches stayed almost wilderness for the longest time. In fact, it wasn't until around the time that Bay arrived there that anything began to change.

Bay was not particularly welcomed by the other boys in his group—all of whom knew one another from summers before, all of whom would come for summers after. But neither did they bully him. They left him a little on his own, and on his own he fell in love with the blue wind and rock of the place. He loved the cool green depths of his plunges from the swimming dock. He loved the tall, bent pines. He loved the canoes. And he loved his teenaged counsellor, Peter Larkin.

He woke them up in their cabin in the morning. He took them swimming, took them jumping at High Rock, took them on their overnights. He played the guitar at campfires, and told ghost stories, and flirted with the prettiest of the sun-browned waitresses when she brought the yellow Mel-mac bowls of stew to the table in their dining hall. Lark, who had his moods. He taught them how to pitch a tent, make a fire, paddle a canoe. He sometimes took a canoe out, alone, in the wildest weather just to see if he could handle the storms, "just to see what it's like out there." He told Bay about paddling at night on canoe trips through the black maze of islands on the north shore of the Reaches and about arriving, just at sunrise, at the fiery, mist-rising mouth of the Skin River.

Bay remembered Peter Larkin all right, remembered him, as a matter of fact, vividly. All his life he could see him, naked, holding Bay's wrists, looking into his eyes and saying, "Don't move." Lark, who was bitten by a rattler then, on the back of his arm of all places, and who was sick in the infir-mary for the last three days of camp—the same three days, as it happened, that Bay missed when he had to go home early.

It happened on a rock beside some juniper, in the sun, at the canoe pond. The other boys were sailing. Bay did not enjoy sailing—the luffing sails and the swinging boom frightened him. The sailing instructor took the group, and Lark took Bay swimming for the afternoon. That was when they encountered the snake.

And that evening, after dinner, Bay was asked to go see Mr. Tobias, the camp director. Bay knew that Mr. Tobias was an old friend of the Larkin family's; he had a cottage in the Inlet that, now that he ran the camp, he used only at the very beginning and the very end of the summer season. He'd spent all the summers of his boyhood there, about fifty miles to the north of the camp. Bay expected the director to ask him about the rattler.

Tobias was, in some ways, an unlikely camp director. The camp had no fake Indian lore and few sappy camp songs, because he couldn't abide them. The camp had no competitions, no prizes, few campfire rituals—not even, as a matter of fact, a name. These did not seem important to Mr. Tobias. It was just called "the camp" because, as the director used to say, that's what it was. The year Bay was there, one counsellor—"a keener," he recalled—launched a campaign to have all the groups be given the names of different North American native tribes. Mr. Tobias had listened patiently; apparently such proposals came along every few years. And he said what he had always said. "I think, given most of your family backgrounds, that it would make more sense if we gave each group the name of a law firm, or a stockbrokerage, or a bank."

Bay remembered the director with great respect. Without any apparent bitterness, he blamed him for what became his own fearsome addiction to cigarettes. Mr. Tobias was a two-pack-a-day man, and, apparently, looked mighty good when he stood on a rocky point in the calm of a northern evening, striking a wooden Eddy match, bending his rough-hewn outdoorsman's head to his cupped hands, and sucking in the first deep drag of his zillionth unfiltered Black Cat.

Bay took the wooden matches and the lack of a filter to be "woodsy," a word the director liked to use—although the application to tobacco was entirely Bay's. His father had smoked a pipe, and his mother had gone through the better part of a carton of DuMauriers every week. But somehow, it was not until he was away from his parents, at camp, that he ever thought of smoking, himself.

There was hardly a counsellor on the island who didn't—either cigarettes or a pipe. This had something to do with the times: the most dire warning about smoking that Bay ever heard in those days was that it might interfere with a career as a long-distance runner.

Mr. Tobias wore faded, open-necked army shirts, baggy grey flannels, heavy wool socks, moccasins, a windbreaker. He had a mournful, deeply wrinkled face, and a voice like rumbling thunder. And—as it was variously put by boys in their infrequent and uninformative letters home—he smoked like a chimney, like a fiend, like a furnace, like a five-alarm fire.

Often, after supper, Bay saw him, standing on the point outside his cabin, the smoke of a cigarette curling up into the still air. The director was looking across the water. He was listening to the fall of the evening, watching the shifts in the dusk. It was understood—without the director ever saying so—that what the boys at the camp were expected to learn from him was how to pay attention to what he was paying attention to. He didn't care, particularly, if his campers became white-water experts and regatta champions. In an odd way—odd for the director of a camp—he seemed to regard such achievements as silly. He bore an intense dislike for the word "activity." It was the broader context—the Reaches and places like it—that was important. The only statement that appeared to be a camp motto had been painted by the director on one of the rafters in the dining room. To most boys it was inexplicable. "Summer is the stillness between things."

Mr. Tobias smoked so incessantly that, when he spoke, his words fell slowly from his lips in the thin, punctuated clouds of whatever nicotine and tar had not been absorbed into his lungs. This was so permanent a feature of his speech that it seemed at times as if he was producing the smoke

inside himself, and Bay had often peered at him closely—
watching his smoky words emerge long after the director
had drawn on his cigarette—to see if the supply would ever
run out. So far as Bay could see, it never did.

The most striking occurrences of this phenomenon were
at the rare and irregularly scheduled outdoor chapel services.
Mr. Tobias was a Presbyterian minister; somewhere in Pitts-
burgh, there was, apparently, a congregation he left in mid-
June, returned to in mid-September, and that knew him in
a context which had nothing to do with an old family cottage in the Inlet, or with the cabins and canoes and campfires
of the boys' camp that he ran. At Knox Presbyterian, he was
the Reverend John Tobias. But at the camp, he was either
Mr. Tobias or "the director," and at camp it was actually difficult to discern where, beyond his love for the natural
world, his religious beliefs lay. There were no rituals to the
camp's chapel services—no set order of worship, no camp
prayer or hymn or blessing, no apparent denomination. The
services frequently made no mention of God, and, as a result
of this rather broad definition of spirituality, they were always unpredictable. In fact, the only rules of the chapel services were that they were held after dinner; that they took
place on the same point of rock where the waitresses sunbathed in the afternoons; that they were exceedingly brief;
and that nobody—not even the director—was allowed to
smoke.

This injunction did nothing to diminish the visibility of
the director's deep, kiln-dried, tobacco-rumbled voice. He
waited until the boys were assembled on the rock before he
emerged from the dining hall. He stopped at the railing of
the veranda and took one last drag on a Black Cat. His eyes
and cheeks and throat seemed at these moments to be joined

together at the end of a chain that was yanked hard and tight
by something down inside him. His face collapsed around
the intake of his lips. He butted what little was left of the cigarette out in the tin ashtray he kept perched on the veranda
rail for this particular purpose, and then stepped down the
steps, over the wobbly pipe of the water-line that the boys
were never supposed to stand on while they were milling
around the wooden bell tower, outside the dining hall, before a meal—but always did. The director passed between
the junipers, heading stiffly toward the point.

Bay would remember one chapel service in particular.
Mr. Tobias stood directly in front of where Bay was sitting
on a lip of rock.

"Not all that long ago," the director began, "we used to
have scavenger hunts here. Groups were sent out with a list of
things to find. A leopard frog, a painted turtle, a milk snake."

Bay watched the sad, sagging face the deepening birth-
mark in the cavern at the base of his throat the veiled, grey
tumult of words.

"Every group always got their list. Then, it started to get
more difficult. And then, three years ago, we had to stop the
scavenger hunts. No one could find a leopard frog, a painted
turtle, a milk snake."

The director gulped some air. "So I'd like you to sit and
think about what 'nothing' means. I want you to try. To try to
think of what happens when something that once was ceases
to be. Extinction. When something is gone. For eternity."

That was all. Mr. Tobias stood perfectly still. He folded
his hands together and bowed his head.

It was after a minute, perhaps two, that Bay noticed one
of the legs of the director's shellac-stained grey flannels beginning to jitter. The jittering increased as another minute

passed in this strange, extended silence—silence, mostly, although, from within one of the clusters of younger boys there came, once, a squeaked fart and then a few giggles. The director ignored them.

Finally, he cleared his throat. He said, "For ever and ever, amen"—and even then, long after his silence had begun, Bay was certain that his words came out wrapped in the faintest grumbled bursts of their own pale gauze of smoke.

There were rules, of course, about who could smoke and who could not at the camp. In general, the staff could, and the boys couldn't—but these rules were loosely enforced; it was hard to imagine anyone except the very youngest campers being reprimanded very severely for smoking when the director was sucking down almost two packs a day and when every counsellor had a pipe in his buttoned breast pocket or a Lucky Strike or a Pall Mall tucked behind his ear.

Most of the waitresses smoked as well, and part of the abiding pleasure Bay would gather around the act of smoking a cigarette was the memory of the rock where they sunbathed: their lissome, cocoa-buttered limbs, their flattened wet sheens of hair—and the perfect white poise of Craven Menthols.

But what rules there were about smoking disappeared altogether on canoe trips, once canoes were out of sight of the camp island. And it was on his group's first overnight— the occasion, as it happened, that Bay picked up the nickname "Baby"—that Bay first tried a cigarette.

He was sitting alone on the shore. The rest of the boys were still in the water, splashing and shouting. They'd been in for hours.

Already the split between Bay and the other boys in the group had become apparent. It was not a big problem; there were no fights, there was no bullying, really. He just kept to himself, mostly out of shyness, and mostly they ignored him.

Lark's clothes and his hunting knife and his watch and his smokes and his matches were on a rock, in a pile beside where Bay was sitting.

Bay picked the cigarettes up idly, out of little more than boredom.

It was the whiteness of the papers that first impressed him. In the sunlight, in the bright heat of the day, the thin, perfect cylinders, offset by the elegantly folded, illusionary solidity of foil, were pristine and unblemished—white, like breaking surf, brilliant against the sandy brown of the filter.

He drew a cigarette out. He half expected the whole fragile construction to crumble, but there it was: still whole, still perfectly formed, between his thumb and forefinger.

There was something pleasing in the way a single, chosen cigarette slid so neatly from the regimen of double rows. The narrow gap it left in the opened half deck had its own appeal. It spoke of a kind of forbearance, a maturity, a measured pace of appetite. Bay liked the fact that this pleasure was undertaken sparingly, that even the heaviest smoker didn't reach into a pack and grab a handful. There was an adult-like restraint in the specific pinch of thumb and finger.

He ran the length of the cigarette under his nose, from the speckled-tan brown of the filter, over the two, fine, vaguely military-looking gold bands, to the packed, precisely circumscribed open end. He breathed in deeply.

It seemed to him a wonderful smell—something like autumn colours, something like sun-warmed pine needles, something like high dried grass. The smell had a bitter, serious quality—a similar aroma to the one near the coffee grinder in the otherwise odourless, gleaming aisles of the supermarket where his mother sometimes took him when she had to do the shopping. He imagined that there was earth as brown and rich and promising as the packed furls of tobacco.

"Can I have a smoke?" Bay called.

"It'll stunt your growth." Lark was standing, waist deep, on a ledge of rock just off the shore.

"Ah. Come on."

In those days, the boxes of Eddy wooden matches had "Facts about Canada" printed on their backs. "Did You Know: That a Loon can stay underwater for more than three minutes; that the granite of the Canadian Shield was formed 2 billion years ago; that a White Pine can reach a height over 200 feet; that there are more than 250,000 lakes in Ontario?" Whenever Bay picked up a box of matches, he read these. Unlike the fronts of these matchboxes—which had a solid, old-fashioned look—the backs were not designed very well. They seemed an afterthought. Bay was faintly troubled by the amount of unexplained emptiness that surrounded the undersized, ill-chosen print of "Facts about Canada."

He read: "Did You Know: That the Fox Snake can imitate a rattler by vibrating its tail in dry leaves?" As a matter of fact, Bay did know. Mr. Tobias, the director had told them. "They are majestic but harmless. Pretending to be a rattler is their only defence," he said.

Bay scratched the head of the match across one of the two pale sidestrips of grit.

He liked wooden matches. He liked the imprecision of their squared shafts, the uneven sizes of their red bulbs and white centred heads. They had an unfussy dependability. Wooden matches, as the matchbox claimed, could be struck anywhere—on the brown iron frames of camp cots, on rocks, on zippers, and, with practice, using only one hand, on a thumbnail. They made having a smoke seem like a useful, perhaps even necessary thing to do. They became part of the only souvenir he kept of camp. All his life, Bay insisted on buying American cigarettes and went so far as only to have a cigarette if he could light it with the satisfying scratch and wreathing flare of a wooden match.

The tiny explosion of the match's sulphur diminished in front of the amateurish-looking thrust of the cigarette, pursed in the very middle of Bay's puckered lips. He moved the steady yellow flame closer and, in the hot stillness of that afternoon, took a certain delight in seeing the cigarette paper curl brown before its end actually touched the fire. Bay sucked in deeply.

He coughed for half an hour, and felt sick for the rest of the day. That night—still feeling queasy—he was chosen, along with one other camper, to sleep in their counsellor's tent.

He remembered the strange proximity of bodies. And he remembered that, for the longest time, he could not sleep; that the night had grown colder. His sleeping bag (so it felt to him, wide-eyed, nervous about rustlings in juniper, hoots in woods) grew thinner. And finally, as he turned into what became slowly the folds of sleep, the night had passed.

And ended abruptly. When Bay opened his eyes to the green light of morning sun through canvas, he saw the other camper—blond brush cut, sunburnt nose (Derek: he would always remember the name) staring at him, grinning. Lark was still asleep, and Bay, in the night, had turned into the warmth of his counsellor's side. He was curled there, one arm over Lark's sleeping-bagged shape. "Cuddled" was the word Derek used when he told the other boys.

"Baby," they said. "Way to go, Baby."

Bay wrote one postcard home that summer. The picture showed a few white sails against blue water, and a red canoe. His note said: "Dear Mom and Dad: I am having lots of fun. I forgot my camera when we left. We went on an overnight last week. My counsellor's name is Peter Larkin but we call him Lark. I have a nickname, too. All the guys call me Woodsy. Love, Bay."

"Woodsy" was a word the director used. It implied, at its essence, an enthusiasm for canoes and a disdain for all other forms of water transportation. The term was broadened at the camp to include anything that accorded with the direct, uncomplicated, economic, and silent passage of a gracefully paddled sixteen-foot wood-and-canvas Chestnut canoe. The camp was very big on Chestnut canoes. It had dozens of them.

A canoe gave no sign of itself on the water—no rainbow pool of oil; no loon-chasing drone; no gush of grey bilge— and so it was woodsy to conduct oneself the same way: to leave a campsite without a trace of visitation. No flags of bumwad, no squats of shit, no tin cans in the junipers, no half-burned boxes of Kraft Dinner in the ashes of a campfire.

Canoeists were obliged to hold the balance of things—in their angled stroke, in their unwavering course, in the way they moved through the landscape. To do this, canoeists were obliged to pay attention to things: shifts of wind, alterations of current, hints of advancing new weather. And so it was woodsy to be attentive: to the poise of Jupiter, to the pendant arc of a morning moon, to the meaning of August crickets, to the dew on an overturned canvas hull, to the sprays of purple and red and yellow wildflowers that grew from the cracks in the granite shoreline, to the snow-like dusting of spiderwebs that could be seen on the pines and cedars only when the sun was just rising, and the early mist retreating like a train of silk

across the calm, slate-grey water. This was the great beauty
of the canoe: like keeping a box score in a baseball game, it
was impossible to paddle one without paying attention to
important things: the water, the rocks, the trees, the sky.

Clothes, too, were either woodsy or not. Only a certain
kind of clothing suited the canoe: loose-fitting, dun-coloured,
unfancy. Canoes were not fashionable. They were perfect.
They were always the same. They required no annual mod-
ification of style. And so, new clothes were out.

Bay knew nothing of this before he arrived for his one
summer at the camp. Pudgy in his brightly striped T-shirts;
his perma-creased Bermuda shorts; his spotlessly white, plastic-
peaked, anchor-crested captain's hat; his thin cream socks and
his brand-new, navy blue, white-soled runners; he looked
like the newcomer he was. Immediately, he admired and
deeply envied the boys who were returning to the camp for
their second, third, fourth year, and who had scoured army
surplus stores for their camp attire: army shirts, baggy shorts,
heavy grey socks, red neckerchiefs, floppy khaki sunhats,
moccasins or, more dashing still, constantly unlaced mukluks.

The word, "environmentalism" was not yet in popular
use when Bay was a boy at camp. Rachel Carson's *Silent
Spring* had only just been published, two years before. The
director had a copy. As it happened, it had been given to him
by Lark's mother, Felicity Larkin (who had read and clipped
the excerpts in *The New Yorker* and who had mailed copies to
all her fellow cottagers in their Inlet). The book sat in the
director's screened porch, just outside his office, where he
occasionally met with boys, after dinner, to talk in grumbly,
deep-drawn and visible syllables of cigarette smoke about
important things: how to make porridge over a fire; how to
patch a tear in a canvas hull using pine gum and a piece of a

shirt; how to read white water. During these talks the director often referred to *The Outdoorsman's Guide*.

When Bay was asked to report to the director after dinner, Mr. Tobias was standing on the rocky point where he often stood. The director was smoking, as always. And he was staring at something he had never seen near the camp before: at the bottom of the bay, white against the dark forest of the far shore, was an anchored cruiser.

When he saw it he never doubted what this vision meant. This was the thing that amazed Bay about prophets: even more than the seeing into the future, there was the business of actually believing in what was seen. On that calm evening, from that placid and unblemished vantage point, a future of polluted water and fast, noisy boats seemed an unlikely prediction. But that, somehow, was what Mr. Tobias saw.

He felt that some long-held rhythm was changing. He felt on the brink of something new—something he didn't like. He understood that summers would soon cease to be like the summers he could remember. He considered the distant cruiser. Moulded fibreglass deck. Fat waddling stern. He could read the name: *Robber Baron*. He sucked down almost a quarter of a cigarette on a single haul.

He was a man of patterns. That was why he understood the weather. That was why he could predict things.

The summer before, and the summer before that, he had heard the distant rumbles. "What is it, sir?" the boys had asked. "An H-bomb?"

"Blasting," he had said. "New roads. From the highway."

He turned when he heard Bay approaching. His voice was a low, gentle rumble. He put a broad, nicotine-smelling hand on Bay's shoulder. "I have bad news," he said. "About your sister."

Bay listened. He nodded. "Yes," he said after a while, he was all right. Bay gulped back a thickness in his throat. Yes, he would pack. Yes, he would be ready, on the dock, after breakfast the next day.

And it was not until the next morning, when he was on the transport boat, looking back over the widening wake, watching the camp grow more distant, that he realized he had not gone to the infirmary to say goodbye to Lark.

In Toronto, when Bay climbed down from the bus, he saw his father at once. Sandy Newling was standing apart from the little cluster of people at the Toronto bus terminal. He looked like a cut-out. Bay, who had a paddle, who had a fishing rod, could not remember whether he and his father were supposed to hug or shake hands.

They walked together over pavement, over rising, bright heat, to the parking lot. The gleam of all that hot metal amazed Bay after only a month away. He felt he had been in a different world: hush of trees, of lake, of lichen-mapped rock.

His father said that it was a blessing really. He said the little funeral had been a perfunctory, official affair.

They said little else. When they were on the highway, on the way to Cathcart, all Bay could think to ask was whether his mother would be going to church on Sunday. This seemed important. It would make things feel normal.

Bay was playing with the button of the glove compartment with the toe of his running shoe as his father drove. He was telling his father about camp. About his counsellor. About learning to paddle a canoe. "Stop it, Bay," his father said. "With the foot."

Cathcart was an hour from Toronto. Bay watched telephone poles go by: slowly approaching through the windshield. Slowly, slowly. Then, flit, they were gone. Like cartoon

characters, vamoosing. One by one by one. Until the highway ended, and Cathcart was around them, and they were
home, and Bay, having been ushered nervously to his mother's
bedside, having hugged her and said he was sorry—because,
he guessed, that was expected of him—was back, at last, in
his little basement room.

Even without his father's approval, Bay loved his basement. He particularly loved the darkness of it. Upstairs, at
night, the hallways were lit. The open bathroom was always
bright in case of his mother's frequent nocturnal emergen-
cies. But once Bay moved to the basement, he said his good
night, and descended slowly into darkness.

Except for the periodic click of the thermostat and the
comforting ignition of the furnace, the basement was quiet.
It was also private. No one could approach on the creaking
stairs without being heard; no one wanted to come down
at night anyway—which suited Bay. He liked his strange
little corner in the cinder-block cellar. He coveted darkness
before he knew why.

It happened the Sunday night of the Labour Day weekend. The day had been far less eventful than he had feared.
His mother had gone with them to church. She had gone—
a little blankly, a little adrift—through the narthex, down the
side aisle, taking her place in the pew. It appeared that there
had never been any question of her not going. His father had
insisted. He had said, "Marj, we should get back on track."
She sat between Bay and his father as she always did: hands
clasped, hat perched.

Dr. James had just returned from his summer holiday.
He sported a red and flaking nose, and a slight darkening of
the liver spots on the backs of his hands where he customarily clamped them over the lip of the pulpit. Behind him, the

choir was assembled, black surplices fresh and ironed from their summer laundering. The soloist sang "Lead, Kindly Light." The sun fell through the stained glass, directly across her shining, vowel-rounded face, the sheen of her hair, the folds and the shadows of the folds of her black gown.

Nothing had changed. Bay told himself that nothing had changed. Bay noticed that his mother was repeating no responses, singing no hymns. But she was there. That was the main thing. He saw that her cuticles were bitten raw. Her fingers crawled over themselves.

He waited: through the Processional, through the Introit, through the first gospel, through the Offertory hymn, and through the psalms and responsive prayers. He waited, beside his mother, until the Sunday school was called forward.

There was always a momentary traffic jam between the baptismal font and the door beside the pulpit. There, a gaggle of demurely ribboned girls and a jostle of smirking boys passed beneath Dr. James's upheld palm. They passed beneath his deeply intoned, transparently unenthusiastic blessing of the children.

Bay could never remember exactly what happened during Sunday school that day. He often wondered whether David had spied Bathsheba from his roof. Or whether the two rotten friends of Joakim were watching Susanna bathe. Or whether helpful old Sarah had ushered Hagar into her drunk husband's tent.

Likely, nothing much happened. Nothing much ever did. Probably Miss Rathnaby, tremulous, fluttering, had excused herself. She was always excusing herself "for just a quiet moment please, boys."

Miss Rathnaby had mottled skin. She possessed gun-barrel grey hair that seemed not so much arranged as permanently

ingrown in a tight, crustaceous bun. She had a peculiar, dim
scent that Bay took to be toilet water because it was faintly
reminiscent of the septic smell of the bathroom after his
father shaved in the mornings and had his amazingly regular
bowel movements. And Miss Rathnaby had a problem. She
excused herself because she suffered from frequent and inexplicable nosebleeds.

Miss Rathnaby had a voice that somehow possessed all
the qualities of a strained upper-class English accent except
the accent itself. She read from her own zippered, leather-
cased bible. The class sat. The class fidgeted. Then, suddenly,
with Lazarus apparently down for the count, or with Legion
ranting among the tombs, or with the unconvinced disciples
contemplating five loaves, two fishes, and five thousand
empty stomachs, Miss Rathnaby would stand, assume the
posture of a circus performer spinning plates on the end of
her nose, and head for the door.

And so, in its way, that Sunday must have passed as the
last Sundays of Bay's summers always did, with church in the
bright, sunny morning and lawn-mowing in the afternoon—a combination of weather and activity that always
left Bay with a slight, empty headache by the enervating last
hurrahs of the weekend: Sunday dinner, Walt Disney, and
the Ed Sullivan show. Cunningly planned to make Monday
mornings look like a good idea by comparison, Sundays
always dripped thinly to their finish, as if the promising sweet-
ness of a Saturday had been steadily watered down until its
taste was gone altogether.

No one had to tell Bay to go to bed. By eight-thirty or
nine o'clock, with the house still redolent of the creamed
corn the Newlings had had with chicken for dinner, he just
gave up. He had told all his camp stories to his parents during

commercials—stories that seemed, somehow, to be less funny, less thrilling than they had been a few days before. His mother said little, and ate three helpings of ice-cream pie. Once it seemed as if she was almost crying, but since that was the moment that Bay's father became suddenly curious about camp—"Tell me, where were your cabinmates from?"—Bay was never exactly sure. Finally, his mother said she couldn't bear another minute of the television. She said she wanted an ice pack. It didn't seem too much to ask. Under the circumstances. Sandy. His father got up. His mother rested her head back and closed her eyes. And Bay went down to his place in the basement because it seemed that not in the entire universe was there anything else to do.

It would later seem remarkable to him that a shift of such importance could occur within his body without being immediately noticed. When had it actually, finally, occurred? Possibly in his father's car, with his toe on the button of the glove compartment. Possibly that Sunday afternoon, out between the Northbound Caravan trailer and the back hedge, pushing the irritating, clod-catching hand mower over the parched lawn. Possibly earlier in the day, with the wedding guests gathered, the water not yet turned to wine, and Miss Rathnaby standing in the Ladies, staring heavenward. He would never know.

That night, he read for a while. By then, Frank and Joe Hardy were beginning to pale a little as bedtime companions. But Fenton Hardy's remarkably companionable relationship with his sons continued to hold Bay's interest. He used to try to picture his own father looking up from his sheets of incomprehensible figures. He imagined Sandy Newling speaking in the collegial tone that the famous detective always used when he was about to entangle his boys in some great mystery.

He imagined his father—his direct gaze sparkling—suggesting, through the convivial smoke of his straight-stemmed pipe, that perhaps Bay could help him with a difficult and possibly dangerous actuarial problem he'd been working on.

Then Bay closed his book. He turned out the light, and lay for a time, enjoying the darkness. He could hear air-conditioners, like distant industry, humming away upstairs.

He closed his eyes. He remembered Peter Larkin holding his wrists, saying, "Don't move."

He had been seated on a spread towel, on the slope of smooth rock. He was startled by the sudden command. There was a dry, rapid sound behind him.

The sound was something like a cicada. Something like the release of an over-wound toy. Bay looked into Lark's widening stare.

A moment before, Lark, his underwear off, had crossed his arms in front of himself. He had pulled his T-shirt over his head. The shirt rolled up over the flat muscles of his stomach and the lean definition of his chest. As if a wrinkled layer of skin was being peeled away from his summer tan. He angled his shoulders and ducked into the coil of faded blue cotton. Then, pulling the shirt away with his left hand, he tossed it toward a juniper bush, behind the flat rock where the young boy was sitting.

The shirt seemed, briefly, suspended by the rising heat of sunshine and the smell of pine needles on stone. Then, as the shirt fell, Lark's attention seemed to be caught by something on the rock a couple of feet from the boy. Bay had seen it too, without comprehension. The movement he saw was a grey flicker, a sudden compacting. A shrinking.

It was the worst coincidence. The snake was just under the spread of the juniper. It was coiled at the edge of the shade.

"Don't move," Lark said. "Stay still."

And moving very slowly, Lark drew forward. He lowered himself to his knees. The gleam of his brown hair flew off into the blue sky and into the brightness on the water. His arms—slowly raised, slowly reaching forward—had the smell of heat and sweat on them. His veins were the veins of garnet in the rock. His face drew closer. He gripped the boy's wrists, tightly.

A rattlesnake can strike no farther than its own length, and Bay's backside was just within the range the coiled snake had established. The way he was seated—knees up, hands down, rump on the upward slope of rock—was such that no unassisted movement away from the snake would take place without first some slight movement toward it. Lark could see all that. He reached forward.

It was as if he were sliding a hand down the inside of a cage. He reached slowly around Bay's soft body. He moved as carefully as he could. Lark's arms drew round, and his skin filled the summer, and the boy slowly closed his eyes and turned his head.

Bay turned in his narrow cot. This was still months before the morning when his father, peering intently into the steamed-up bathroom mirror, carefully carving a path of Rapid Shave around the corner of his lips, told Bay: Of course not. They couldn't possibly afford to send him back for another summer at camp. That had always been clear. The one summer had been an exception. An anomaly. The circumstances were such.

And so, on that Sunday night, it was unclear to Bay, as he shifted from memory toward dream, whether he was recalling the summer that was just over, or looking forward to the ones that he still expected to come.

He may have been thinking about what it had felt like to arrive at the camp—standing uncertainly on the dock in a throng of unfamiliar boys, smelling the creosote and the sunshine on the wood, staring into a placid little bay where the grey rocks slipped into the calm water. The sunken logs looked like relics from an ancient civilization. The reflected green of the pine trees and the rippled openings of russet light made the rocky bottom appear the colour of verdigris.

He may have been thinking of the summer to come. He may have been thinking of seeing Lark again, of the canoe trip they would go on together, arriving at the campsite on the Skin River at dawn. Or perhaps, that night, in his little cot in the basement, he was thinking only of the deep, cool weightlessness of water.

He turned to his front. He expected to curl into sleep. He slid comfortably against the smooth, fitted bottom sheet.

The freezer hummed in the storage room at the bottom of the basement stairs. His father's slippers creaked slowly across the floorboards of the hall above.

Bay moved against the mattress. He imagined the darkness as folds, and as the shadows of folds. He imagined the dark drifting around him. He moved, then moved again. His eyes opened with some surprise. On the floor above, his father's steps suddenly quickened: "Marj? Marj? Just a minute, Marj." The anxious voice was muffled and far away. Then, slowly, Bay's eyes shut, and his hand closed on what he had never done before.

That his imagination was not intent on parted lips and unbuttoned blouses, but rather on images of innocence—summer camp, of all things—was not as strange as perhaps it seems. He was new to the strokes of this unimaginable ascent. He had not yet perceived the need to develop the cast—the beautiful movie stars, the sexy girdle models, the gorgeous strangers glimpsed on the street—who would later help him spin the brief and ludicrous scenarios of lonely adolescent desire. Bay didn't yet know he needed anything beyond the clutch and soaring of his own body. He was rushing too fast to think of anything. He was ahead of himself, or at least ahead of the connection he would soon make between verb and object. Irreversibly on his way, he had no idea where he was going. No amount of playground knowledge or cabin whispers can prepare a boy. He reaches into emptiness. He rises—through the fall of dew, the shadow of pines, the refrain of stars. And so Bay rose, forgetful of everything, unconcerned with returning, not coming so much as going—as lonely and ignorant of his resolution as someday he would be again.

FIVE

B AY TOLD CAZ that the moment when he recognized Elizabeth Larkin hadn't been like a premonition. It was more a sudden, surprisingly complete recapturing of something he thought he must once have known, but had long forgotten. As he spoke he was staring into the campfire, noticing how the scaled, charred branches had begun to look like the bones of ancient animals. He noticed how the soft grey ash under the cavern of coal and flame moved rapidly in the slight but violent eddies of heat. He was peering as intently into the fire as Nebuchadnezzar once had when the fourth figure had so mysteriously appeared, along with Shadrach, Meshach, and Abednego. Bay was reminded of the grainy films of nuclear test blasts he had seen as a child: the roofs torn off the model homes that had been constructed in the desert for this very purpose; the walls blown to smithereens in the furnace of the epicentre. He lit another Marlboro, tossed the match into the flames, and said that in the vestibule of the Caldicott and Son Funeral Home, having just been informed that they would have to wait another twenty minutes for the remains of their loved ones to cool, ". . . it just came to me. Absolutely out of the blue." Somehow, as soon as Mr.

Eugene Caldicott had said, "So. Miss Larkin. Mr. Newling. If you will excuse me. . . ." Bay had realized who she was.

"It's how hypnotists work when they're trying to solve a crime," he said. "We did a story on it once at the magazine. Dreadful piece of writing. But I gather that what they do is try to use memories as stepping stones. Sometimes very inconsequential memories: the shape of a mouth, the pronunciation of a certain word—the odd bits of things that you hold on to: an old Beatles song, for instance; a canoeing lesson at camp; a bowl of Cheerios. These kinds of ordinary things.

"They take one ordinary memory, and that memory leads to another, and to another, and so on, like a game of playground tag, until something quite vivid and complete has been constructed entirely out of what once appeared to be forgetfulness. Do you see what I mean?" Bay asked.

Caz turned his head on his knees. The firelight caught his clear, narrow features, his fall of straight blond hair. He said he thought he did.

Bay told Caz that he suddenly saw his counsellor's face in the face of his sister, Elizabeth Larkin: her horse-like but somehow handsome looks, her strong white teeth, her eyes. He heard Peter Larkin's voice in her swooping "God's teeth."

"It just came to me," he said: the memory of Lark talking to them about himself one night in the camp cabin—the kerosene lamp lit; the smell of the wooden match and mosquito repellent in the piney night air; the copy of *While the Clock Ticked* open on Lark's lap; the tuck of Bay's feet into the sand-gritty, flannel-lined bottom of his sleeping bag. The group had pestered their counsellor to tell them about himself; he had always been a little mysterious on this count. And so, flicking his brown hair away from his face, he closed the Hardy Boys book he'd intended to read to them, and said, all right. He told them that his father, an eye surgeon, had died of a heart attack when Lark was seven and his sister, Elizabeth, was ten. That Lark's mother had supported the family by teaching at a private school for girls in Toronto. That the camp director, John Tobias, had been a friend of his mother's since they were children, and that Tobias and the Larkins both owned old family cottages in a place called the Inlet, a day trip to the north of the camp, on the way to Moriah Island and the Skin River, on the north shore of the Waubano Reaches.

Bay told Caz, "The moment I heard her name—Miss Larkin—I looked at her across that coffee table, and I knew she was his sister. Had to be."

"How extraordinary," Elizabeth Larkin had said.

And so, for twenty more minutes, while the remains of Laird and of Felicity Larkin dropped steadily in temperature in Mr. Caldicott's refrigerator, Elizabeth Larkin and Bay Newling sat in the vestibule of the Caldicott and Son Funeral Home, and talked. And it was later that night—very much later—after Laird's memorial dinner at Nora's apartment. After the martinis, and the hors d'oeuvres, and the lamb, and the creamed spinach, and the wine, and the Stilton, and the Armagnac, and the cigars. After Laird's favourite records—Pollini, Jessye Norman, Casals—and after the outbreaks of tears, and of stories, of giddy jokes, and of slightly drunken speeches and toasts and eulogies, Bay was lying in a hot bath.

Sarah was in her slip, removing her earrings, leaning over the counter, in front of the bathroom mirror.

Bay was saying how odd it was to learn that someone he had always thought—for thirty years—"Thirty years," he said, "can you imagine?" Islanded by bubble-bath and steaming water, Bay looked ceilingward, contemplated his level of drunkenness, smacked the still-rich taste of the Monte Cristo in his mouth, and said again how odd it was to learn that someone he had always thought was some-where—growing older; getting married possibly, working at something; maybe having children; becoming, no doubt, less magical, more adult, less perfect, less beautiful, less re-markable as time went by—how very strange it was.

"But surely," said Sarah, "you must have known. You would have heard from someone."

"I don't know anyone from there. From that time. It was never my circle. And I suppose, after a while, when I never heard anything of him . . . I suppose I didn't want to know. All this time," Bay said. "It's weird. It's as if he hadn't."

"Died," Elizabeth Larkin had told him, rather bluntly. "Oh, yes. Years ago. Up at the Inlet." In the vestibule of the Caldicott and Son Funeral Home, Elizabeth Larkin told Bay that her brother had drowned at their cottage. "A canoeing accident. One night. There was a terrible September storm in 1964. Peter had come up to the cottage, after camp. He came up to the cottage to rest before school started. God knows what he thought he was doing out in that storm, in the middle of the night. The idiot."

In the bath, Bay contemplated his belly and his toes, emergent in the foam. Sarah was brushing her hair.

"Laird's dinner seemed to go pretty well," Bay said.

"Yes. Once you got there."

"What could I do?"

"Oh, I don't know. It sounded so silly. Waiting for the ashes to cool."

Quickly, a little too loudly, Bay spoke. "By the way. I may have found a place for us. A cottage. The Larkins'. For our holiday. For a month, or even for six weeks. For this coming summer."

Sarah stopped drawing the brush through her thick blond hair. She turned slowly.

"An island," Bay said. "We can rent. In the Waubano Reaches area. For a month. Or more, actually, if you want."

Sarah said, "I beg your pardon?"

"A cottage to rent. For a summer holiday. Up north."

"I know where the Waubano Reaches are."

"I could teach you how to canoe."

"I didn't realize we were looking. For a place. To rent. Up north." She stared at Bay for a moment or two. Then she turned back to the mirror.

The cottage had been sitting there, on the island, in the Inlet, so Bay told her, for seven years. Unused. Unrented. Unoccupied. Because old Mrs. Larkin—Felicity Larkin—had been unable to go up any more.

It was Felicity's parents who had built the place. But it was Felicity whose mark was most apparent on the cottage: Elizabeth had described it for Bay: her mother's quilted Chinese cosy on the teapot, her kerosene lamps still on the mantel, her books—*Wayside Ferns and Wildflowers*, *Random Harvest*, *The Nine Tailors*, *Ten Little Indians*—still on the shelves. Her yellowed First Aid guide still tucked in beside the hand-labelled, brown bottle of peroxide above the kitchen doorjamb.

Felicity Larkin had summered there all her life. She was seventy-three when she stopped going up. She was eighty when she died.

During her last few summers at the Inlet people noticed that she stumbled over things. "Names, to begin with," said Elizabeth. Then they noticed that on occasion she was momentarily confused by the function of everyday objects. A can-opener. A fly-swatter. Things got worse. Now and then she would say things that seemed unconnected: "I can't. The thing is. On the top."

Eventually, she forgot what hands and chairs and hours were.

And the cottage had remained unused for those seven years because Elizabeth had found it too distressing to go up. Partly because the cottage was so sadly rich—with memories—of her father and her brother, of course, but mostly of her mother. Everywhere Elizabeth looked—at the rocky point where Felicity swam every morning, at the veranda steps where she sat and shucked corn, at the black woodstove where she baked her blueberry treasure, at the *New Yorker* poem tacked to the wall of the outhouse—she could see what she could no longer see when, visiting in the stale, overheated air of the nursing home, she looked at her frail, faraway mother.

But also, so she told Bay, Elizabeth Larkin stayed away because she found that the Inlet had changed too much. Elizabeth said that it had once been extraordinary. "Perfection itself," she had said to Bay during their conversation in the funeral home. "We really had the most perfect summers there." But gradually, she said, things had begun to change.

At first, they had tried to limit the access of the new motorboats, the new cruisers, the new runabouts to the Inlet. Felicity had launched campaigns to keep the water clean; to preserve the quiet; to protect the loons, the minks, the frogs, the fox snakes; to limit boat speeds, and wakes, and engine size. And Elizabeth had joined her mother in this ongoing battle. They joined committees. They circulated petitions. They sent letters to government officials. All, of course, to no avail. Of course, they had been unable to turn back the tide of outboards, hydro lines, telephones, marinas, cabin cruisers, bilge. People. The area began to be (as it was called) "opened up."

Elizabeth said that at first they had felt protected by the fact that there were plenty of lakes inland that were more commodious to vacationers—lakes where the water wasn't so cold, the rocks weren't so dangerous, the storms so severe. "And those lakes quickly surrendered," Elizabeth told Bay. "They became festooned with cottages and boathouses. With housekeeping bungalows. Resorts on the American plan. With shores bulldozed for lawns. With beds of geraniums. With gaily waving water-skiers and whining runabouts."

But as the pressures of the summer population increased, even the Waubano Reaches began to give way. Roads were blasted through. Marinas were built. And since the people who took the new roads to the new marinas were heading out to new cottages in new boats, the government decided to mark a seventy-mile channel through the Reaches' islands and shoals—from well south of the camp, to well north of Moriah Island. This meant that even the most inexperienced navigators—and there were, as it turned out, a surprising number of them—could steer their erect speedboats, their galumphing cabin cruisers from buoy to buoy without fear of striking anything so untoward and natural as a rock.

"The Reaches remained daunting," Elizabeth had said. "They remained gorgeous. But as the summer population increased steadily, as the boats multiplied, as the electric lights came, as the loons and the mink and the rattlesnakes disappeared, as the wildness of the place diminished, the Reaches became—for those watchful enough to see the change—not quite so extraordinary as they once had been. And that was truly heartbreaking."

Elizabeth told Bay that one summer they all had diarrhoea. "For weeks," she said. They thought it was this. They thought it was that. Finally they realized—"It seems so obvious now, but it was almost unbelievable then." It was the water. They had to boil the water.

"It's like a theme park now. We've allowed God's country to become Funland," she said to Bay. And in the end, having watched what she had always thought of as perfection become less and less so with each passing summer, she had decided that returning to the family cottage—the cottage she loved so much—simply made her too unhappy. "It made me too angry, actually," she said. "It was an anger that didn't diminish. It simply kept growing." Over the coffee table, in the vestibule of the Caldicott and Son Funeral Home, Elizabeth Larkin shot Bay a brave, sad smile.

So it sat there, the cottage. "Out of indecision, I suppose," said Elizabeth. For seven years. For the seven years her mother drifted through her lost backwaters of time in a nursing home in Toronto. But Elizabeth couldn't bring herself to sell it. "I simply can't, although I don't know what else to do with it now." And that was when Bay, on an impulse, leaned forward and said, "I'm not sure I believe that coincidence has any particular meaning, really. But still . . ." And he asked Elizabeth Larkin if she would consider renting to them.

"And so," said Bay to Caz, as he poked a half-burned branch into the campfire's bed of coals, "there we were. Six years ago now. Your mother, extremely dubious about the entire undertaking, sitting in the front seat of the car with the life jackets on her lap because the trunk and the back seat were so full. Dubious, but in agreement with me on one crucial point: that we needed a break. We'd never had a real summer holiday together, and so she'd managed a six-week leave from Children's Press."

Bay was surprised that Bunty Brownlea, "my beloved publisher," had been so amenable to his request for six weeks off. But, as it turned out, Bunty had plans. She had marketing strategies. She'd been sitting down with focus groups and reps from ad agencies. She was happy to have her useful but unnecessarily literary and vaguely old-fashioned editor out the way for a while. She took the opportunity of Bay's absence that summer to hire a social columnist, an "advertorial consultant," an "interiors" editor, and a marketing director. She suggested to Bay that he do a piece for the magazine. "Summer stuff," she had said. "You know. Something on 'Northern chic.' Rattan chairs, antique rowboats, Hudson's Bay blankets, summer soups, willow-pattern china, old paddles on the walls. That kind of thing."

"Of course, it was a preposterous assignment," said Bay to Caz. "An exercise in missing the point by as wide a margin as was journalistically possible. But I tried to write the damn thing. I filled pads with notes, but eventually I realized that I could describe boathouses, and docks, and screened-in verandas, and sleeping cabins, until the cows came home, and it wouldn't get anywhere near what I take to be the great, sad, overlapping beauty of northern summers. Hard as I tried to make it something else, the story became exactly like her goddamn magazine—an isolated thing about isolated things, and I never did finish the bloody piece.

"But I won't quibble; Bunty let us go on that holiday. That one, long holiday. And there, suddenly, we were: the family Newling, turning off the secondary highway and onto the Inletter Road, with you, six years old, having thrown up twice on the highway, asleep between the bedding and the food and the rain gear and the beach toys and the books and the clothes for warm weather, the clothes for cool weather, the mosquito repellent, the wine, the gin, the towels and the water bottles in the back seat."

Turning from the pavement of the highway to the gravel, waiting first for two southbound timber trucks to roar past, Bay had thought: These narrow, rutted, lakebound roads; these gravel roads that lead from the secondary highways, down slopes of bush and forest—they are almost never noticed. By the time people turn onto them, their thoughts are already ahead: predicting the summer shorelines that lie beyond, guessing at the happy future of their holidays. No one sees the wet green depths of ditch sedge and rushes. Spray of daisies. Fall of hawkbit. Burst of summerbright. The road's primrose and foxtail, their banked mallow and laced buttercup. Their spread of fern. No one thinks of these roads as the beginning, although they always are.

The road was marked—as Elizabeth Larkin's neatly typed instructions had said it would be—by a sign, posted to a tree, for "Inletter Lodge." The road twisted for three bumpy miles through the woods to the northern shore of the Waubano Reaches.

The Inletter Road had been built in 1965, to the dismay of many of the cottagers. Felicity Larkin and her daughter, Elizabeth, along with Felicity's old friend John Tobias, were among the handful of Inletters who uselessly protested its construction. They circulated petitions. John Tobias, who spent part of June and part of September in the old Tobias family cottage in the Inlet, but who spent July and August running the boys' camp he owned, fifty miles to the south, wrote letters to the influential parents of his campers. Felicity telephoned members of the provincial legislature from her little office at the girls' school where she taught English and history.

They prized their unpopulated, unchanging summers. They prized their shore lunches, and their regattas, and their favourite blueberry patches. They prized the water that could be drunk straight from the lake, and the silent, unelectrified darkness that settled over the Inlet on the star-sprayed, loon-calling nights. They prized their old recipes for blueberry treasure, and their old canoes, and their campfire songs, and their morning pancakes. They prized their stories of summer after summer: the time the rattler somehow got into old Quentin McCormack's rowboat and how he, deaf as a post to the dry, dangerous buzz between the varnished thwarts, discovered it only when he reached underneath himself for the coil of what he thought was the anchor line—the bite left him sick for days; the accidental explosion of a crate of dynamite on the headland toward Moriah Island in 1959—an awesome, echoing "thundration" (so Albert French, the captain of the supply boat, called it) that shook china off the shelves in the Inlet's cottages and that led more than a few of the summer residents to the conclusion that the Third World War had begun; how Dr. Larkin—Felicity's husband, Elizabeth and Peter's father—used to stand placidly, in his old khaki hat, at the end of the dock, casting for bass for hours. And how, when the weather was bad, he told his two young children to watch the sky for enough blue to patch a Dutchman's breeches.

The Inletters prized their traditions: raising their flags when they arrived at the beginning of the season; attending the annual tea party and regatta that marked the summer's zenith; picking their blueberries; taking their morning swims and sunset paddles; watching the children grow from summer to summer; opening in spring, closing up in fall, always, on the last day of the Labour Day weekend, emptying the john boxes from the outhouse—a procedure that, because it marked the very end of the summer and because the john box had the shape and the weight of a small casket, was called by everyone in the Inlet "the funeral procession."

These—the summers that reached so far back into their families' past—held the promise that summers would reach, unchanged, just as far into the future. And it was this expansion of time that held the present of their sunny days, and their swims, and their picnics, in balance. This was what Bay, notebook in hand, would come to realize: his lists for his magazine story were beside the point entirely. It wasn't the objects. It wasn't Northern style. It was the way memory curved back through time, the way hope reached forward, that made summer seem enduring. It was the steady accumulation of summers past and summers yet to come that saved the present from being over as soon as it began. Past, future. Past, future. It made the holidays seem—hiking windward on a blue and whitecapped day, paddling through the sundown sheen of an evening's calm, reading a good book on a crib-lapped dock, lying on a rock in what was once the wholesome, health-giving sun—as if they would last forever. And the Inletters treasured this poised moment, this skilfully held angle of time, this balance—as if it were a cottage handed down through the family, as if it were an inherited cherry paddle, as if it were a battered khaki sunhat passed, miraculously, from grandparent to parent to child.

They prized these little things: the way they always dropped the articles when speaking of cottages (We're going to Larkins' for a singsong. We're going to Tobiases' for a cookout); the way they waved to one another from passing boats; the way children chanted the old counting rhyme that someone in the Inlet had made up long ago to choose the teams for the games of capture the flag that were held at Larkins', summer after summer.

One for shores of cedar stands.
Two for blue and cloudless hands.
Three for birch leaves in the wind.
Four the hole the rattler's in.
Greens as green as green can come,
And in this circle, you're the one.

In the old days, there had been no road. The Inletters were accustomed to arriving at their old log cottages by the supply boat that left from a government wharf at the southern end of the Waubano Reaches; the trip took a long day, maybe two—depending on the weather. They feared that the new road would end their splendid summer isolation. And of course they were right. This, after all, was the point—the unstoppably modern point of the road: to end the perfect privilege of the few and to open the area up to the money-spending democracy of the many. This was why the Inletters' petitions and letters were ignored. The road went through in no time, and it brought new cottagers, and new fishermen, and new boaters—and, eventually, new renters. The road was a great convenience. It was a boon to the area. It led to the Inletter Lodge, and it led to the dock, and it led to the water taxi that would take cheery, Eddie-Bauered

Bay; sceptical, nervous Sarah; and wide-eyed, life-jacketed, six-year-old Caz, along with their mountain of luggage and supplies, to the Larkin cottage.

Caz stood. He wobbled for a moment in the darkness, on the uneven rock, and for a moment Bay feared he was going to fall toward the campfire. Caz pulled his clenched fists back to the height of his shoulders, arched out his slender chest, and stretched. He stepped cautiously away, past the juniper, into the shadows. He unzipped, stood there, and said, "I'm listening."

"It was much the same kind of road," Bay said, "as the road you and I took to Walt's three days ago. The road I took to get on the boat to camp when I was twelve."

The road that Bay and Caz had taken, on the way to the point of departure for their one canoe trip, was the same dirt road that Bay had taken in 1964, on his way to his one summer at camp. "Absolutely unchanged," Bay had said, as he and Caz passed the pellet-riddled sign: "Walt's Cabins and Fishing and Sundries."

"Sun-dried what?" Caz asked. Bay seemed not to hear his son.

In 1964, at the docks of the single-gas-pump marina at Walt's Cabins and Fishing and Sundries, five rumbling wooden transport boats were waiting to take the boys out to the camp island. There were teenagers with clipboards, and teenagers who heaved dunnage bags, and teenagers who shepherded the boys toward the docks. Everything was done with great dispatch, and soon the boats were heading out from Walt's across the dreary, open bay, into the gorgeous spindrift maze of islands of the Waubano Reaches, with boys holding their sunhats, singing, into the wind, above the rumbling inboards: "You Can't Get to Heaven"—

a song young Bay Newling did not know. He had never been to camp before. He was shy and quiet and seated toward the stern of one of the five boats. He did not yet know that the west wind shapes the pine; that every island has a lee; that sister helped to trim the sails; that River Jordan is chilly and cold; and that if weight is distributed properly, and if the bow is kept into the wind, a properly paddled canoe can proceed against the force of almost any storm.

He said to his son, "But it was odd. The boats crossed the bay, out of Walt's. They went around the final red marker. And then . . ."

They were in the rolling, whitecapped open. They were passing through the maze of wooded islands.

The sun was in Bay's eyes. He wore perma-press shorts. He wore a captain's hat—white, with the badge of an anchor—that made him feel new and ridiculous. He shielded his eyes, both hands cupped at his brow, under the shiny black peak of his cap. And he was astonished—as astonished as he had ever pretended to be when, during the Easter pageants at Greystone Church, he felt the nail holes, or had peered, dumbfounded, into the empty tomb.

From the stern of the boat, he stared at the smooth, bone-like rock of the islands. He took in the deep green of the trees. He could see the brown shade of the gaps between the junipers and the darkness of shadow on the sunless sides of the pine boughs. There were flocks of tumbling whitecaps.

"It was odd," said Bay to his son, who was carefully picking his way through the darkness, back toward the campfire. "Well, it was odd for one thing because I was really struck with how beautiful it was, and I'm not sure that twelve-year-olds normally pay much attention to beauty."

"We're not morons," Caz said as, with legs crossed, he lowered himself, akimbo, to his seat on the rock.

"No, of course not. I didn't mean you. . . . But, anyway. What was really odd was that I'd never been to this place before. Never. I'd never been up north. And yet I remember that I had the distinct impression that I was very familiar with everything that I was looking at: the islands, the rock, the trees, the water, the sky."

"Weird," Caz said.

"Well, not quite so weird," Bay said. "It took me a while, almost thirty years actually, to figure it out, but eventually I did. Eventually I realized why I knew that view so well. It was very much like a stained-glass window I used to look at, at church."

Caz looked blankly at his father.

"My father insisted that we go to church. To Greystone United Church. He was an elder. You know what an elder is?"

Caz shook his head.

"Lucky you," said Bay. "My father was one of the twenty-four men at Greystone who took turns greeting on Sunday mornings. Who drove lilies and poinsettias around to invalids at Easter and Christmas."

During Sunday services, Bay said, the elders on duty gathered, even on the coldest mornings, at the back door, outside the narthex, for a smoke. They all smoked. Some of them—grey faces, tight, leathery skin—looked like they never consumed anything else. Sandy had his pipe.

They huddled there, gauging the declension of their cigarettes against the rumbling hubbub of responsive prayers, against the intoned Scripture, against the warbled hymns. Then, with cheeks red, with starched white cuffs cold as hard snow, with the gold of wristwatches gleaming in the sanctuary sunbeams, with the air they passed through ruffled faintly with the smell of aftershave and tobacco, they passed the wooden collection plates up and down the hip-hoisting, pocket-jingling pews.

For years, Sandy Newling was the treasurer at Greystone Church; for years, every April, he stood at the pulpit and projected the gloomy figures of dwindling revenue and rising expenditures into a bleak and churchless future. He was the Jeremiah of the fiscal year, and during his tenure he stood at the pulpit and warned that there was coming a point in the not too distant future when the donations and collections of an ageing congregation would finally and irretrievably slip under the rising flood of the church's expenses.

"I try to see what's ahead" was how Sandy described his work when Bay, a little boy, asked his father what he did at his office. "I try to look ahead and see what's going to happen before it happens."

As a boy, Bay dreaded budget Sunday. This was partly because he disliked the season. Budget Sunday was always in early spring, and the weather in southern Ontario was like the chill of a lingering flu. But mostly Bay's discomfort was due to the peculiar intensity and passion his father brought to this task. Budget Sunday was the most important date on Sandy Newling's calendar.

He worked on his budgets throughout the fall and winter. He took enormous pains. He was minutely precise in his review of expenses. He hunted down every nickel of revenue. He bothered everyone, from Dr. James to Mr. Gruber the janitor, with his rigorous inquiries. He calculated depreciation. He initiated long-term projections—projections that turned out to be absolutely accurate.

From the pulpit, Dr. James peered down, looking over the pages of the huge, gold-edged, purple-bookmarked bible. Once a year, he called upon the treasurer, and once a year, Sandy Newling, in his double-breasted blue suit and crisp white shirt—worn at Christmas, worn at Easter, worn on budget Sunday—rose in the pew from between his wife and son.

He sidled out, portfolio under his arm. His carefully shined black shoes clicked up the chancel steps to the pulpit. Sandy Newling unfolded his glasses. He opened his ledger. And, without introduction, he started reading from his neat columns of figures.

Sandy Newling had a prophetic vision. He was able to pinpoint a tiny speck of visibility beyond the murky blur of the present. He believed in this. He believed without question that the distant flicker that he could see was an approaching conflagration. He tried to warn the congregation of what was bound to come. There would come a time when the church could no longer sustain itself. He said: If we're not careful . . .

And no one listened.

"No one listened to him," Bay told Caz, his yellow teacup of Rémy Martin poised between his knees, the coals of the campfire shifting.

Sandy Newling's voice always trembled with emotion when he addressed the congregation, and Bay always shrank in the pew beside his mother. His father's emotional display humiliated him, and he tried to pretend he was somewhere else. He tried to imagine himself not in the pew at all, but travelling back through the panels of stained-glass windows that, on budget Sundays, he stared at so intently: from the road to Damascus, to Gethsemane, to a mountain in Ararat, to Creation.

Bay squirmed: As his father's voice grew thick and teary; as Sandy tabled the always disappointing revenues of offerings, of church bazaars, of fellowship pledges, of bake sales; as his hands shook at the edges of his neatly ruled pages; as beads of sweat appeared beneath his dark, unreceding hairline; as his voice cracked, and the tears welled at the cost of the new slate roof, of the congregation's ongoing contributions to the Overseas Student Mission Service, of the unendurable insurance for stained-glass windows.

Bay's discomfort was not relieved very much by the knowledge that not very many people noticed Sandy's emotion. People slept. People drifted. People paid no attention. They ignored the moments when Sandy Newling's voice cracked with the unbearable sadness of shortfalls and debits and unanticipated expenses. Sandy spoke as if he were delivering a eulogy, but people thought these momentary unravellings were a nervous tic and nothing more.

Sandy was an oddity. His lack of professional progress, in the most materially progressive of times, added to the aura of eccentricity that surrounded him. It was a cruel fate—for he was the least eccentric of men.

He regarded himself as a failure in the land of success. But he was the bearer of dire warnings to the congregation of Greystone Church in a time of optimism and two-car garages. So of course no one listened.

No one listened to Sandy Newling because the church's foundations were sunk too deeply for anyone to imagine them ever shifting. They were embedded in the Sundays of old Mrs. Proctor's extravagant hats, and in the lavender scent of fox-wrapped widows, and in Dr. James's joyless benedictions, and in the folds of the choir's black gowns, and in the shadows of folds, and in Mr. McPheter's snores from the back pew where he had been slumping, sound asleep, since the Flood. Nothing so settled could ever change.

"My father was troubled that catastrophe could be so clearly revealed to him, and yet not be believed by anyone else," Bay said to Caz. "I guess he felt a bit the way environmentalists must feel today."

Caz looked at his father. There, in the light of the campfire, was the strain of the day. There was the sadness that was sometimes so audible in his voice. There, visible above all, was Bay's age. Caz turned away from the fire for a moment, as if intent on something in the dark. He looked toward the spot where his father had pitched the tent, but he could not make out the shape of the canvas. He looked back to the shock of thick grey hair, the blustery, red face, the tired eyes. Bay was looking straight into the fire, and Caz saw the same profile he'd seen when they were driving on their way up for the canoe trip—northbound on the busy highway from Toronto; northwest from the highway onto the secondary; west from the secondary onto that bumpy, unpaved, lakebound road.

The gravel had sprayed up under the rust-proofed bottom of the car. The brush blurred by. They passed a second sign for Walt's Cabins and Fishing and Sundries. "Sun-dried what?" Caz asked again.

Bay glanced over to the passenger seat. He heard, this time, but he didn't know what to make of the question. He actually didn't know his son well enough to know if "sun-dried" was a joke, or if this was a word, like so many words, that Caz did not see clearly enough in the tutor-fanned glimmer of his education. ("Caz is well below grade level in his reading skills. Remedial attention is required.") Bay remembered one meeting they had with the child psychologist they saw once a week—Thursdays at four-forty-five—for a year and a half after the divorce. "Sometimes I feel like a stranger to him," Bay had said. "I can't recall when I last heard him laugh."

Bay shuddered round a dusty turn. "Does that mean your mother still makes that pasta?" he asked Caz. "The one with the olives and sun-dried tomatoes?"

"About five times a week."

"Cutting back, is she?" Bay, as ever, hopeful of friendship, casting with a joke.

Caz stared straight ahead through the dusty, bug-splotched windshield. Bay could hear the tinny little ruckus of his headphones.

Bay had decided not to buy clothes specially for the canoe trip—partly because it was only going to be a five-day outing, but mostly because Bay expected to be several sizes smaller again, before too long. There was another diet looming. He was reluctant to give his current weight and girth the imprimatur of permanence by purchasing any more clothes to fit what he viewed as an unhappy and soon-to-be-corrected state of affairs.

In fact, the canoe trip was part of the correction. The canoe trip was the result of an unlikely convergence: of Bay's state of health and of his dreams. This was not exactly predictable. Bay had a rather remote view of his own physical well-being; anyone who could consume a tub of ice cream *before* picking up the telephone to order, cigarette in hand, a deep-dish deluxe from Papa Cicca's was not exactly rigorous in his approach to health. Nor was he the sort who normally paid much attention to dreams. But these were the two unlikely tributaries of his life that would find their flat, reedy, deer-fly-buzzing delta at Walt's Cabins.

They parked there. Bay weighed his promise to Sarah not to smoke in front of Caz against the jittery after-effects of a nicotine-deprived three-and-a-half-hour drive from the city. He patted his pockets for his cigarettes as he got, stiffly, from the car. He concluded that weakness revealed was preferable to headache unleashed. He lit up.

They shuffled down the gravel from the parking area. They stepped over the white-painted rocks. The cabins were green frame, with peeling white porches. The forest loomed around the clearing.

They inquired at a cabin with a sign that said Inquiries. "We saw the sign," Caz said. "We've come to inquire." Bay, the well-trained smoker, had taken a last drag at the screen door, had flicked the last third of the cigarette toward the gravel.

No expression came from the man behind the counter. He looked to be in his sixties. He wore a green work shirt, green work pants. His skin was brown and tough.

Bay said, "I called a few weeks ago. About a canoe."

"Nawling, is it?"

"Newling."

Bay pulled his wallet from his khaki slacks. He handed over a credit card. Caz turned away and was modelling fishing lures. Dangling them from his nose. From his ears.

"The weather should hold for you now," the man said. "Maybe a bit of a storm. But last week was the bugger." The place smelled of wood and Doublemint gum.

"A jigga-popper through the navel would be pretty cool," Caz said.

Bay spoke. "Put it back, Caz."

They were led out behind the office. They crossed a dusty lot strewn with bits of old trucks and cars and rusted road machinery. Their feet scrunched in unison across the gravel. They were led to a weathered red shed at the edge of the pines, where the rental canoes were kept.

Caz asked the man, "So, are you Walt?"

"Nope."

"Who's Walt?"

The man pronounced it "Disiney." He opened the shed door.

Bay realized immediately that his expectations had been unrealistic. He was outdated enough to have imagined that either elegant cedar-strip Chestnuts or classic wood-and-canvas Peterboroughs would be awaiting them. He was dismayed by the half-dozen banged-up aluminium hulls stacked on the wooden arms of the canoe cradle.

"Years back," the man continued, "when the township was talking about another new road, my father figured to put in a theme park idea sort of thing."

Bay was eyeing the canoes. "This is it?" he asked.

"That's the lot of them," the man said to Bay. To Caz, he said, "But they put the road in further up the shore."

"Too bad," Caz said. "We could have just checked out the water chutes and then gone home."

Grunting, Bay bent down. He placed his hands on his knees. He crooked his head, and peered up, underneath the overturned hulls. He wasn't sure what he was looking for—ribs, thwarts, gunwales, gut—but whatever it was, it wasn't there.

"You'll find them pretty much all the same," the man who wasn't Walt said.

"So I see," said Bay.

"You done this before?" asked Not-Walt. "Canoe camping?"

"Yes," said Bay. While, at the same time, Caz was saying, "No, we're beginners."

"A bit more than that," said Bay.

But Caz, in fact, was correct. Practically speaking, they were beginners. It had all begun that spring.

It so happened that one day that spring the two elevators in Bay's apartment building were out of order when Bay, light-headed with hunger, got home from work. He had stopped at the little variety store on the ground floor for some ice-cream.

Amid the mirrors, the plastic ferns, and Chinese-food flyers of the lobby, he pressed the up button, and waited.

And waited.

Finally, conscious of the time constraints put on him by the unseasonable heat, by the lack of air-conditioning in the lobby, by his hunger and the slowly melting contents of the white plastic bag he was holding, he set himself to calculation. He estimated the height of each of the building's floors, the distance to climb.

He could handle one hundred and twenty feet. One hundred and twenty foot-high steps. It would be a disgrace if he couldn't.

Who knows how we manage to sustain our illusions: that we are thoughtful, that we are responsible, that we are not wasteful, that we are not polluting? How do we so completely ignore the consequences of our actions?—so Elizabeth Larkin had asked Bay when he went to pay her a deposit against the rent and to receive her carefully typed instructions for the opening up and closing of the Larkin cottage. In her living room, Elizabeth had passed him a glass of sherry, and asked: "How do we continue to believe, against all evidence, that things will work out, that endings will be happy, that the planet will survive, that we will not reap what we have sown?"

Who knows? Bay had replied. And who knows how, on that hot May day, with the elevators broken, Bay managed to convince himself that although he was overweight, although he had smoked a pack and a half a day for decades, ate none too well, drank too much too often, and almost never did any exercise, he was, basically, in pretty good shape?

A week after he fell through the doorway of his sixteenth-floor apartment—his knees awobble; his thighs on fire; his chest heaving; his face flushed and glistening; his throat raw; his temples pulsing; his vision wavering into negative images (his hallway at last; his door not a moment too soon; his diminishing, darkening, ear-ringing view of the keyhole)—Bay sat on the cold white paper of Dr. Jane Virgil's examination table and told her what had happened.

Dr. Jane (as Bay always called her) was almost the only remaining point of intersection in Sarah's and Bay's lives, other than the rigorously shared custody of their son. They had both been going to her for years—ever since Bay's crewneck-sweatered, Wallaby-shod doctor had been found, so Bay was dumbfounded to learn, hanging accidentally in his bedroom. "Accidentally?" Bay had asked.

Suddenly physicianless, Bay turned to Sarah, and she suggested that he see her doctor, Dr. Virgil, for his weight problems, for his sciatic nerve, for his persistent rectal itch, for his high blood pressure, for the cold he couldn't shake. After the divorce, he lost friends, he lost the accountant, he lost the cleaning lady, but he continued to see Dr. Jane.

Apart from the initial uncertainty that attended having a beautiful, deep-voiced brunette poking and prodding him, it had worked out well. Never having enjoyed a relationship with his physician, Bay found himself enjoying Dr. Jane. They talked. They gossiped. She was the one who, thwacking on a pair of surgical gloves, rolling him onto his side, and getting up much higher than her predecessor ever had, said,

"Yes, accidental." Dr. Jane kept Bay's mind off the discomfort and humiliation of her probing finger by describing the wardrobe of Bay's former physician's final auto-erotic fling. (A bias-cut satin gown; black high heels that could not, apparently, quite find their way back to the top of the chair.)

Because Dr. Jane liked the occasional night of cigarettes and Scotch herself, she tended toward leniency when it came to Bay's habits. He had seen her often enough at parties—fag in mouth, drink in hand, peerless legs swivelling under her short skirt—to shrug off her examination-room admonitions. Dr. Jane always said he should lose a few pounds, cut down on his smoking, join a health club. Bay always smiled. Always shrugged. He always said he would, someday.

But Dr. Jane had listened to his description of his May ascent to the sixteenth floor of his apartment building with a humourless severity that he had never encountered at a checkup before.

He told her how he'd collapsed coming through the door, that he'd been incapable of moving from his sofa for more than an hour. He lay there, he said. Heart pounding. Splayed. Breathless. Shaken. Watching a pint of death-by-fudge ice-cream melt into an appalling mess on the floor.

Eventually, he had made his way to bed. Eventually, he could feel his extremities. And eventually, later that night, still dressed, he had what he took to be a strange dream.

He could hear the sounds of the building. His refrigerator. The humming Exit light in the hallway. A voice somewhere. A radio somewhere. And far away, far below his apartment, he could hear the rumbling of traffic, the whooping of sirens through the ramps and collectors of the city's outskirts.

But the strange thing was, the noises were diminishing. It was as if someone was slowly turning down the volume.

Bay lay there. He felt he was asleep. He thought, for a moment: I am going.

At Dr. Jane's he shifted his bulk on the cold white paper
of the examination table. "It was a strange night," he said. "I
thought I was dying."

Dr. Jane locked her beautiful grey eyes on his. She said,
"Look. The first thing is. Under no circumstances. Ever. No
sudden, intense exertion. You're a prime candidate."

He nodded, like a reprimanded schoolboy.

"You're going to have to stop smoking, stop eating like
a teenager, and you're going to have to start getting some
exercise." She suggested something gentle and steady. "Like
walking."

"I walk," said Bay.

"Or cross-country skiing. Or swimming. Or bicycling.
Something. Anything to get you moving."

Dr. Jane's warning had frightened him. She had, at one
point, in a most undoctorly manner, placed the palms of her
hands on his cheeks and forced him to look directly into her
stern, no-nonsense face. "Bay," she said, "you have to get
serious. This isn't a joke. You're not looking after yourself.
You're almost fifty."

And so, as part of his new regimen—as a way, actually, of
starting his new regimen—Bay had decided on a canoe trip.
The planning, the scheduling, the preparing, the buying for
it—for weeks that summer this activity gave Bay the impression that he was following his doctor's orders.

He had decided that they would set out from Walt's. This
was a convenient point of departure. It was also a harmless
exercise in nostalgia for Bay: like looking at photographs,
like playing his scratched old Beatles records.

They would head north for three days, before looping

back. The halfway point would be past Moriah Island, at the campsite on the Skin River that Peter Larkin had told him about so long ago—the campsite just beyond the portage at the river's mouth; the campsite that looked, if you approached it at sunrise, as if the red air was on fire, as if the mist rising from the water was swirling steam.

The route that Bay had chosen was not a particularly adventurous or ambitious route for a canoe trip. This was made abundantly clear to him by the young man at the outfitting store when he went in to buy a backpack, a tent, and the cooking gear that they would need. There were trips, Bay learned—his learning having mostly to do with declining further purchases—that required transportation by float plane to the chosen point of embarkation. That required survival suits. Freeze-dried food. Arctic sleeping bags. Bug hats. Everest-ready tents. Graphite tent poles. And vigilant radio contact with the nearest outpost of civilization lest— lest what? An emergency amputation? An avalanche? The discovery of Franklin's grave?

On these ambitious canoe trips, there were portages so long they could have supported collector lanes. There were woods that did not end at a road, a marina, or the back of somebody's cottage; as far as anyone lost in them was concerned, they did not end at all. There were rivers that looked like rivers when you looked at them on a map. When you looked at them in reality, they looked more like waterfalls. These rivers were so fast and wild that the canoeists crazy enough to go on them had to wear helmets. "Helmets!" Bay said. "Can you imagine?" He was astonished. This was not the kind of thing he had in mind.

When Bay told the young man in the outfitting store where he and his son were going, the response was not enthusiastic. "The Waubano Reaches? Well, that's maybe not a bad place to try the equipment out. I guess."

Caz was equally unimpressed. "Not exactly the wilderness," he had said when Bay called to tell him of his plan.

Not exactly. Although it had almost been wilderness´ when Bay had gone to camp there. He had to remind himself how long ago that was. As long ago as "All My Loving." It was so long ago that the tents they had slept in on their overnights with Lark, the billies and the cutlery they had used, the blackened reflector ovens they had burned their johnnycake in, and the enormous leather-tumped green canvas packs that they had lugged over the little portages looked as if they might well have seen active service in Italy, North Africa, or Normandy. The tents always leaked so much, it seemed possible they had been sprayed with Nazi machine-gun fire. The songs they sang at campfires—"Hitler, has only got one ball"; "My eyes are dim"—were also army surplus.

It had been almost wilderness, way back then. As long ago as the Kingston Trio. As kapoks. As filterless Black Cats. When few motorboats went by. When few cottages marked the granite shores. But Bay had arrived for his one summer at camp in the Waubano Reaches—as indeed he had arrived for life on the planet—at the crest of a demographic tidal wave. Everything was going to change.

It was almost-wilderness no longer. The enormity of Bay's generation had washed over everything. The area, as people said, had been opened up—an expression that always and immediately brought to Bay's mind the image of a pair of resistant but helpless knees being shoved apart by big hands.

The young salesman had suggested a more distant and remote route. There were charts for sale. There were useful topographical maps. But Bay's sense of adventure, extending to the point where he was willing to take Caz on a canoe trip, was not going to extend beyond the only part of the Canadian Shield with which he was vaguely familiar—however tame the landscape had become, however well-marked the boat channel. He knew the Reaches weren't exactly wilderness anymore. But the truth was, he wasn't exactly keen on exactly wilderness anymore. Unlike people who pointed their bows intentionally down churning, thundering, forty-foot vertical drops, he did not think near-death experiences would be fun, or character-building, or otherwise illuminating. He wanted to get some steady, gentle exercise. He wanted to talk with his son. What he did not want to do was end up stranded on some remote line of latitude, supplies running low, weather closing in, Swiss Army knife brandished against the circling wolves.

At Not-Walt's dock, they had loaded and lashed the packs between the thwarts—as per the instructions of *The Outdoorsman's Guide.* This careful procedure had tried Caz's patience. Then Bay had lowered himself carefully into the stern. He looked up to where Caz stood, slender as a reed in his baggy shorts, in his orange Fender Stratocaster T-shirt, in his black high-top running shoes. With his Walkman still on.

Squinting into the sun, Bay said, "So. Caz. Before we get going, let me show you a few things."

Bay pushed the canoe away from the dock. He shifted his weight cautiously to one side. There was a sudden, almost catastrophic wobble—the food pack slipping suddenly to one side. Bay corrected himself. The embarrassed, good-humoured dad. Bay steadied himself. And began the demonstration he had been planning for weeks. "The first thing to remember. . . ."

"I think I know how to paddle."

Bay stopped, blade poised. "Well, I know. But there's a little more to it. . . ."

"You pull the thing through the water, you take it out, and then you do it again. The same thing, over and over. About a zillion times."

"There are a few things I'd like . . ."

"Then, when we're tired and hungry, we build a smoky little fire and eat real shitty food . . ."

"Hey."

"Eat real crummy food. Then we sing 'Michael, Row the Boat Ashore' and 'Kumbaya,' and you do Sitting Bull in front of the fire and tell me ghost stories or something. Then we try to sleep in a cramped, farty little tent that probably leaks . . ."

"Hey."

"And then after six days of nature and stuff we return the canoe, drive back to the city, and have a bath and a large pizza. With double cheese, no anchovies. I think I got it figured. It's pretty simple."

"Sometimes simple things aren't so simple."

"I guess," Caz said.

This was about as far as Bay got in the lesson of the day. There, with Caz standing above him on the sun-bleached planks of Not-Walt's dock. With the waves lapping through the cribs. With the minnows drifting in the green shadows. The little lesson in canoeing Bay had planned—had researched in *The Outdoorsman's Guide*, had remembered from Lark, had looked forward to giving. Bay stumbled badly, at the end of his imagination.

He paddled back to the dock. He said, "Well, I guess you'll pick it up."

"I guess I will."

Bay had stumbled here before. It was, so he thought, the most familiar terrain of his fatherhood. His attempts to teach. To teach anything. To teach Caz to read, for instance. He was never able to keep down a slowly mounting fury— "Goddamnit, Caz. Where. Where. Where. W-H-E-R-E. How many times . . ."

It was the same with swimming: the summer at the Larkin cottage. Caz coughing, sputtering. Caz in tears, in the shallows; Bay standing waist-high in the water, saying, "I give up."

Sarah furious, of course. "He's only a little boy."

Bay couldn't teach anything to save his life. It was a curious flaw. He had no idea how to catch a child's interest. He didn't know how to spark a boy's enthusiasm. This was something that good teachers, somehow, knew how to do. This was what Lark—more than anyone Bay had ever met—had, somehow, known how to do. Lark had understood how to make boys laugh, how to make them listen, and how to make them learn without realizing they were learning.

Bay had no idea how to pass things on. He was troubled by this: no cottage, no battered old summer hat, no boat, no favourite swimming place, no memory for Caz of a quiet, summer-happy father floating halves of peanut shells at the shore of a lake on a picnic, of the old man pumping up a Coleman stove on a cookout, of Dad in a checked Viyella shirt, of Dad at an old Viking outboard, of Dad in his baggy green Jantzens, of Dad pulling on creaking oars. Of Dad saying, "Just remember. Always keep your weight low in a canoe." No memory left to a son of a perfect summer outing. Bay had not managed to take his son's face between the palms of his hands and to say, "Look, whatever you do. The first thing is. Remember summer days like this one. Always. Protect them. Pass them on."

Quite by accident, Bay had recklessly wasted it all. Bay had squandered everything: only because Bay had paddled Kathleen Hagan back to the cottage where she was staying that afternoon; only because later, he returned. And only because, for the rest of their holiday, Sarah had not noticed that something had changed.

And because then, too soon, the season turned, the weather shifted. The wind changed. The water cooled. The taxi boat was called. The bags were heaved. The summer place went quiet.

At the end of their time at the Larkins' cottage, after the rooms were swept, and the blankets were folded back into the cedar chests, and the heavy black frying pans were oiled and hung above the woodstove, Bay's last chore—clearly stipulated in Elizabeth Larkin's typed instructions—was the funeral procession.

Bay opened the hatch at the back of the outhouse. The wood was damp and soft. He pulled the full wooden drawer out from beneath the two seats. He set it down. He moved as cautiously as an explosives expert.

He had white plastic buckets of ash and peat moss ready. He had a sand shovel. He covered the evidence of their month. First with the ash. Then with peat. Then he slid a fitted piece of plywood over the upper rim of the drawer.

He lifted the drawer to about waist height. He held it in front of him, and he walked away from the back of the outhouse. He was not on the path. He headed back through the bush, through the grass, through the juniper. He worried about snakes. He worried about stumbling over a root or a rock.

He held the box carefully in front of him. Its size and weight forced him to walk steadily, as if at slow march.

He went well back, into the buggy thick of things, almost to the very centre of the island. Someone, years before, had found the hollow; had dug it deeply away; had filled it again with sand. Unused for seven years, it was still a visible anomaly in the juniper. It looked like a small crater. The place had always been dressed with peat and ash.

Bay slid the plywood off. He held his breath. He lifted the box. And then, with waist and legs thrust back as if a drink had been spilled, he dumped the contents.

He checked: nothing on his shoes, nothing on his hands. He was back at the outhouse, lining the drawer with fresh newspaper, pushing it back under the seat, when the water taxi came around the point. Caz saw it first. Caz, entrusted for some reason with the camera, took a picture of the luggage piled on the dock. Beyond the suitcases and the life jackets and what was left of their supplies, Sarah, out of focus, looked out to the Inlet.

She was thinking: that the boats would be lugged back to their cradles, the swim rafts pulled up, the shutters banged back into their winter places; that the summer places would go quiet.

And then, abruptly it seemed, unexpectedly somehow, they were actually going: their view of the flagless cottage from over the widening wake of the water taxi; their last glimpse of open water, just before the boat turned down the Inlet toward the lodge. Caz was holding his hat in the wind. Sarah clutched the waistband of his shorts. Caz was calling out: Goodbye, tree; goodbye, rock; goodbye, sky.

Then they heaved their stuff up the path from the lodge's dock to the car. And then they were on the dusty, bumpy gravel road.

These roads, Bay thought. These roads are all the same. They are the last people see of their summers: with their cars packed, their patience thin, their children's hair still damp from one last swim. Cinquefoil, loosestrife, turtlehead, speedwell—the beautiful abundant sides of these roads go by unnoticed.

Sarah's hair was pulled back matter-of-factly. Her face and arms were tanned from the swimming lessons she had given Caz. Her eyes, behind her black-framed glasses, were still patient from the stories she had read to her son—the brave little mouse; the amazing spider; the swan that lived in the northern woods. Sarah was still content from the endless games of crazy eights, still peaceful from the tucking in, the unhurried waking up. She had not expected it, had never imagined it, but the holiday had turned out to be a kind of perfection for her: her morning swims, the afternoons reading on the veranda, the blueberry expeditions, the wide blue days that sometimes seemed as if they would never end. She was still happy from the walks along the back trail of the island, picking wildflowers, watching clouds, hunting for frogs with her son, who was already asleep in the back seat.

Bay drove slowly. Sarah took long sideways looks out the window: she couldn't identify plants, but she loved the names she'd read in Mrs. Larkin's old illustrated copy of *Wayside Ferns and Wildflowers*: yarrow, knapweed, bluebur, larkspur, gaywing, summergone. Sweet Caz, she thought: like the name of a flower. She said, "I suppose these ditches are never more lovely than they are at the end of the summer."

Bay stopped at the rise to the highway. A flatbed of logs roared by, on its way to the south. He looked over at his wife. She turned, and smiled, and he said, not lying at all,

"Like you." Her tanned face; her sun-blond hair. She had never looked more beautiful.

He thought: The house in the city has been empty for weeks. The roof will have leaked. There will be mice in the cupboards. We have been robbed. There will be mail in the hall. He could see it, there, scattered, like leaves blown through a smashed-in door.

She patted his knee. She said, "How are you?" and he said, "Oh, fine," and the car rose up, as if over a wave, and they turned from the narrow, rutted gravel onto the wide, paved highway.

A few feet from Not-Walt's dock, Bay was sitting in the canoe. Everything was loaded and lashed in. They were ready to go. His blade was poised hopelessly. The aluminium hull slapped gracelessly on the choppy little waves.

Caz climbed lightly down from the dock. The canoe scarcely moved under him. He rattled his paddle up from the riveted bottom of the canoe where Bay had placed it for him. He adjusted his weight on the bow seat.

And there, pointing slowly into the wind, they were. Caz high in the bow. Bay low in the stern, heading out toward the red marker. Father and son—bound to bring smiles to all the tanned, gin-leathered faces in all the swank, leatherette-cushioned cruisers that passed them on their first day out. Such stupid names, Bay thought: *Highball, Fastlane, Greased Lightning, Fatboy, Chugalug*. "Look at that," the people on the cruiser would say, pointing their cigarettes, their ice-rattling plastic tumblers, their long red nails at the quaint sight. "Look there," at a wobbling aluminium canoe, rolling up and down and over their precipitous wake.

fig. 1

J UST as the real smoker can, through the un-
pleasantness of initiation, see the approaching
glimmer of habit, we sometimes can look ahead
to a time when everything will change. It would have been
possible, even then, to see a glare of light through brittle
leaves, a swirling of hot grey dust, sunset after sunset of the
same bloody red. After all, there were people saying, "Look,
there. Look ahead." But you would have had to push your
stroke hard, without correction. You would have had to
veer into the future to see the heat wavering up from the
concrete of bare white streets. To see the pall of smoke hanging over the endless cities. The streaming, shineless traffic
in the haze. It would have been difficult, certainly, to see
how things would be when finally we met. But even Bay,
had he put his mind to it, might have been able to imagine
the dusty rattle of wind in a parking lot, the gentle knock on
Caz's office door, the handshake. Even Bay might have pictured an encounter that, however delayed, however long it
took finally to happen, would have always been inevitable.

"The thing that saddened him about his summers," Caz told me, "was that he felt there had to be many of them. Summers made sense when one became part of another. When they lay folded on top of one another. If there was only one—as there was when he went to camp, as there was when we rented the Larkin cottage—it was just an isolated little moment. But if it was summer after summer after summer, he believed it came to mean something much more, I think. That was what he always envied."

In his office, high above expressway and shopping mall, intersection and warehouse, parking lot and gas station, Caz stopped speaking. The rush of air-conditioning filled his neat, little space. The blueprint on his desk rustled slightly. I asked him about the smoking, and Caz laughed. "Hopeless," he said. "I asked him about it. I probably asked him that night when we stayed up talking, because by then he had completely given up on his four, or six a day, or whatever it was supposed to be. He must have smoked a pack while we sat in front of the fire. American cigarettes, always—you knew that? And always lit with a wooden match. Funny, eh? It was his camp souvenir, that's what he said. And what he told me about smoking was that, for every ten cigarettes, there was one really good one. One that, from start to finish, was something all on its own, like a little story. That was always the one that made it hard for him to quit."

"Tell me, please. I'd like to know."

"Sometimes I can hear his voice. There were words he used. Sometimes I can imagine him talking."

fig. 2

SIX

B AY's lies about his summer holidays began with the stories he told when he was a young boy. That was what he told Caz that night, with the new moon rising over the blackness of the pine trees, and the night water of the Skin River lapping at the shore. Bay told his son that there had been a boy in his class at Sir Douglas Haig Public, a gimpy-legged kid named Rigby O'Connel. "He was the one I told all the stories to," Bay said. "Because this kid, Rig, was the only one in the schoolyard who would either believe them or, if not quite believe them, at least find them entertaining."

Rig was the only boy in Bay's class whose claim to have had a real summer holiday would have been less believable even than Bay's. Lakes, cottages, canoes, summer camps— they might as well have been on Mars as far as Rig was concerned. Rig never went away. The O'Connels, so Bay's father said, were poor as dirt.

Rig lived in the South End of Cathcart, and the South End had a reputation as a dangerous and impoverished part of town—as dangerous and impoverished as things got in Cathcart. Firecrackers were for sale there. Jackknives. Caps. Stink bombs.

Tough kids lived there. Rocks, they called them in those days. They slouched, these rocks, in front of drugstores. They leaned on Orange Crush bike racks. They flicked butts end over end into the gutter, and whistled at the white-socked, black-slacked, teased-haired girls who clattered past in their pointy shoes. The rocks swore. The rocks played hooky. The rocks drank arcane, rebellious soft drinks: RC Cola. Tab. Squirt. Without straws.

In the South End, kids were sent at dinnertime to get their dads out of the Canada House, or the Maple Leaf, or the Empire. Women read *Screen Gems* in the laundromat. Young men in undershirts listened to transistor radios and worked on cars in the alleyways off Locket Road—cars that were back-jacked and dice-dangled. Locket Road: the street of the Keystone Grill, and Filoni's barbershop, and PeeGee's Pizza, and Sally's Smoke and Gift; Locket Road, between the Catholic school and the stands of the baseball diamond, where the O'Connels lived and where Rig's father, Two-Bit O'Connel, ran a disreputable bicycle shop.

It's hard now to imagine how a bicycle shop could be disreputable. But in those days—before fitness, before helmets, before mountain bikes—O'Connel's Bicycle Sales and Service was a dive. The store itself—its stale, oily smell; its bare wooden floors; its dusty, disorganized shelves of inner tubes and handle grips; its sign scrawled on cardboard and posted on the front door as if to make clear not store policy, but the injustice of the world: "No Free Air"—gave the impression that a bicycle was a kind of beginner's motorcycle. So did the gang of kids who hung out in front—with the noisy flaps of cigarette packs pegged to their spokes, with their banana seats and ape-hanger handlebars.

It was, by Cathcart standards, a notorious sort of place—

not that the notoriety did the O'Connels much good. The O'Connels' poverty was the poverty of walls insulated with newspaper, and of plastic sheeting tacked over curtainless windows. It was the poverty of fingernails that needed cutting and socks that needed darning and hair that needed washing. It was the poverty of smoky kitchen pots, and oily rags, and garbage that didn't get taken out, and of scrap lumber collected from vacant lots to keep the woodstove at the back of the bike shop going.

O'Connel's Bicycle Sales and Service was cobbled together, a frame building with tar-shingle additions teetering out the back. It stood on the edge of a tangled embankment of old tires and empty oil cans that fell to the deep trench of the railway tracks. Trains shook the place.

The O'Connel family lived behind and above the shop. There was a Mrs. O'Connel, thin and pale and out of sight. There was a vast and troublesome family. Rig was, by far, the youngest.

Bay encountered Two-Bit O'Connel a few times. Once or twice he went into the cluttered shop to try to buy streamers for his handlebars, or a mirror, or a dynamo-hub headlight—none of which was ever in stock at O'Connel's Bicycle Sales and Service.

Bay stood there, thinking that Two-Bit's quick, suspicious eyes were from a distant past. In their way the O'Connels seemed far more deeply rooted, far less wrenched out of history than the more middle-class families of New Cathcart, with their unremarkable betterment. Bay had the impression that the O'Connels had been poor for centuries.

Two-Bit seemed shrunken. Stunted, Bay figured, by a lifetime of poor breakfasts and bad hygiene. A dribbled old pot of something that smelled like motor oil steamed on the woodstove behind him. Glue for inner-tube patches? Tar for the roof? Melted-down tires? Bay had no idea. But the crackling heat and the thick, black smell were always there.

Smoke drifted up from the flat, brown, hand-rolled cigarette that hung from Two-Bit's lips. His eyes were watery and unfriendly. He was cleaning grease from his hands with a rag. "No, sir. No streamers for no handlebars here."

Bay and Rig were both in Mr. Penson's class, and once, at school, Mr. Penson asked Rig, "Will your mother and father be in for their parent–teacher interview this evening, Rigby?"

Rig hated speaking in class. He always blushed. He always stammered. "It's. That. Only. Ma. She don't like to go out, Mr. Penson."

Mr. Penson seemed to enjoy Rig's discomfort. A trace of a smile on the smooth roll of his lips. "Your ma don't like to go out, do she? And your father? What's your father doing?"

Rig looked down at his hands.

"Six months in the county jail," whispered the boy behind Rig. He spoke loud enough for everyone to hear. Even Mr. Penson laughed.

"But Rig was OK," Bay said to Caz. "I liked him. To tell you the truth, I liked him more than I really let on."

There was a gentleness to Rig. He had a slow, dazed smile, and a shy, secret drift of intelligence behind his close-set eyes. He kept a lot of things to himself. He never said much. When he did speak he employed a flat, ungrammatical accent.

I seen ya. I would-uh. No I never.

Rig was short and had a face that made Bay think of a muffin. He had a stale smell, and crooked teeth, and a black solid mass of hair that was always slick and duck-tailed. A comb jutted out of his back pocket. And on his left foot, under the wide-rolled cuffs of his jeans, there was a heavy metal brace. *Clicka. Clicka.* It was fitted over a thick-soled, round-toed, black boot.

Rig's black pants and frayed sweaters had a kind of antiquity that distinguished him from the white jeans and desert boots of his peers. His shirts—too big, pale blue, uniform-like, and often with someone else's name scrolled in black thread on the breast pocket—linked him to the bowling teams and jobs of several long-gone older brothers. In fact, Rig's only possessions that were not hand-me-downs were a few LP records. His oldest brother, Earl, played drums in a band that was, apparently, forever on the road: at strip clubs in Detroit and Buffalo, at roadhouses in between. Through some association between the talent agency that booked the "Fireballs" and a local Cathcart radio station, complimentary copies of LPs would occasionally be sent to Earl O'Connel, care of O'Connel's Bicycle Sales and Service. Earl was never there; he'd punched his father in the mouth the last time he had been. And so, in a gesture of not very useful generosity to a kid brother he hardly knew, Earl told Rig that he could have the records. So Rig kept them—mostly to read the lyrics on the liner notes. The O'Connels didn't own a record player.

On the playground at Sir Douglas Haig, Rig clicked up and down the concrete sidelines, watching the games of tag the boys always played before and after school and at recess. He stopped sometimes. He flicked his comb out of his pocket. He cupped a hand behind the path of its teeth and swooped back his hair.

The boys always played tag at school. There were no other sports—apart from the sessions of Danish rounders and bean-bag tosses and lumpy tumbling-mat pyramids that they were required to endure in the school's small, fusty gymnasium.

The real games were always played outside, in the concrete schoolyard. The girls' skipping ropes thwacked out double dutch. In the unused bell tower, pigeons flapped away from heaved, sky-high India-rubber balls. And when the boys played tag, they ran in great stampedes. Their charges rippled through the playground. The high, chain fences at the ends of the yard were home, where you were *"home free."* And Rig's daily role was to start every tag game. He did the counting rhyme. He chose who would be "it."

The games always had one boy starting in the middle: he had been chosen to be it. He waited, and all the boys would race from one fence to the other. If the boy knew what he was doing—if he didn't panic and try to chase everyone at once—he drifted backward, edging from side to side, closing in. He picked out the slowest.

This was usually Bay. He was not a good runner, although he sometimes dreamed that he was. He was a little overweight. His toes splayed outwards. He moved awkwardly. The boy in the middle chased him down, and when he was touched, Bay joined him. The two of them cornered a third boy on the next pass.

It worked the way hypnotists help people recall a memory: first one detail, then from the first to the second, and then from the first and second to the third. And on it went.

Bay admired and envied the best runners. They could sprint. They could dodge. They could, it seemed, throw whole shimmies of feints and counter-feints into their bold accelerations. They always lasted until the end of the game— their windbreakers flung gallantly open, the tongues of their running shoes lolling, their crew cuts slanted back as if thrown that way by their speed. They never gave up, and when, finally, they were surrounded by a dozen boys, there was something brave and beautiful in their doomed twists and their last futile circles.

Rig never played, of course. On the sidelines, he clattered—*clicka clicka*—up and down, like a coach. He was usually on the playground by the time the other boys arrived for school in the morning. He was often there when they left at the end of the day.

It was accepted on the playground that Rig always did the counting in. He was often ridiculed in the classroom; everyone poked fun at his old clothes and his greasy hair and his dirty hands and his odd smell and his hopelessly messy printing. But on the playground his position was clearly established. His announcement was always calm and unshouted: "All in for tag." And the boys came running. They jammed the toes of their Keds, their Converses, their Hush Puppies, and their desert boots into a circle around him.

Rig didn't use the usual counting rhymes. There was no "One potato, two potato," no "Engine, engine number nine," no "My mother and your mother were hanging out the clothes."

Rig waited while the boys jostled their shoes into position around him. He seemed to be thinking something over; he was picking up a pulse no one could ever predict.

He clicked his brace against the concrete. *Clicka clicka.* He established a little fragment of rhythm.

Then, tunelessly, he would count out on the circled toes with bits of lyric, plucked, Bay always thought, from the alleyways and smoke shops of Locket Road: "Mama she done told me. Papa told me too. Son, that gal you're foolin' with, she ain't no good for . . ."

Rig was never consistent in his counting. He changed the words whenever he wanted, but even when he repeated himself two games in a row, his rhythm was unpredictable. Sometimes he stretched out syllables. Sometimes he clipped others suddenly into staccato bursts. His pointing finger danced around the circle of feet in an improvisation that no one could ever guess. But no one ever complained about the outcome. Everyone understood that Rig's syncopations unfolded according to their own internal laws of metre and beat. They had nothing to do with whose toes were where. Rig was always fair. He had no interest in manipulating the counting. It never mattered to Rig who ended up being it.

"You don't like crazy music. You don't like rockin' bands. You just wanna go to the movie show. And sit there holdin' . . ."

For some reason peculiar to his own private sense of ritual, Rig always left the last word of his little riff hanging there, as an unspoken beat, when he counted a boy out. He silently pointed at the toe on which the conclusion of his tuneless verse had fallen, and the boy would then remove himself from the diminishing circle.

When there were only two boys left, the rules changed. At this juncture, skipping his finger back and forth between the two remaining shoes, Rig counted out. The rhythm unfolded. Then he raised his index finger from the shoe of the boy who was going to be eliminated and pointed it like a pistol at the chest of the boy who was going to be it. But here, the word Rig spoke was never the concluding "you" that rhymed with "too" or "hands" with "bands" or "alley" with "Sally." Rig always said the same thing. He said, "Fuck."

He said this out loud, with a certain dramatic flair. It was as if the word, pronounced with a certain unequivocal seriousness, would forestall any protests and would bestow an irrevocable stamp of finality on the decision.

Bay liked this about Rig. He liked this eccentric self-invention. He liked the absurd tradition. There was a bravery to it. The ritual of counting in was entirely Rig's and came, it seemed, absolutely out of the blue. It had no connection with anything else—not with the long, polished hallways of Sir Douglas Haig; not with bellwork or opening exercises; not with cloakrooms or foolscap or Gestetner machines; not with the tartan skirts and resplendently ribboned hair of the girls who always sat at the front of Mr. Penson's classroom. And so, careful not to form too close a friendship with someone who, when he wasn't starting the tag games on the playground, was often the butt of classroom jokes, Bay sometimes walked partway home with Rig. Together, with Rig's clicking boot keeping time, they made their slow way past the neat little houses of Civic Avenue, past the smaller and less neat homes of Kitchener Street, to Locket Road. There, they stopped and talked for a while—until they said, "See ya." Then Rig turned down toward the South End, and Bay, crossing at the lights, started over six busy lanes of traffic toward the carports and treeless front yards of New Cathcart.

It was on these walks that Bay entertained Rig with extravagant lies about his summer. He told Rig about the drive north, and about the bats in the cottage when they opened up. He spoke of how cold the water was on the 24th of May weekend, and how warm it was by the last week of July. He told Rig about mahogany launches, and creaking rowboats, and marshmallow roasts, and casting plugs, and high, steep grey rocks where the water was deep enough for "Geronimo"-shrieking jumps. He told Rig about the girls in bikinis on the swimming raft, and the water-skiers, and about the rich people at the end of the lake who came in for

their weekends by float plane. It was never exactly clear to
Bay whether Rig believed him, or whether he just enjoyed
the stories as preposterous entertainments. Bay was often a
little unclear on the distinction himself.

The fact was, Bay found it all miraculous: that people
could, with confidence, head up the highway from the city
every year; that after driving for three or four hours they
would come to the same, unchanged dirt road, to the constant marina, the inevitable lodge. And that from there they
could point the bows of their familiar boats through the passages between islands unshifted by the ice of winter. They
would cruise calmly past tumbled crags of granite that had
not budged in millions of years. They would find the way to
a place where the flagpole, and the dock, and the shelves of
paperbacks, and the faded regatta ribbons, and the ancient
bottle of Halazone above the doorjamb in the kitchen were
as they always were. Undiminished somehow—the smell of
hooked rugs, of the inside of blanket boxes, of a cake of
Sunlight soap, of unpainted wood.

It seemed to Bay an improbable coincidence: that the
earth, in its annual revolution around the sun, would arrive
at the same point in space each year where the same angled
light would so fully find an upturned, smiling face of a child
in the water of a late afternoon. He found it remarkable
that the early-morning blueness would always illuminate a
woman returning barefoot from her daily swim with her red
towel folded once over her breasts, wrapped around her like
a gown.

These were summers that came and, while still coming,
went, but miraculously came again: year after year, decade
after decade. With the water gullaping at the shore. The men
tapping the barometer. The rushes growing. The rowboat

leaking. With fathers shouting, "Life jackets. Don't forget your life jackets." With mothers calling to children not to go out too far.

"But where," asked Caz, looking over at his father, "did all this come from? This summer stuff?"

"I don't know," said Bay. "From books, I guess, or magazines. From what other kids at school told me about their summers at cottages or at camp. Or from what my mother told me about my parents' annual visit to Timberside Lodge with the company."

"Weird," said Caz, stretching out his bandaged foot toward the light of the fire. He stared down at it, making sure that the tensor and the gauze were still in place.

"Well, not really. I think I just took my summers and invented their opposite. I sometimes think that I knew the details of a summer cottage because the house that I grew up in was a kind of anti-cottage."

Old cottages were often brown or grey—the brown and grey of logs, of faded wood stain, of old paint, of creosoted lumber. They usually blended into the trees, the rock, the saplings and juniper that surrounded them. The single storey of Bay's parents' house, on the other hand, was yellow brick and flash-trimmed white. It didn't fade into anything; there was nothing to fade into.

It stood out like a billboard on the subdivision lawn. The plants were squat, marshalled annuals—impatiens, petunias, pansies—black as death by the end of autumn, and left in the ground under shovelled snow, under tire-spun rock salt, under windblown advertising flyers, under frozen dog shit, until the earth made its way around the sun once more and Bay's father, responding to the majestic and eternal cycle of lengthening days and rising temperature, stoked a bowlful of Amphora Aromatic into his pipe, got into his four-door Impala, tuned in to the Saturday-morning marching bands, and drove to the parking lot of the local supermarket. There, for a few weekends in the spring, plastic flats of flowers were for sale, along with weed killer, lawn booster, aphid spray, ant poison, and slug powder.

Sandy bought what he needed. He went home. He killed the weeds. He boosted the lawn. He sprayed the aphids. He poisoned the ants. He powdered the slugs. Whistling "Colonel Bogey March" as he worked, he plunked in the garden.

The cottages of Bay's imagination had shutters that had to be taken off at the beginning of the summer, and windows with long, unravelling blue views. The windows opened on snug latches and let in the morning freshness, the afternoon breeze, through the sleepy old shadows of the place—lifting the regatta ribbons, rustling the papers left on the pine table, banging closed the bedroom door if no one remembered to put the rock behind it. The views included a foreground of the plain wooden windowsill with a milk bottle of wild daisies, or sundews, or buttercups. The middle distance was divided into scenes that were like the titles of paintings: *The Swimming Rock, Summertime; Dock with Overturned Canoe; Moored Sailboat on a Calm Day*. And from there, the view extended on to the background of dark green islands. To the narrowings between shores. Bay imagined he could see the royal sash of water, the meandering windstreams, the pale horizon.

On Ardell Crescent in New Cathcart, the windows in the Newlings' house did not open. They were caulked tight against cold weather, fresh air, and (so Bay devoutly hoped during the Cuban missile crisis) against the fallout of

H-bombs. Several of the windows had their lower halves filled by grey air-conditioners that hummed like cicadas in rising bursts, in falling diminuendos of freon and hydro from June to September.

The views from the windows were not impressive. They featured the inside of the carport; the back-patio flagstones; the upper branches of a young, unhealthy red maple; the aluminium lawn-mower shed; the parched swamp cedar; the chain-link fence at the end of the flat expanse of plotless yard. The view from the living-room picture window—a vast and modern plate of glass around which the house seemed to have been constructed—was of the lawn, the privet, the absence of sidewalk. Across the wide black-topped suburban road was another absence of sidewalk, more privet, more lawn, another carport, and another, nearly identical, picture window.

The interior design of the Newlings' house was not schematically complex. They put a kitchen table in the kitchen, beds in the bedrooms, a TV in the TV room, a living-room couch in the living room. The size of the picture window, however, did present some difficulties. When Bay was four or five, his father clipped an article in *Popular Mechanics* and undertook the making of his own hi-fidelity unit—a task that took months of sawing and planing and wiring and countersinking and sanding and staining and varnishing in Sandy Newling's carefully organized workshop. But when the glossy, walnut-stained hi-fi was completed, it nearly threw the living room into chaos. No matter how Marj Newling had her husband move things around, they could not find the correct arrangement of furniture.

The sheered picture window simply took up too much wall space. There was no getting around it. Sandy moved the round wooden table with the cut-glass vase and bouquet of artificial lilies and ferns to the hallway. He replaced it with the record cabinet. This meant that, for all of Bay's growing up, the central fixture of the Newlings' living room—as viewed from the front lawn—was the drilled, wired, unstained, plywood back of Sandy Newling's handiwork.

As viewed from the living room the hi-fi looked more suited to storing liquor bottles than a turntable. There was a small compartment inside for records. And there, stacked behind Ray Conniff, Perry Como, and *The King and I*, was Bay's favourite record, one of the four records he owned. It had a black-and-white cover with four oddly unsmiling, half-eclipsed faces. Rig had given it to him.

They had been standing on the corner of Kitchener and Locket when Rig had pulled the records out of a rumpled paper bag he had carried to and from school that day. One Fats Domino, two Chubby Checker, and the record Bay loved from the first time he put it on. "Here," Rig said.

"What's this for," Bay had asked.

"I dunno. Just felt like it."

Cathcart was a year or two behind London, a year behind New York. But according to the record's jacket sleeve, the Queen Mother liked them. So did *Time* and *Newsweek*—recommendations that, for some reason, carried no weight with Bay's parents.

Bay knew every detail of the cover. He had read it, inspected it, looked it over a thousand times. The calm, old-fashioned logo: Capitol Records, High Fidelity, 6000 series. The bold black letters of a single word. Beatlemania. Exclamation mark. The white type on black background: With the Beatles.

He played it over and over on his father's hi-fi, bending into the cabinet like an auto mechanic into the engine of a car. Fourteen songs—six covers, eight originals. But the song he loved the best was the third on the first side, the Lennon and McCartney "All My Loving," and he played it over and over. With his thumb, he lifted the arm deftly and placed the needle back accurately at the band of the song's beginning. And back again. Two, three, four, five times before he let the album run its course: on to "Don't Bother Me" and "Little Child" and "Till There Was You" and "Please Mr. Postman."

It was the pause in "All My Loving"—the instant of silence between the end of the last bar of the second verse and Paul McCartney's suddenly clear, suddenly unaccompanied vocal introduction of the song's refrain—that Bay found irresistible. He loved the way everything stopped. He couldn't get enough of it.

At the break, the verse hung there, in memory. The refrain, not yet arrived, was irreversibly on its way. And Bay, stretched out on the living-room carpet, running shoes in the air, belt-buckle in the broadloom, felt the pause to be entirely his own. It trembled with something he could not quite explain.

Many years later, reading a paperback on an anonymous Caribbean beach, while on a lonely, recently divorced, rum-washed winter holiday, Bay came across Nabokov's explanation of his lifelong passion for butterflies. "This is ecstasy, and behind the ecstasy is something else, which is hard to explain. It is like a momentary vacuum into which rushes all that I love." And Bay, shifting his pale weight on a hotel towel spread on the hot sand, thought, "That's it. That's that old song."

Bay imagined everything rushing into that second of perfect emptiness in "All My Loving." There he was: twelve years old; briefly happy; in an ordinary house, in an everyday city, balanced precisely between his childhood and whatever came next.

Once, he had played "All My Loving" for his parents. He insisted they listen to it. His mother was in the early stages of her pregnancy, and never felt well. His father was worried about work. But Bay had pestered them. They sat in the living room, finally. They sat together tentatively, on the Scandinavian living-room couch.

In the first two verses of the song, the rhythm guitar has an ordinary progression. Then comes the exclamation mark of the pause. And when the guitar returns, it abandons the everyday strumming of the song's beginning, and comes in on the slice of the downbeat. Bay loved this. This was his perfect brightness. And when he looked up happily at his parents, they looked at him blankly, and he realized they had missed it completely.

That was in the winter—the winter before Bay was sent to summer camp. Everything changed that year, and when, late that spring, he told Rig about the camp he would be attending, Rig accepted this information as part of Bay's ongoing anthology of summer tales: an island, canoes, cabins, campfires—all described in the brochure that Mr. Tobias hurriedly sent to Sandy Newling with the clothing list and fee schedule—all these seemed to Rig as fantastic as any of the other things Bay had told him of his summers. If anything, the camp seemed more improbable to Rig than any of Bay's other creations.

But for Bay, among the pleasures of the camp—perhaps even chief among the pleasures—was his anticipation of the stories he would tell Rig when he got back. Although he was often lonely and homesick, and although he did not have any real friends among the eight other boys in his group, Bay loved the place because he loved the idea of telling Rig about it. While he was there—at the outdoor chapel services presided over by Mr. Tobias, or waiting, in the rain-rattled cabin, for a storm to pass—Bay kept a growing inventory of the descriptions he would bring back: the red-brown path around outcrops of rock and the sheltered clusters of the wooden cabins of the camp. How they all ran, through the maze of juniper and over the granite span of that northern island. He would tell Rig how, after the first week, he knew every rock and root and turn and drop. How they all made a hollow sound as they ran, as if passing over a roof of rock and shallow loam: racing up, around, and over, along to here, then across, just so, past and down, and through the grass to the sneaker-rattled wooden dock on the shore of the calm little bay.

Hey, come on.

Hey, wait up.

Peter Larkin, on his bare knees, kneeling in a red canoe, saying: "You see, you guys. At the most basic level, there are two forces at work when you paddle a canoe. There's the forward stroke of propulsion and there's the backward stroke of course correction. Essentially, that's it. A positive force. And a negative force. One to push you forward. The other to pull the canoe back on course. And the trick, the real trick is to find a balance by combining the two. Make them overlap. See what I mean, you guys?"

Lark had a skill as a canoeist that was uncanny. No one, not even Mr. Tobias, had seen anything like it. Lark seemed to inhabit a canoe, as if it had been fitted around him to the exact specifications of his strength and size. He could glide forever on the smoothest calm. He sometimes went out alone in the worst weather, even at night, just to prove that it could be done, just to show everyone that if you distributed your weight correctly, if you stayed low and paddled steadily, you could hold your course against the strongest wind.

Lark could move around in a sixteen-foot Chestnut— adjusting a pack, shifting his position to accommodate a change in the wind—so easily that the boat seemed balanced on its tumblehome by some magic.

He could paddle with remarkable speed. His group often asked him to show them how fast he could go. And, during his canoeing lessons, he sometimes complied—the way a piano teacher might occasionally remind a beginner of the Bach, the Beethoven, the Mozart that lies ahead.

Lark pushed away and, heading to the opposite shore, bent steadily into his stroke. There was no splashing. No furious motion. No grunts. It was all silent, all controlled. The stroke's power seemed completely internalized—and the canoe shot across the calm.

He stopped the canoe instantly. He made it turn, as if something was swivelling it from below. He headed back toward them.

Even a good solo canoeist cannot help but steer a course that is, however skilfully controlled, a series of over-reaches and corrections on a bearing. But Peter Larkin was much more than a good canoeist. He was able to chart an unflickering, perfectly straight line across the water: a stroke that was neither pull nor pry. There was never a waver. There was never so much as a tremble in his bow.

Bay would tell Rig about these canoeing lessons. As he would tell him about the jute-wrapped diving board, the smell of baking peanut-butter cookies from the camp kitchen, the campfires, the pretty waitresses, the way Lark played the guitar. These were the things Bay planned to tell Rig on the very first day of school.

Lark had an old Martin six-string with a well-scratched pick guard. He often sat on the end of one of the cots in the group's cabin, his dark brown hair hanging over his long, expressive face. Trousers rolled. Bare feet tapping. Fingers working out some simple blues progression.

"A neat guy," Bay was going to tell Rig. "Neat" being the big camp word that summer.

There were other counsellors at the camp who had guitars. Although Bay had never been to the camp before, it was apparent to him that there had always been counsellors with guitars and ukuleles.

There were campfires once a week, and during the summer that Bay attended the camp, Lark played a prominent role in these gatherings. He told ghost stories; he wore a costume of a toque and suspenders and sat at a rickety little table and, by the light of a kerosene lamp, read "The Cremation of Sam McGee." And he helped out with accompaniment on the old camp songs.

But there was something about Peter Larkin that was different from the other guitar players. His guitar had steel strings, and tended, with its beautiful jangly, carefully tuned sound, to overpower the flat nylon strings of the other counsellors. The other counsellors strummed with open hands, looking always like actors who were only pretending to play. Lark used a few finger-picking techniques: descending lines of bass notes that ran between the chords; twanging flourishes of sevenths in the treble; the occasional, curiously sad bent accent.

Lark sometimes shut his eyes and let his head fall back when he was playing—which was, in itself, a departure from the solicitous, cheerful, singalong faces of his fellow counsellors.

There was something about him. The other counsellors must have felt a little upstaged, for when he stood to tell a story or to adjust his guitar strap or fiddle with his capo, the young boys who attended the camp, as well as a good many of the waitresses who worked there, couldn't take their eyes off him. He wasn't good-looking in the manner of many of the other counsellors. The most square-jawed, frat-handsome of them must have thought him a little homely. His brown hair was straight and thick, a little long, unparted. His teeth were a little crooked. He had the kind of slender, slightly horse-like looks that were on the brink of fashion that summer, but were not quite universally established yet. They might still prove to be a brief, passing fad. These looks were not yet in absolutely everyone's imagination: appearing everywhere above collarless jackets, not yet bending over Rickenbacker guitars, not yet keeping the beat with pointed toes and Cuban heels in front of a set of Ludwig drums.

The tradition of the campfire songs was drawn, in those days, from groups such as the Kingston Trio, the Lime-lighters, or the Mills Brothers. Most of the counsellors at the camp emulated this collegiate fashion. They wore school sweaters, or football jerseys. They sang "The Wiffenpoof Song." They wore their hair short and brushed and parted. They shaved every day: their lean, first-team torsos resplendent in the morning light as they swished their badger-hair brushes in their enamel bowls and jutted their lathered chins toward the mirrors that hung from the pine trees in front of the staff cabins. They smoked pipes. On their days off, they took waitresses out in canoes, to nearby islands, for cookouts, for swims, for feels, French kisses, fingers. They joshed one another about second base, third base, home. They talked about different private schools and fraternities and colleges. They said things like "Neat-o," and "Way to be," and "Good man."

Lark was not like this. The waitresses liked him—liked him because he was sometimes moody, and because he was shy. He kept his distance. The other counsellors weren't sure about him, but they thought that he was all right. He was cheerful enough, usually. Occasionally a little blue, it was true. But a good man. His athleticism was respected—in the slapping, straining, naked free-for-alls on the main dock when the counsellors struggled to throw one another into the camp bay, it was often Larkin who was left standing. And, without question, he was the best canoeist in the camp.

But there was some slight element of disapproval that attended his appearances at the campfires. Nobody said anything, of course. Nobody, then, would have known quite how to articulate an objection. He dressed a little too sloppily—shirttails untucked, jeans faded—and he took his performances a little too seriously.

His hair had a shining weight. His hips a jut. There was a brightness to his uneven grin, and a glimmer of excitement in the insistent beat in which he seemed, almost imperceptibly, to move.

Peter Larkin introduced new songs to the campfires. This was a slight impertinence—although not so bold an impertinence that anyone would actually object to it. There was no official canon of campfire songs, and the whole idea of these gatherings was for people to take part. But Lark's songs were not drawn from the same repertoire as the others. They were not about the quartermaster's store. Or the food in the army. They weren't about Joshua fighting the battle of Jericho; or about Shadrach, Meshach, and Abednego standing in the fiery furnace. They weren't about a-grieving the Lord and not getting to heaven.

Lark's songs came from someplace else—a place Bay often tried to imagine when he lay silent in his cot in the cabin, pretending to be asleep while the other boys talked.

After dark, and after the story Lark read to the eight boys, in their cots, in the cabin, after he blew out the lantern and said, as he always said as he closed the cabin door on his way to staff hour at the rec hall, "Keep it down to a dull roar, eh, guys," night gathered round the unknowable sadness of children, and the wooden cabin disappeared. Into trees. Into rock. Into juniper. Into the darkness of the island. Into the blackness above the rafters. And sometimes, as it did, Bay was silently crying. He hardly knew why.

Bay curled into his sleeping bag. He thought of his house, and his mother and father, and he thought of the things he'd tell Rig on the first day back at school. He stretched down to the untouched reaches of the flannelette liner with his feet, and pictured the world of Lark's songs.

Where there were rivers to cross that were deep and cold. And mockingbirds. And bands of angels. And candymen. And kisses sweeter than wine. It was a place where there was hair that came down, and ribbons tied up, and where there were ramblers, always ramblers who, with winter coming and a young girl's heart to break, always knew they had to keep moving on.

Bay lay still, listening to the secrecy of crickets, a distance of loons, the monotony of hushed wind in birch that gathered round the creosote-stained walls of the cabin. There was the rustling of sweetgrass, and at the shore the pebbled lapping, and away in the darkness of the camp bay, there was often a mysterious, recurring splashing that Bay used to think was the paddle of an Indian ghost, but that, years later, he would realize was only the sound of fish rising to the lure of a yellow moon.

Then, suddenly, one of the boys in the group would say, "Hey, Baby. You awake?"

"Yes."

"So, do they have any sports where you go to school? In—where is it again?—Cathcart?"

The boys in his group were always talking about their private schools in Toronto: about football teams, and hockey games, and about championships, and team colours.

Frightened, turning in the dark, Bay said, "Sometimes we play tag."

"Tag! Hey, guys, Baby plays tag. And what are you? Captain of the first team?"

There was laughter. And there were jokes and farts and a little cruelty. And eventually, there was the rustling of sweetgrass again. And soon, away in the dark, there were the spooky little splashes of fish rising to the lure of a yellow moon.

His cheeks still wet, his cabinmates finally asleep, Bay lay in his cot and thought about Rig. He imagined what he would tell him on the playground, on the first day of school: about the beautiful islands; the shimmering water. About how popular he was.

When he got back, he'd tell Rig about canoes. About swimming. And about the place where, if you weren't careful, you could gamble your money away, or break your heart, or owe your soul to the company store. Where you could end up without a penny to your name. Riding the rails. Denying your Lord. Wandering like the Israelites. Doing her wrong. Where you could hang your head and cry. Hundreds of miles from your home—on your knees in the valley, at the crossroads, in the garden—a long, long way from the glory where we all are bound.

Rig's idiosyncratic counting rhymes were established as a playground tradition at Sir Douglas Haig long before four-letter words became commonplace, and his final pronouncement had to be made carefully in order that the teachers not hear it. At recess, the teachers' strolling passage through the playground was one of the things Rig had to take into account as he worked out his rhythms. One of the rules that Rig set for himself was that if he miscalculated—if a teacher turned in a way he hadn't predicted and headed toward him—he would not disrupt his rhythmic creation with an arbitrary delay. He would carry on, come what might.

And once, Mr. Penson—his hands clasped behind his open overcoat, his rubbers walloping loosely beneath the soles of his black oxfords, his stomach stretching his white, unwisely tapered shirt—had executed one of his abrupt about-faces on the playground at the beginning of a recess. And Rig was, at that very moment, down to two boys.

Rig's face took on the seriousness of a sea captain spying an approaching gale. But he stayed his course.

Mr. Penson came closer. He drew up. He stopped.

Rig pointed his finger.

Then he said it.

But nothing happened. Nothing at all. Mr. Penson did not react.

Mr. Penson often had a slightly bored and distracted air. He was a terrible teacher—a man who held his pupils in such stiff and ill-tempered disdain, and who was so uninterested in finding the place where the passion of the instructor met the curiosity of the instructed, that his failure was obvious, even to children. They couldn't have quite put this observation into words, but at some level—the level of being thrilled whenever he was sick and a supply teacher arrived in his place—they recognized that the gloom that followed him was there because he had somehow chosen the wrong profession.

He stood there, on the playground. His hands were behind his back. His face was vacant. The angle of his flabby gaze was supercilious. He looked out over the dun toques and jostling cloth coats.

Children's voices rose and fell. Mr. Penson was daydreaming—possibly, of the sweet scent of "My Sin" that lingered in the hallways when Miss Kittersley *click-clacked* past in her pencil-skirt and high heels. Possibly of the pink satin panties that everyone had seen when the wind caught her tennis skirt at sports day. Possibly of the toasted westerns he liked to get when he walked the three blocks to the Keystone Grill on his lunch hour. But somehow Mr. Penson didn't hear what Rig said—loudly, clearly, bravely, as if the word had been printed solid and black, suspended in the clamorous grey air.

At school, Bay walked with Rig in line. In those days, teachers insisted that partners hold hands in lines. There was to be no horseplay. No talking. As they walked, Bay could feel the lurching, clicking rhythms of Rig's gait pass into his hand. And when they arrived at wherever they were going—the gym, the assembly, the tile-cool washroom—Bay could lift his palm to his nose and smell Rigby O'Connel. Warm and sour—like old air, like damp wool, like the corners of the linoleum floor where the sponge-mop always missed. Bay sometimes worried that a faint memento of Rig's limp had been left with him, too.

Their friendship had been based on their mutual slowness, a fact they never mentioned. They both imagined being
fast. Rig, entirely without hope. Bay, with great embellish-
ment of the clumsy truth. At night, both went to sleep with
the same dreams: they both ran like the wind. They feinted,
braked, turned. With bravado, they leapt over the up-
stretched arms of players who had tripped over the intrica-
cies of their dodging. And as they ran, the patterns of their
running grew wider and more elaborate. They ran until the
playground opened up into emptiness. The red brick horizon of the school, the cluster of teachers by the stairs, the
high chain fence—all fell away. The lagging, intent faces of
the boys who were chasing them disappeared. They were
going, gliding without effort, on and on, toward sleep, with
nothing between their running and home-free.

It was one of the peculiarities of the early 1960s that playgrounds at schools were paved. They hadn't always been. In
the school's polished corridors, in the background of black-
and-white photographs of past honour students, bespecta-
cled valedictorians, and terrifying-looking principals it was
apparent that the expanse of concrete where Bay's school-
mates routinely skinned their knees and cracked their skulls
had once been a broad field of grass.

No longer. Except for a single, twisted old quince tree
that stood in a tiny island of green where the girls' side met
the boys' side, at the lower end of the playground, everything—everything the teachers so carefully surveyed at re-
cesses—was covered with a skittery, hard, line-marked grey
asphalt.

An odd bunch, the teachers. Even then, Bay thought so.
They seemed stranded on the rim of time. Even then, Bay
could see it.

Bay could already sense things, dim and unrecognized, beginning to turn. Even before the Beatles were upon him, the gap that their music would fill was already there. It was a little place that echoed with possibility. It trembled with something he could not quite explain. Either you saw it or you didn't. He was expecting something—which his teachers were definitely not. He was excited—about what, he could not quite say. He imagined that something was coming even if his sense of its approach was little more than a shudder of happiness, a gleam of silver light, a shiver he couldn't explain. He was wide open: kicking leaves through the chill dusk of October streets, bouncing weightless toboggans back up icy blue hills, trailing down through the embankments of grass and thistle at the train tracks. It wasn't sex he was waiting for; the idea still appalled him. It was something else. And when for the first time he heard "One, two, three . . ." he braced himself for the takeoff of the expected *"faaaaur!"* It was as if he knew the jangly-chord, hand-clapping backbeat before he had even heard it. It was as if everything was poised, imminent. This anticipation separated him from the teachers, he realized. They were looking in a different direction.

In class, the teachers watched for gum, for spitballs. At recess, they could spot a jackknife at fifty yards. They were always on the lookout for scuffles, and trips, and punches. They patrolled the line that divided the girls' from the boys' side of the concrete playground like border guards. And if so much as the toe of a running shoe crossed it, the teachers blasted their whistles, and sent the offender packing up the stairs to wait until the end of recess.

Rig's stairs. That's what the children called them. This was one of the things the teachers never knew.

They called them Rig's stairs because sometimes Rig didn't go home at night. He hung around the playground after four o'clock. If there was a tag game, he did the all-in. Then he roamed the sidelines, watching. He was still there when the last of the tag players left. And when, the next morning, the children came back to school, they found him sleeping under his stairs.

For all their remarkable powers of observation, the teachers never knew this. They didn't seem to notice that frequently Rig wore the same clothes for days. Bay and a few other kids in their class often bought him Pez and blackballs for breakfast. They admired his nerve. Rig never told them why, exactly, he spent nights by himself, under the playground steps. "I dunno," he said. "Sometimes I just feel like it."

He told them about raccoons that scooted across the playground at night. About teenagers with motorcycles and beer. He told them about a girl one warm midnight in the spring.

The sound of her hard heels awoke him. He watched from under the iron steps. She crossed the playground. She waited by the quince tree.

He could see her flaxen hair in the glance of the streetlight. He could see the gleam of her black raincape. She stayed in the shadows.

Rig said there were other footsteps. They came down the sidewalk, on the other side of the playground.

The man approached. The girl took a step away from the tree. He walked directly toward her. They stood together. She touched her palm against his cheek. They lowered themselves, as if they were going to have a picnic.

Bay couldn't quite picture it. Even though Rig told them. At nights, that summer at camp, Bay tried to think of it. The man's noise, Rig had said, was like some kind of bully. Hers was like an animal crying. Bay lay awake, in his cot in the cabin, but couldn't quite make it out. All he could see, in his imagination, was the splay of flaxen hair, and the black gleam of the raincape shining like oil in the little island of dark grass. He'd have to ask Rig, when he got back from camp. He'd have to ask him to tell the story again when summer was over.

But that September—before nine, on the Tuesday after Labour Day—Bay had looked for Rig in the playground, and had not found him. He looked for him in the lineup, and on the staircases and in the summer-polished hallways. He looked for him in the rows of desks of the classroom.

By some unfortunate shuffle of staffing, Mr. Penson had Bay's class that year, too. And just before the first bell of the term, he came in from the hallway where he had been talking with Miss Kittersley. He had new shoes: Hush Puppies. Brushed carefully, Bay could see, with the little sponge that came with them free. Waterproofed. Spotless.

Mr. Penson came in without expression on his smooth face. It was already hot; the day was more like summer than fall. The school felt clean and orderly. The new textbooks smelled like bleach. There were boxes of red pencils and rubber erasers on Mr. Penson's desk.

Mr. Penson patted a handkerchief across his brow. He stood at the side of the classroom. He didn't say anything special. All he said was what he had always said, every morning of every day of the previous year: "Class."

They stood beside their desks. They stood straight and tall. They sang the anthem. *Centervictoreeus.* They said the prayer. *Thykingdumcum. Thywilbedun.*

Bay would always remember the dark gleam of desktops, the wooden frames around the spotless chalkboards, the windowsills, the unscuffed floorboards, the smell of polish.

Mr. Penson told the class to be seated. He moved to the front and took off his jacket. His armpits were already dark.

He said, "Some of you may have heard. About Rigby."

The fire had started in the bicycle shop. It spread quickly to the attached house. Rig's parents had got out.

Mr. Penson said the firemen thought he had passed out in a hallway. Mr. Penson, sounding official, said, "Rigby sustained some very serious burns."

And so, the school year began. And so, for a while the class sent Rig a letter in the hospital once every few weeks. Naomi Fisburn, who was the best student and the door monitor and who sat in the first seat of Row One, always wrote the letter. Bay decided girls seemed most beautiful in the fall. In the equinox of crisp sunlight. Their shiny foreheads, their plaid skirts, their perfect cursive.

Naomi completed her task. "Yours sincerely, Room Nine." She turned primly in her seat. She placed the foolscap on the desk behind her. It passed up and down the aisles. Everyone signed.

But as the routine of tests and projects and math quizzes and book reports filled the wall-clocked periods, the timetabled days, the test-marked weeks, and as Mr. Penson became more tired and impatient and bored with their slow progress, the class stopped finding the time to write their letters to Rig. And forgetfulness spread: from desk to desk, from windbreaker to windbreaker, from mitten to shoulder in the games of tag on the playground. And as the sharp days of autumn turned grey and cold and dull as concrete, nothing more was heard about Rigby O'Connel.

He did not come back after Christmas. He did not come back after Easter. And one morning, early in the spring, when there was still a low ridge of dirty snow at the edge of the sidewalks, Bay and a few other boys rode their bicycles down from New Cathcart to Locket Road.

They raced through the leafless sunshine. They stopped at the empty lot by the railway tracks. They could see the crusty black joists, the flaps of charred tarpaper, the remains that looked as if they might still be warm. Then, full of some game, intent on their speed, they whirled away to somewhere else.

For a while, Bay always expected to see him. Somewhere. On a corner on Locket. In an alleyway in the South End. Coming round the boys' side of the playground. Bay was always sure he would recognize him. There would be a bandage, perhaps. A scar. A new angle to his old limp. But it would be Rig.

Years passed, and as they did, Rig's face, then his face and his voice, then his face and his voice and his smell, and finally, joining the rest, his peculiar clicking, lurching gait disappeared.

Bay shifted his weight on the rock in front of the campfire. He sipped his cognac. He let it burn for a moment in his mouth before swallowing. He looked up, following the faint plume of grey smoke into the darkness. His face turned up to the swath of stars, he worked a few kinks out of his neck. The afternoon had been bad—he could still feel the burning in his flat, soft biceps—but the truth was the three days of paddling had been more difficult than he had imagined.

On their first day out, heading away from Not-Walt's dock, across the chop of the wide bay, out into the open and toward the islands of the Waubano Reaches, in the first quarter-mile, aware of his son's Walkman, Bay had encountered the difficulties of beginning a canoe trip. They were sitting up on the seats, instead of kneeling (and who, Bay wondered, other than the uncompromising outdoorsman of the uncompromising *Outdoorsman's Guide*, was going to kneel for five or six hours a day of paddling?). But this meant that their weight was too high in the canoe. This would not be catastrophic in flat, calm water. But it meant that everything felt a little uncertain, a little wobbly. The lower, the better, the *Outdoorsman's Guide* maintained. "As if in prayer which, all things considered, is an appropriately humble position to take during a canoe trip through God's country."

Bay had read this particularly poetic bit of instruction out loud to Caz. "Un-huh," Caz said, rolling his eyes, miming barf-bulged cheeks.

But Bay felt the strain of their incorrect centre of gravity. In his lower back, he felt the shifts of his constant adjustment against waves, against wind, against the changing placement of his son's presence in the bow. He wondered if perhaps a boy was so flexible and so untight that the roll of the boat just passed through his body without confrontation—without running into stiff bones, dry cartilage, tight joints, hardened positions, set ways. Maybe that is the way everything— a beautiful day, a piece of music, a glance of light, a shudder of ecstasy—passes through a body when it is young: unopposed, as unremarked upon as air.

Less than twenty minutes from Not-Walt's, Bay was dismayed to realize that he felt uncertain about continuing. He was surprised by the unpleasant strain in his back, in the slag of his stomach, in the pull of his neck. (In the light-headed need for a cigarette.) And Bay felt, felt again, and dammit, as soon as he forgot, kept feeling the squish of thumb between wooden paddleshaft and aluminium gunwale.

He felt the weakness of his arms. He saw the weights at the back of his closet in his apartment. He remembered the forgotten pushups. He regretted the paid-for, unattended aerobics classes. He wished, in the steady, irritating onset of headwind, that he was in better shape than he was.

He felt the reality of distance. A few power boats whizzed by. He felt like a horse on a freeway. He considered the absurd, self-inflicted slowness of their progress. He had not prepared himself for this.

But what he thought of, as they paddled, was: the red-brown path, around outcrops of rock and the sheltered clusters of the wooden cabins of the camp. They ran, through the maze of juniper and over the span of that northern island, to the wooden dock on the shore of the calm little bay.

Hey, come on.

Hey, wait up.

And what Bay imagined was something like this: the perfect brightness of fatherhood. It was Bay who was kneeling; it was Bay in a red canvas, cedar-hulled Chestnut canoe—a classic; Bay on a perfect angle, on a perfect summer day; Bay on the calm water. And his son crouching on the dock, watching, listening to Bay who was saying, "You see. At the most basic level, there are two forces at work when you paddle a canoe. There's the forward pull of propulsion and the backward pry of correction. You see? They have to be combined into something that is neither from nor toward. You see?"

In front of the campfire, Bay's eyes were closed. He listened to the little cracks at the back of his neck as he slowly turned his head back and forth. He hunched his shoulders, and breathed in the fresh coolness of the night, and said to Caz, "And you know—" He blinked open his eyes and looked directly into the fire. "You know, I don't think I'd given that kid a thought in ten, twenty, twenty-five years. Not until, for some reason, it came back to me—his face, his voice, the sound his brace made on the concrete—when we were at the Larkins' cottage that summer. Hadn't even thought of his name. Not for years."

The lodge's water taxi had dropped them at the Larkins' dock. It was raining. The old wood was slippery underfoot, and almost immediately, Caz, aged six, fell in. Bay fished him out.

The taxi's engine was still receding over the water, down the Inlet, when Bay got the cottage open. Elizabeth Larkin had warned them: bats, spiders, mice, porcupines under the veranda. Sometimes a fox snake in the cupboard.

The latches were stiff. The place smelled damp and chill and airless. The shutters covered little cracks of light at the windows.

Bay's eyes adjusted to the darkness. Sarah and Caz stood behind him. Caz was soaked and shivering. Sarah was slightly drier, equally miserable.

Bay saw, beyond the kitchen, a dining area. A sideboard. A long country table. Spindle chairs. And beyond that, over varnished floor, over hooked rugs, another, larger room. An iron-framed sofa. Wicker armchairs. A stone mantel. Tucked into either side of the fireplace were two child-size beds.

In the kitchen, Bay had said. "Now. If you'll just give me a couple of minutes here. I'll get the shutters off. And then I'll get a fire going. And we'll feel a lot better."

"Daddy," Caz said.

"Just a minute, Caz," Sarah said. "Let your father get a few things sorted out."

The shutters came off more easily than Bay expected. The expected flurry of bats from behind them did not materialize. Flat, grey light did though, sifting window by window, like opening eyes, through the cottage.

"Daddy."

"Just a sec, Caz."

In the woodshed Bay bundled up four logs against his polo shirt. He lugged then to the scarred old stump that served as the splitting block. He dropped them, without breaking any toes. He returned to the cottage and got the axe.

Caz followed him out. "Daddy."

He lowered the blade. "What is it?"

"I need to go to the bathroom."

"Now?"

"Now."

"Number one or number two?"

"Number two. And I need to go."

"Up that way," Bay said.

"Outside?" Caz asked.

"Well, you'll be inside. When you get there. It's an out-house. It's like a little house. Right on this path."

Sarah was at the kitchen door. She said, "Bay. For God's sake. You can't send him by himself."

"He'll have to get used to it."

"But it's his first time."

But Caz, suddenly brave, turned and said, "It's OK, Mom."

"I'll go with him," Sarah said.

"It's OK," Caz called back.

"I'll go with him just the once," she said.

"Suit yourself," said Bay.

Caz's scream was audible, Bay was certain, throughout the Inlet. Had anyone missed it, there was—three seconds later—Sarah's for the Inlet to contemplate.

Bay came running, axe in hand.

Caz was frozen. He was pinned against the base of a pine tree by his fear. He was pointing to a spot in front of him. A brittle, angry buzz came from the grass. The snake was under a branch of juniper at the side of the path.

It was over in an instant. Bay could hardly remember doing it. He felt, as best he could remember, as if he had not been running so much as chasing the axe blade down the path. He could not remember swinging it.

It was like cutting through gristly sausage. And the blade continued, into the ground—clanging into the rock beneath the shallow turf and the pine needles, sending the clang up through his forearms. The snake writhed in two for a few seconds.

Caz was in tears. Sarah could hardly breathe. "I thought rattlesnakes were extinct up here."

So did Bay. He stepped closer. He looked at the two halves of what he had done. Leaning forward, bending down, he remembered something he'd learned at camp. He thought: Christ.

"Look," he said. "No rattles. No rattles on the tail. It's only a fox snake. They can do that. Move their tail in dry leaves to pretend they're a rattler. Because they're harmless. They don't have any other defence."

It rained for most of those first two days. Bay said, "It was odd. It was a funny thing. But, for some reason, your mother and I ended up assuming that it would stay damp and grey and chilly the whole time. Because that was the way it was when we found it."

Bay remembered this assumption clearly, because he remembered how surprised they all were when it changed. It stopped raining partway through the second night.

Bay woke early. It was still dark. He went outside, peed into the juniper, gazed upward. When he came back in, he lit a coal oil lamp in the kitchen. Then he crumpled up some newspaper and some birchbark. He lit the woodstove.

He had prepared the battered aluminium percolator the night before. He had packed in the ground espresso like gunpowder. He jammed three splits of birch into the stove's open burner. The convection of flames huffed around the wood. The branches were untouched, for a moment, by the flames: like Shadrach, Meshach, Abednego. Bay put back the lid. He put on the coffee. He blew out the lantern, and sat at the long pine table in the main room.

Caz was sleeping in one of the two little beds by the stone fireplace. Sarah had tucked him in the night before. She sat beside him, in the old cane rocking chair. There was a fire. She had found a half-dozen children's books on the shelf. She had brought books for Caz herself, of course. But she was delighted with her find; one of the books was a favourite. And she read: "When Mrs. Frederick C. Little's second son arrived, everybody noticed that he was not much bigger than a mouse."

Caz had slept right through. He had not awakened in the middle of the night, as he had the first night. He had not called out. He had not been frightened by the dark and the quiet of the island.

Bay watched the morning lighten. He listened to the coffee spurt. The islands emerged across the way.

As the sun rose, the trunks of the pine trees became briefly red. Across the bay, the stone shore went white as bone. The clucking lap of water seemed to increase with the light.

Inside the Larkin cottage, the unfinished wood was turning the colour of butterscotch. He saw the kerosene lanterns. The china in the sideboard. The books. The life jackets. The entangled fishing rods. The old, tattered, floppy khaki sunhat.

Bay sat, drinking coffee. He watched the morning drift like smoke through the cottage. The faded regatta ribbons appeared slowly from the shadows. He imagined a lost memory revealing itself, memento by memento, like this.

Caz moved beneath the blankets. The little boy lay for a moment staring into the dark rafters, remembering where he was.

He climbed out of the bed. Tousled and sleepered, he said good morning. He crossed the cottage. He pushed open the kitchen door. The day appeared.

Sun was shining through wet leaves. Light was finding its way through openings of green. Even from inside the cottage, Bay could smell the cool wetness in the sunlight.

The light fell in great shafts across the juniper.

Caz said, "Look." And Bay rose and moved to the doorway.

Bay was remembering the colours, the mossy smell, the lines of water beyond the trees, the lightness of the air. He was, for an instant, running along a path. He was remembering the hollow sound his footsteps made. He was thinking children run so perfectly. It's as if they make the path up as they go.

Caz was racing down, barefoot, to the dock. "Look," he called back. "Look. It's a shiny day."

"And that," Bay said, "was really the beginning of it. The beginning of our summer holiday. I remember your mother went for her first swim there that day."

He would always see himself sitting, in the sun, on the veranda of the Larkin cottage that morning. The wind was high in the pines.

She was coming, through the blue, over grey rock, around the grass, returning barefoot from her morning swim. Red towel, folded once over her breasts. She was coming from the point where Felicity Larkin had always bathed before break-fast. So he had been told by Elizabeth Larkin. Elizabeth had said, "Rain or shine, my mother never missed a morning."

Sarah was picking her way carefully over the rocks. He was aware of her sunlit blond hair. Her freckled shoulders.

She was on the veranda steps. She was looking up. "What are you thinking?" she asked.

He said, "Oh, nothing. Just about a kid I knew at school."

Bay hadn't thought of him for years. But as his wife stepped past him on the Larkins' veranda, as the smell of her wet hair slipped through the morning sunlight, as he absently reached out, just missing the red towel, his fingers falling through the gentle eddies she left in the passing of their summer, he realized that long after he had forgotten about Rig, an expectation had remained. Expectation of what, exactly, he couldn't say. It was a little gap that had never left him—a sudden feint, a two-beat rest in an old song, a crack of silver air. It was a vacuum into which everything rushed. It was a story he had never told. It was the emptiness that lies between an outstretched hand and someone who is no longer there.

SEVEN

I F THERE WAS ANY TRUTH to the notion of a life passing before your eyes at the moment of death—so Bay guessed; so Bay said to Caz as they sat in front of the campfire—it would have to be a single image carried, like a snapshot in a wallet, from one dimension of time to the next. Bay imagined that when whatever else happens when you die happened, this image would suddenly and surprisingly unfold. It would be illuminated, in extraordinary detail. "Like sunshine coming through a stained-glass window," he said. He pictured, as a matter of fact, something quite specific. "You could never really guess what moment it would be," he said to Caz. "Only a prophet would be able to know that. But if I could choose a moment to keep, it would be a moment at your grandparents' apartment, at that last family dinner with Laird and Nora, when your mother looked up at her stepfather and said, 'What a sweet thing.' That's what she said. And what I remember is that she wasn't just sad and she wasn't just happy when she said it. She was both, at once. She had such a stillness to her. She looked so beautiful to me. And I can imagine being able to see my whole life in the way I remember her face that instant. 'Laird, what a sweet thing to say.' I can imagine being able to see everything that came before and everything that came after that one memory."

Bay was late for the Thursday family dinner at Nora and Laird's, the night before they left for their winter tennis holiday in Florida. He was always on deadline, it seemed, and at *The Weekender*, in his cluttered office just down the hall from Bunty Brownlea's frozen, demanding smile, Bay was always kept late—composing heads and decks, rewriting leads, reworking conclusions, cutting stories because a two-page, scent-strip ad had fallen through at the last minute.

He arrived at Laird and Nora's, his battered briefcase full of manuscripts and page proofs, his tie loosened. He was out of breath and full of apologies. Sarah and Caz were already there. In the kitchen, he greeted his mother-in-law, hugged his son, kissed his wife. He was eager to have a drink and a cigarette—Bunty had recently banned smoking in the magazine's editorial offices; but not, Bay noted bitterly, the thick clouds of sweet, fruity perfume that followed her back from her lunches and her mid-afternoon hair appointments and her massages and exercise classes.

Laird was in the living room of the apartment, listening to music. This was the tradition of the Thursday-night family dinners at Laird and Nora's. Bay would arrive, be handed a martini. Sarah and Nora would talk in the kitchen, young Caz underfoot. Bay would visit with them briefly, then, lighting a cigarette, he would go down the hall and join Laird.

Often they didn't speak if the music was on. Laird nodded when Bay entered, and Bay sat to sip his drink, to smoke his cigarettes, to listen to Laird's Chopin, Laird's Schumann, Laird's Wagner.

If they did talk before dinner, it was usually to argue—sometimes about politics, sometimes about baseball. This was a kind of entertainment for Laird. He enjoyed debate. He could be gruff and bombastic, and he particularly enjoyed arguing with Bay about religion for Laird was adamant in his own bleak views. He was always amazed—shocked, so he pretended—that his son-in-law was willing to contemplate the notion of divinity. "Resurrections. Prophecies. Divine intervention into our paltry little affairs. Poppycock. All of it. Invented out of fear of death and nothing more. Why can't you believers see that?"

Actually, Bay was an unlikely spokesman for believers. There was nothing very firm in his religious convictions. Still, he had not entirely renounced belief. Bay trailed his history at Greystone: the voice of Dr. James and Miss Rathnaby, the tunes of old hymns, the rhythms of the psalms rattled around in his memory, and were, mostly, welcome to stay there. He did occasionally show up for Christmas Eve carol services at the neighbourhood church, and every few years he darkened the door of an Easter service. But he had never really settled on what he believed and what he did not. Over the years, he had grown comfortable with his inability to decide one way or another.

This indecision—while not exactly the passion of the martyrs—was enough to set him at odds with Laird. It was enough, as far as Laird was concerned, that Bay was not ready to state, without equivocation, that creation had been an accidental spurt of biology, a spilled beaker of chemistry, an insignificant and incidental inadvertence of the physical universe.

There was an intensity to Laird's arguments that took a little getting used to. But he was not actually as furious as he sometimes pretended to be—so Bay came gradually to realize. "A bit of a softy, really" was Sarah's description of her stepfather. "There," Laird would say to Bay, suddenly interrupting himself. "Do you hear? Listen to this." And, dropping his argument altogether, he would close his eyes, settle back in his armchair, and conduct the Berlin, the Philadelphia, the Metropolitan Opera orchestras with his waving cigar, his lolling head.

His hair was thick and, except for the grey in his side-burns, still dark. His large face was sternly cragged, and not made any less handsome by the bent nose he had been left by a high Glaswegian elbow in a rugby match during his University of Edinburgh medical school days.

Nora and Laird had recently moved to Toronto—from their large Victorian home in the country, and from Laird's rural general practice in southwestern Ontario. They had taken an apartment on the second and third floor of a down-town Victorian row house in the city. Laird had taken a position at a surgical clinic.

The move suited Nora and Laird perfectly well. The gabled, gardened, music-filled home in which they had raised Julia, Pru, and Sarah had felt too large and too empty for some years. The snow-bound country winters had begun to feel long. They wanted to be closer to the children.

There was an unchanging ritual to those Thursday family dinners. At about six-thirty, Nora would appear at the door of the living room, often with her grandson at her side. Coughing pointedly, fanning extravagantly at the blue clouds of cigar and cigarette smoke, she would raise her voice over the Beaux Arts Trio, over the Richard Strauss, over what-ever argument Laird was waging. "Would the gentlemen care to join us for dinner?"

Laird would hoist himself from his armchair, flick the ash from his front. "Ah. You've interrupted at a crucial juncture. Bay was just about to renounce Jehovah and all his works."

But on the Thursday evening that Bay would always remember, Bay remained briefly seated. They had been arguing about Christ's miracles, and a line of debate had occurred to Bay—one that he did not want to have evaporate in the shuffling commodious pleasantries of seat-taking, roast-carving, child-bibbing, wine-pouring, mint-sauce-passing. Bay remained seated and asked his father-in-law a question: had nothing ever occurred in Laird's life that had seemed inexplicable, that might be considered—and here Bay proposed the word cautiously—miraculous?

Laird raised a thick eyebrow suspiciously. But, after a moment, he let his stern countenance relax slowly into something more accommodating, more reminiscent than usual.

Laird turned toward the doorway. Bay could see that an answer would come, but not immediately. They would have to take their seats. They would have to settle. Laird said, "We better get to the table before we incur Nora's wrath. Hell hath no fury like cold roast potatoes."

The Englishness of the table setting that was always featured at Nora and Laird's Thursdays gleamed as proudly, was polished as carefully, tinkled as finely as the Englishness that surrounded much of their transplanted lives. ("English!" Laird would, at this point, have rightly complained. "I'm not bloody English!") Which was true enough. Nonetheless, the table certainly was: in the setting of Sheffield silver, in the etched goblets, the cruet, the gravy boat, the sauce bowls, the crystal decanter, the covered silver serving dishes, the dripping-veined roast platter, the candelabra, the damask tablecloth, the pewter-ringed napkins, the horn-handled carving set, and the Queen Ann Royal Doulton china.

It was Englishness that commanded the empire of Nora's oval walnut table. As it was Englishness (the Shetland sweaters, the inadequate winter macs, the Bovril) that they had packed long ago to bring to Canada with them: she a war bride from a village that had been near a Canadian air base in Suffolk; he a young Scottish doctor.

And it was Englishness that had always dictated Nora and Laird's approach to Canadian summers. They were happy to let summer come to them; to their garden overflowing with perennials, to their carefully rolled grass tennis court, to their July and August patio of lantern-lit dinners. They were aware, of course, of what many of their Canadian neighbours did during summer months. But they saw no attraction in driving north into the wilderness, into clouds of mosquitoes. They could see nothing to commend suffering again many of the deprivations—tinned food, dubious plumbing, primitive appliances—they had known during the war.

However, there were a few summers, when the girls were young, when they did actually go away. And even here, Laird's Scottish protestations notwithstanding, it was Englishness that came to the fore. With a cultural affinity that would prove as durable as their accents, the seaside remained for them the place of holidays. This was a less than convenient destination for a family that lived just outside a small, landlocked town in southwestern Ontario.

Still, for three or four summers, Laird took three weeks off. He closed his office. They packed up their station wagon with beach toys, Coppertone, and children. In the full heat of August, they drove south.

The idea had always amused Bay. He pictured a lone car breezing southbound along a vacant stretch of American interstate. In the opposite lanes, sitting bumper to bumper in his imagination, he saw a solid, unending jam of automobiles laden with Coleman stoves, fishing rods, mosquito repellent, boat-trailers, outboard motors, tents and sleeping bags, stretching north, from the Pennsylvania turnpike to well beyond the Canadian border.

There were motels with redundantly heated swimming pools. With miniature golf courses. With rattling ice machines in tobacco-stale hallways. The ice machines were irresistible to the children not because they had much use for ice, but because the thrill of scooping a cardboard bucket through a mountain of cubes was to be had, in the United States of America, for free. There were roadside restaurants that served almost nothing but cheeseburgers, french fries, and milkshakes. So they consumed cheeseburgers, french fries, and milkshakes. The only radio stations they could pick up played either pop music or evangelical prayer meetings. Laird concluded that the top-40 was the lesser of two evils, and on they drove. And, after three days of chart countdowns, butterscotch Lifesavers, comic books, and stops for pecan rolls and visits to secret caverns that sat, dark and dripping, in the centre of a two-hundred-mile radius of highway billboards advertising the approaching, not-to-be-missed Mystical Canyons, the pale and wobbly-legged family ended up at a motel on an impossibly hot and, not-coincidentally, deserted Florida beach.

At the dinner table, over Nora's excellent roast lamb, Laird eventually answered Bay's unusual question. He treated it far more seriously than Bay had expected he would.

Laird was stepfather to Julia, Pru, and Sarah, and he said he would tell the story of the day their father died. "If you don't mind," he said to Nora and Sarah. "You'll see why," he said to Bay.

He told the story: of how Sarah's father collapsed suddenly on the sunny patio of a swimming pool when she was five, her sisters were three and one, and Nora, who then, he said, bore a striking resemblance to the young Ingrid Bergman, was twenty-seven. The girls had been left at home in the care of a baby-sitter.

Jim Bishop's death occurred at a barbecue and swimming party at the white-brick, split-level home of someone whom Laird always remembered only as Alderman Kleeve. ("Later convicted," Laird gleefully pointed out, "of embezzlement and fraud.") Laird said people always snapped their fingers when they described Jim Bishop's death. They always said, "Just like that." It had happened while he was laughing at Alderman Kleeve's arm-whirling bounces on the diving board.

Jim Bishop was the generally popular manager of accounts payable at the local wire and spring factory. Compactly built, notably flat-voiced, he was a former RCAF navigator who had been stationed "somewhere in England" during the war. In Suffolk, actually, not far from a pretty village where there had been dances. Eventually, there were visits to Nora's family for Sunday dinners—such as they were, with rationing. When the war was almost over, there was a modest wedding. There were tears at the train station, and long backward looks over the stern of a ship at the disappearing coast of England. And eventually, in Canada, Jim became the father, Nora the mother, of Julia, Pru, and Sarah. "And no one," said Laird, "could possibly have guessed at the events set in motion when Jim bit into a hotdog that day."

Alderman Kleeve executed a ragged front-flip off the diving board, and, a moment later, bubbled merrily to the surface of his new and, as it was later revealed, kickback-financed swimming pool. His hands were raised in hefty, dripping, triumph. But almost immediately his grin collapsed.

Kleeve was bent on becoming the town's next mayor. Thus the poolside barbecue. Thus the forty-two guests. He thought his front-flips very funny. He enjoyed putting on a bit of a show. Which was why he was irritated to find that not one of the forty-two guests he had assembled (at no small cost) was even looking in his direction when he came to the surface of his pool.

Snap, went people's fingers. Just like that.

Immediately prior to the *prongongong* of Kleeve's diving board and the depth-charge of his splash, Dr. Alistair Laird had been talking with Nora Bishop. Laird's four-year-old general practice was already well established and his credentials from Edinburgh made him, at the age of thirty-three, one of the town's most respected surgeons.

He and Nora were standing a few feet beyond the dry, earthen gap that had opened between the strips of sod and the concrete squares of the pool patio. They were under one of the gnarled branches of an old quince tree that the pool contractors had spared but that Alderman Kleeve had recently decided would have to go because he was tired of emptying the fuzzy, pointless fruit from his efficiently gurgling skimmers.

Laird and Nora were talking about music—or rather, Laird was talking to Nora about music, for music was his great passion. He was shocked to learn, as he sipped his gin and tonic and admired Nora's tapered white patio slacks and the bare, tawny shoulders above the flounced bodice of her lemon-yellow blouse, that the Bishops' record collection consisted entirely of two Harry Belafonte, one Patti Page, and a two-record set called "Classics for Skating Parties."

As they spoke, he breathed in the acrid scent of her hair

spray, which, frank and unexotic, seemed excitingly inti-
mate to him. His own wife, a prim and timid Englishwoman
whom no one had ever suspected of either grand passion or
terrible judgement, had left Laird the previous year—moving out with the resolute fury of someone who had never
done anything unpredictable before. She had moved in with
a handsome, if alcoholic, vacuum-cleaner salesman.

Naturally, this had been the subject of much gossip in
the town. But Laird, with a tight-lipped dignity that Nora
greatly admired, never mentioned his wife.

"Scandalous," Laird said to Nora Bishop as he stood in
the dappled July lace of sunshine and shade. He was com-
menting on a household where evenings were spent listening to "Day-O" and Strauss waltzes. "I shall send over some
emergency Schubert at once. Schnabel. You should hear
Schnabel before you listen to anything else."

Nora smiled at him. She smiled less with her mouth and
more with her grey-blue eyes. He looked into them. And
here an unusual thing happened.

Neither Nora nor Laird was inclined toward the idea of
an affair. They were both conservative in such matters. Still,
it couldn't be said that the thought of the touch of the other's
lips had not occurred to each of them. Laird was lonely, and
had been long before his wife had left him. Nora, while
neither miserable nor self-centred, and—with three young
girls—too busy to have acknowledged unhappiness very
clearly to herself, was not happy.

The two of them were aware of something pleasant—an
alertness, a conversational ease, a quickening of good humour—that they shared. Throughout the year, they met at
cocktail parties, and on the awninged veranda of the town's
tennis club, and at New Year's dances. They gravitated to-

ward each other, and within the constraints of what they took to be their own unshakeable decency, they flirted, slightly.

In fact, they had been flirting, slightly, when, beyond the shapely horizon of Nora Bishop's left shoulder, the widening, deeply sagging weight of Alderman Kleeve on the diving board was suddenly released. Laird watched him flap upward, whirling heavily, absurdly airborne.

Laird stood before Nora in his baggy brown bathing trunks. There was a frayed slice of lime aground in his empty plastic highball glass. Nora had never seen him so undressed. She was pleased to discover that his serious, slightly askew face, his rugby'd nose, and the disarray of dark hair had somehow, in the wise medical proficiency these features implied, acted as a disguise for a slender, boyish body. His legs, in particular, were very fine. Her gaze settled on them as he spoke to her about Schnabel's recording of Schubert's piano sonata number 17, in D.

It might have been the gin, for Laird was not, in those days, a very experienced drinker. On that hot afternoon, beneath the branches of the doomed quince tree, he had downed a single gin-and-tonic on an empty stomach. He was on call that weekend, and had performed an emergency appendectomy instead of eating lunch. The operation had gone well; one of the attending nurses had said, "My, you *are* fast," which had pleased him inordinately. Now, with the stitched young farm boy sleeping through blank fields of anesthetic, Alistair Laird stood before Nora Bishop, and for the first time in many months he felt content.

The laughing, poolside conversations around them, the affluent North American sizzle of the barbecue, the smell of recently unrolled sod, the hiss and bang of the aluminium kitchen door, even the boisterous *ya-hoo* of Kleeve, the flying idiot, seemed part of some giddy summer perfection. The New World. He had never seen it so clearly.

Laird considered this. He realized that the moment at hand—shimmering back and forth through time—was one of those that could be carefully turned in its observer's consciousness as it was being experienced. It was a hot July day. It was the summer of 1957. Here was a beautiful woman. There, revolving ridiculously in the air, was the haphazard body of the overweight fool whose gin he was drinking. He felt like laughing aloud. It was an unlikely jewel, a perfectly ordinary suburban scene, burnished by the resplendent light of his own youth and expectation.

When Nora Bishop, responding to the offered loan of Artur Schnabel's legendary and magisterial accounts of the D-major and B-flat Schubert piano sonatas, looked up and smiled at Laird, their eyes met for an instant longer than a normal conversational transaction required. She would not be the one to look away first. But Laird, peripherally admiring her aerosoled and immobile light brown hair, while staring into the depth of her gaze, experienced something that literally staggered him, his weight shifting suddenly back onto his bare heels.

Laird's loss of balance was odd. But odd as it was, it passed unnoticed by Nora.

There was Kleeve's splash at the deep end. But also, at the shallow end of the pool, there was a sudden commotion. It seemed out of place. Nora's head swung toward it, her mouth opening, her drink spilling, her eyes widening in alarm.

But Laird, who was looking the other way, stood where he was. He was transfixed by what had just happened to him.

Laird said that it was not that he had experienced a vision. Even when entertaining the possibility of the intervention of the miraculous in his life, Laird was not the sort to use such a word. He said that it was, more precisely, as if an entire realm of consciousness had been placed, with a snap of fingers, into his own consciousness. Suddenly, there it was: not seen so much as known. "The way," he explained as he dribbled the mint sauce over his roast lamb, "without having to work through a sequence of remembered events, we know that we know the details of a memory." Out of the blue—"It was," he said, "exactly that, for I remember having the strong impression that this came to me like a bolt out of the sky." Suddenly, unaccountably, completely, he was vividly familiar with a life that he could have had no reasonable expectation of experiencing. It was a life in which he married Nora Bishop, became the stepfather of her three daughters, and moved with them to a rambling old Victorian home just outside the town.

Laird said that he saw it in the most minute detail. "In a flash," Laird said, "I saw it all. Exactly as people are supposed to see their lives pass before their eyes at the moment of their death. That's exactly what it was, I suppose. Except, of course, that I had veered wildly into the future. The life that I was seeing had not yet happened."

Nor was there very much likelihood that it ever would. Not, that is, until a second later—when everyone on the patio realized that the surprisingly loud crack they had heard had been Jim Bishop's forehead splitting against the mosaic at the side of the pool.

Jim Bishop, drawing in a fierce gulp of laughter, had inhaled a small plug of wiener and, as if tackled by an unseen linebacker, had abruptly collapsed. An almost instantaneously fatal combination of asphyxiation, concussion, and coronary seizure. Laird snapped his fingers. "Just like that."

At the dinner table, Laird skewered a piece of roast potato and placed it thoughtfully in his mouth. He looked toward Nora, over the lamb. He continued to look at her, over the candles, the wine glasses, the cruet, the silver, the china. His mood seemed entirely changed.

He swallowed. He paused. He said to his wife, "Perhaps I shouldn't have raised this. . . ."

Nora said kindly, "It was quite a while ago."

"But I wonder," said Laird, speaking straight across the table, directly to Nora. "But I wonder, do you remember what you were thinking the instant before?"

Nora, silver-haired, pale in the winter and in the candle-light, was scooping out the last of the green beans for Bay. She chased them momentarily around the silver serving dish, then scooped them up.

"Yes," she said. "I do remember what I was thinking." She met his eyes placidly.

"And?"

"I was admiring your legs."

Laird's gentle mood passed. "Ha," he said. He turned to Bay. "You see."

"See what?"

"Women have a much clearer view of these things than we do. A man might have been impressed with the little revelation I thought I'd had. He might have thought the heavens had opened."

"Maybe they had," said Bay.

"Ah, there, you see. That's the great idiocy of men. We think the universe turns every time we do."

Nora said, "There you are, Bay. Careful, Caz, passing the plate, please."

Laird continued. "A man might have imagined that, as a

result of such a revelation, he was some kind of prophet. That God had allowed him to see the future. He might have built a shrine to the miracle beside the bloody swimming pool. But Nora, a member of much the wiser sex, thinks nothing of the sort. You see. She knew what was going on."

And here, a new softness entered Laird's voice. His face softened. His low, grumbly voice actually wavered slightly. He looked intently and seriously toward his wife at the other end of the table. "You see. Nora knew. She knew that we were falling in love."

Sarah turned with surprise toward her stepfather. He was not given to such emotional avowals. "Laird," she said. "What a sweet thing to say."

The room fell silent.

Bay stared at his wife in astonishment. He had the sensation of everything stopping. There was such a stillness to her. He felt he had never loved her as he loved her in that innocuous, quiet moment.

Nora was smiling at Laird. Her eyes glistened in the candlelight.

Laird, too, seemed overcome. He cleared his throat. Then, as if to cover suddenly exposed tracks, he reached forward and swooped up his wine glass. He turned to Bay. "You see. An entirely earthly explanation. Nothing spiritual about it. Nora was admiring my legs."

Nora looked steadily at her husband. She said, "I still am."

He gave his wife a little toast. Their eyes met again. And then, returning to the more familiar footing of bluster and debate, Laird said to Bay, "And you? Any miracles? Any glimpses of the future? Any moments of divine intervention in your life?"

Bay waited a moment. He felt that Laird's story required

a further beat of silence. It needed an empty moment to settle in. It had indeed been a sweet thing to say; he could see
Sarah smiling, dabbing at her eyes with her linen napkin.
And then he said, "Well, sort of, I suppose. Or at least for a
long time I used to think so."

"Unequivocal as always," said Laird.

Bay shrugged, and sipped his wine, and said that when
he was twelve he had been sent to summer camp. He had
never gone up north before.

Bay sat in the stern of the motor launch that took them
from Walt's to the camp island. The other boys held their
sunhats. They sang songs he didn't know.

The sun was in his eyes. He shielded them, both hands at
his brow. And he was, he said, astonished by the smooth,
bone-like sculpture of the islands. The deep green of the
trees. The tumbling whitecaps.

Bay said, "I was certain I'd been there before. Somehow
I knew that place."

"Ah," said Laird, "a rent in the veil of time. A revelation."

"I guess I thought so," said Bay.

He had thought so, in fact, until the day of his parents'
funeral. Until then, he had never been able to explain to
himself the coincidence of returning to somewhere he had
never been.

As the last guests were leaving the wood-panelled memorial room of Greystone Church, as Sarah stood outside the
church on the curb with old Mr. Morton, waiting to help
him into a taxi, Bay decided to stop, for a moment, alone, in
the sanctuary. The reception had gone smoothly enough.
His parents' friends, their neighbours, their bridge club, their
fellow congregation members, secretaries and actuaries—
all had been in solemn attendance. But in the three days of

police reports, funeral arrangements, and phone calls, Bay had not had an opportunity to let the reality of his parents' sudden, accidental extinction sink in. Preoccupied with the service, and the announcement in the newspaper, and the reception, he had not really got very far beyond the moment when he had stood, dripping, wrapped in a towel, staring at the half-stripped wallpaper of their bedroom, and asking P.C. Warburton, "They've been what?" He had not yet entirely accepted the fact that a single moment of absent-mindedness had changed everything. (Gas-pump, match.) No one could anticipate a death like this. In the parking lot of another gas station, almost half a mile up the highway, people had seen the rising ball of flame and black smoke— so the small story on page six of the Cathcart newspaper had reported.

It would be Bay's last visit to the church. Even if it had not later been sold. Even if what was left of the Greystone congregation would not soon be crossing town—on stretchers, Bay imagined, in wheelchairs with IV units rattling along beside—to merge with that of a newer, younger, slightly more populated church. Even if the building were not soon to be turned into a restaurant—"Il Paradiso," Brad, the young minister had told Bay at the funeral reception. "Rather clever, I suppose."

"I suppose," said Bay.

Even if the church had lasted forever—on one foundation, in hope eternal, with Christ the head and corner-stone—Bay would likely have never returned.

The sanctuary felt empty; the voices, the mysterious dimensions, the solemn echoes that he remembered there were gone. It smelled of lemon oil and wax. He sat in his parents' customary pew.

There was the marble baptismal font. There were the old regimental flags, ornamental staffs. There was the dark walnut of Dr. James's pulpit. There was the chapel door that was always opened by the invisible caretaker when it was time for the children to go to Sunday school. And there, directly in front of Bay, were the stained-glass windows.

There was one window in particular that he had stared at—so intently, so often, during budget Sundays: on the north wall, behind the choir stall, above the honour roll of the congregation's war dead. It was a window illustrating the story of Creation. The darkness upon the face of the deep. How had he not remembered?

Bay sat and stared. There it was, hanging above him: the view from the stern of that rumbling, old launch. There were the bone-like granite rocks. There were the flocks of open waves. There were the green, wind-bent trees. There was the blue, cloud-rowed sky. Bay considered the shafts of mystic light. He sat in the vast, cool air, and remembered that the firmament was heaven, and God had dominion, and time had always turned in the darkness above him. And he remembered that on the morning of the seventh day his father always pinched his neck while helping him with the top button of his white shirt when it was time to get ready for church.

EIGHT

THEY BROKE CAMP after their second night a little later in the morning than Bay had planned. "A truism of canoe trips," stated *The Outdoorsman's Guide*, "is that unless you set an inflexible time of departure and work single-mindedly toward it, the mornings at a comfortable, well-established campsite will slip away." But the weather was fine, and the breeze, out of the southwest, was almost behind them.

The day before, the wind had chopped against them—not heavily, not in a threatening way. The weather had stayed fair, as Not-Walt had promised. The days had been bright and blue. But the wind had been steady, slowing them so that when they came to the mouth of the Inlet they did not turn in to explore—as Bay had thought they would when he had planned the trip. They could see the white frame of the Tobias cottage on the long point to their right, they could make out the opening of the Shelter Narrows, but they stayed outside the reefs and continued on, northward.

Today, though, the wind was with them. It would help them pick up time. Bay guessed they'd be at the Skin River by late afternoon.

Bay sat in the stern of the canoe, staring at his son's narrow shoulders and the back of his head as they paddled. They were not speaking very much. Contrary to his hopes, the canoe trip had opened up wide, hull-slapping passages of silence between them. Bay had been left to himself. He watched his son. He thought: How terrifying to love someone so much.

He thought: Perhaps I will not be forgiven this. Perhaps this is all I will leave you: my impatience, my failure. Not faith: just the lack of it. Not belief: just its absence. Not beauty: just the emptiness it leaves when it is gone. Not summers at all: just funland; just poisonous sunshine; just a dead, ice-blue lake.

Bay paddled. And he wondered if this was the guilt that awakened him in the middle of all his nights in the city. The bedside, digital flips of anxiety before the dawn came: 2:30, 3:30, 4:00. The apartment hum. The distant wailing of the far-below traffic. The coughing jags. The ashtray by his bed, by his toilet, by the couch where he sat in the middle of the night, playing his scratched old Beatles records, having a smoke, looking out over the lights of the city from the sixteenth floor. Bay remembered the child psychologist saying, "Of course he'll blame you—for a while. His problems at school may well be part of that. Part of a process he has to work through."

Bay watched Caz paddle. The boy's upper hand was not clasped over the butt as it should have been, but wrapped, as if holding a rake, around its shaft. *Cuchugachugachchch*, went the Walkman. This would be the most basic correction of a paddle stroke, but Bay was conscious of the resentment in the orange-T-shirted shoulders and the lank fall of blond hair. Bay could not see a way to say a word.

As he paddled he pictured nothing—a dead lake; an empty church; the hot, thick night of a city; a wasted evening of television; a lonely man and an open lingerie catalogue, a crusty, crumpled Kleenex. O seed of Jesse. From generation unto generation. He could see the flat-roofed, air-vented buildings. The red sun. The howling wind. Sometimes the future scared him to death.

Hey, come on.

Hey, wait up.

What Bay had wanted to do, of course, was exactly what Caz would have thought too silly, too preposterous, too dumb for words. Bay would have been quite happy to have sung "Swing Low, Sweet Chariot" and "Michael, Row the Boat Ashore" with his son at their nightly campfires. It seemed, now, an entirely unlikely expectation. Bay had even planned to tell Caz a ghost story. As he had gone about planning the trip—buying the gear, reading *The Outdoors-man's Guide*, calling ahead to Walt's to rent the canoe—he had actually pictured the fire. Had seen the two of them, father and son, sitting up late, talking. Bay had imagined that he would tell Caz the ghost story he remembered from camp.

"What about that guy?" Caz suddenly asked, without turning his head in the canoe. "Your old counsellor. What was it that happened to him?" But as he spoke, the boy caught the crest of a choppy wave with the blade of his paddle, sending a cold sheen of spray back over the canoe.

"Jesus, Caz. Will you watch it."

It was a ghost story Peter Larkin had told at one of the campfires. Perhaps he'd stolen it from somewhere. It had taken Bay years to figure it out. It was a story that had scared them all to death.

At one of the weekly campfires, Lark had ducked his head under the strap of his guitar. He set it down gently, a burnished old Martin with ivory pegs, bought in a Church Street pawnshop a year or two before everybody wanted guitars. He stepped in front of the fire. His face was aglow. He looked suddenly very serious. There was no glint of entertainment in his eyes. His shadow shot up the dark curtain of trees. There was no indication that he was acting. There was no sign to the attentive boys that he was making something up.

The waitresses sat on a rise of rock, slightly removed from the boys, with their arms around their knees, in their boyfriends' football sweaters, with their socks pulled over their slacks because of the mosquitoes. Mr. Tobias, the camp director, sat on a ridge of rock behind them.

Lark said: There was a princess of the Waubano tribe who was as beautiful as a summer day. She wore garlands of flowers in her long black hair, and her eyes were like the depths of secret pools. She wore moccasins of sweetgrass beading, and she passed through the forest softly, like a gentle breeze.

She also brought with her the luck of good weather. And in the summer campground, along the shores of the Waubano Reaches, all the young men wanted to be with her. For the days were long and warm with her, and her songs were like sunshine, and her skin was as smooth as glistening water.

Now, there was a hunter. And although he stood with the other young men, and although he also admired the beauty of the girl, she noticed, when she raised her head from her beading, that he always looked beyond her, toward the sky and toward the open water. And when, at last, she asked what he was looking for, he said, "You will think ill of me."

And she said, "No. Tell me why you look beyond me to the sky and to the open water."

To which he replied, "The other men say they will love you for ever. But I look to the sky and the open water because if I look at you I am reminded that winter will surely come, and for this reason, your beauty is almost more than I can bear."

And for this answer, the princess gave the hunter her heart.

And when the weather was still warm, and the sky still blue, the hunter left the shore to hunt and to prepare the winter camp. But before he left, he said to the girl, "On the day I look up from the path and see that the leaves have turned red and gold above me in the sky, I will return from the hunt. And on that same day, you will look up, and you will come to the winter camp that I have made. For you will always look for me in the distant sky and the open water. And I will always look for you in the changing light and in the turning of the stars."

But the hunter had a brother who was a thief. He was weak and lazy, and when he heard what the hunter said to the princess, he was filled with jealousy. And when his brother had left for the hunt, he stole the princess, and took her away in his canoe. He took her to the unknown island. And there he kept her.

And she brought to him blue, perfect days, and a still wind, and a bright sun. She brought to him the glistening water. And he ate the ripened berries, and he slept in the sunshine. And he watched her sadly plait flowers in her long black hair. And he lay with his head in her buckskin lap. And he made her trace her fingers slowly on his brow.

But one day, she looked up and saw that the leaves had turned red and gold, and as she traced her fingers on the thief's brow, she began to sing. And her voice swirled round him, and danced before him, and the sun caressed him, and the breeze lulled him, and the song enchanted him, and soon he was asleep.

And on that day, she took his canoe and stole away. And when he awoke, he found that he was alone, and that the sky had turned dark and cold. He had prepared no shelter, put away no food. And soon the wind came howling from the north. And the brittle leaves blew. And he perished on the unknown island.

Lark paused in his storytelling. A log shifted in the campfire, and a burst of sparks cascaded upward into the darkness. Above the pine trees, a yellow moon was rising. The night was so still there was nothing but the sound of crickets and frogs and, from somewhere deep in the woods, an owl. Lark looked upward. Around him, a ring of faces. Not a boy moved.

Lark said: The princess paddled all day, and at night she came to the first portage. A yellow moon was rising above the pine trees. And she hoisted the birchbark canoe to her shoulders and started into the darkness. And as she made her way over the portage, she could hear the crickets, and the frogs, and from somewhere deep in the woods, an owl.

Now, as ill luck would have it, there was someone camped on the portage that night. He was a map-maker who had been sent by the white government into the Reaches. He was a nervous little man, a city man, with poor eyesight and no sense of the woods, and when he heard a footfall on the path, he thought it was a bear. He had a great fear of bears, although he'd never seen one. And he took his rifle and climbed from his tent. He saw a great shape approaching. And when he heard the hull of the portaged canoe rustling against the saplings of alder and birch, he was very frightened.

He raised his rifle. He fired into the darkness. And the next morning, when he discovered what he had done, he took the body of the princess and weighted it with rocks and sank it in the deepest part of the lake. And he set the birchbark canoe on fire on a rock in the open water, where the first big waves would wash the charred ribs away. And no one would ever know.

And that, Lark said, would have been that. Except.

And of course, in ghost stories at campfires, there was always an *except*.

The boys waited. The red coals of the campfire glowed. Except the hunter's love would not die. And it is said that he is still looking for the princess among the islands of the Waubano Reaches. He paddles in the darkness, and still, on summer nights like this, when the moon is yellow and the wind is calm and the stars are turning, it's possible to hear him. Sometimes, on nights like this, he paddles by.

When Lark stopped speaking, he didn't move. He seemed frozen there, and none of the boys dared move, either. They listened their way through the darkness.

Their cabins were behind them, through the woods, across the spine of the dark northern island. The black skin of water lay in front of them, past the coals of the fire. They sat still. The silence stretched on. And then . . .

They all heard something. They all, absolutely, heard something. It was a gentle splash. Then another. It was perfectly distinct, soft, irregular. It was as if someone was out in the blackness, dipping the blade of a paddle into the motionless water. It was as if someone was paddling, gliding, coming closer, taking another stroke.

And after the campfire: flashlights through the woods, along the paths, they hurried back to the cabins.

The story had frightened Bay. His fear sat in the same hollow of his stomach that he felt while brushing his teeth at night on the shore in front of the cabin. Squatting, toothbrush in hand, he looked up from the black surface of reflected stars. He considered the night sky. Smelling the familiar pyjama'd smell of himself, spitting Pepsodent, thinking of the cold, empty galaxies that spun above him. "It goes on and on and on . . . ," he said to himself. Said it until the incompleteness of the sentence became too much for him. Said it until he gave his toothbrush a last swish in the disrupted constellations.

Hey, Baby, they would say. Hey, Baby.

In the cabin, the boys always talked. They always whispered from cot to cot. And of course, that night, they tried to explain what they had heard.

They had all heard it: a gentle splash, then another. It was perfectly distinct.

It must have been another counsellor. Someone out helping Lark with sound effects. That's what they decided. That must have been it: another counsellor, out in a canoe. Out on the black water.

Because it couldn't have been a camper: the director would never have allowed a boy out in a canoe, after dark, by himself.

"He'd of had a bird."

"A total hairy."

So it must have been a counsellor. "But who was it?"

"Hey." A voice came from the darkness outside the cabin. "Knock it off in there. Get to sleep." Then the tread of footsteps on the path fell away.

There was always a time in the cabin at night when the last conversation trailed off into even breathing. When the last story or joke disappeared into the rush of night breeze. The cabin was hushed by the pines above the shadowed rafters. Sometimes someone would makes some last sleepy comment, or, recognizing the comic potential of this long, last pause, just let one rip.

"Nice one, Fraz."

"Gross me out."

"Gas attack."

But on the night Lark told his story at the campfire, as the eight boys in the cabin cuddled down into the flannel of flying ducks, of casting fishermen, of leaping pike, as they all drifted to sleep, Bay stayed wide awake. He was thinking: "You Can't Get to Heaven."

It was one of the camp songs. It was sung at every campfire—always introduced by the same keen, crewcut counsellor. Always sung the same way, even though the director and the other counsellors found this campfire tradition a little tiresome.

Nobody noticed the song's meaning any more. Probably nobody ever had. It was a song about the necessity of faith. "Faith," Miss Rathnaby had said. "Think of the faith of Shadrach, Meshach, and Abednego. The faith to refuse to pray to Nebuchadnezzar's golden image. To step into the furnace and to know that the angel of the Lord would walk with them in the flames and protect them."

At the campfires, the song's improvised but relentlessly tedious verses endlessly listed the uselessness of trying to get to heaven by any means other than faith. You can't get to heaven in Lark's canoe: because Lark's canoe needs too much glue. Not in the director's car: because the director's car won't go that far.

And on it went.

And bloody on, Mr. Tobias always thought. Everyone groaned when the hairy-legged, football-jersey'd counsellor said, "Okay, everybody. How about 'You Can't Get to Heaven'?" The director sighed. He pulled his Black Cats and his Eddy matches from his breast pocket. He ducked his cragged face into his cupped hands, and lit up.

The way the song worked at the camp was this: every member of the staff had to make up a verse, and each verse had to refer to another member of the staff. It was a chain, and the chain continued—interminably, it seemed to the director—until, without a single omission, the last verse linked back to the first. When every member of the staff had been named, the song was complete.

And so, that night, in the darkness of the cabin, like a detective checking alibis, Bay was able to go backward in time. This required some concentration. But it proved to be possible. Bay found that with some effort, he could remember from verse to verse, from link to link.

Simon had sung about Matt's boat that don't even float. Matt about Paul's road that's way too slow. Paul about John's shoes that are worn right through. And in the cabin, on that yellow-mooned night, remembering his way back to the song's beginning, Bay was able to remember exactly which staff members—promising not to grieve their Lord no more—were present.

One by one. The faces were called up: fire-lit, singing out, happy.

So he lay in the darkness, working his way around the campfire's circle, eliminating names one by one. Skate, gate. Boat, float. Skis, trees. And as he came in sight of the song's conclusion, Bay felt a familiar sad hollow in his stomach. It was like homesickness. He lay in the darkness, wide awake and frightened to death. Because the thing was: everybody had been there that night. No one was missing.

He thought of this as the aluminium canoe slapped through the waves. Caz still did not turn around in the bow. He continued, incorrectly, to paddle. He said, "Hello."

"Hmm?"

"Earth to father."

"Uh-huh."

"That guy? Your counsellor? What happened to him."

"Larkin? Oh, your mother heard the story first. For all her worries about going up to the Inlet, your mother was much better at meeting people there than I was that summer. Someone told her. She seemed to just pick things up—stories, old recipes. She knew whose children were whose. Somehow she got the details of the place. Someone told her, at the lodge, I think. I'm not sure anymore what she told me and what I've invented. I just kept trying to picture it."

"Picture what?"

The time, one night, early in September, in the Inlet. "Oh, more than thirty years ago, now," Bay said. "Apparently it was a terrible night." The night when the wind woke John Tobias up. It was unusual for the wind to wake him.

Unhurried, unruffled, unmarried, John Tobias—the Reverend John Tobias, although he almost never used "the Reverend" in the Reaches—John Tobias was sometimes roused by a loud and simultaneous fracture of thunder and lightning. He was sometimes awakened by an explosion that was, so he always noted as he turned beneath the old English-wool blankets on his iron-frame bed in the old cottage, right on top of the place. Sometimes, the rain wakened him—if it was heavy enough and persistent enough to find its way through the warm depths of his customarily sound sleep. Rattling on the shingles, as his father used to say, like gravel on a casket.

But the wind—the wind rarely interrupted his nights. He had been coming up to the Waubano Reaches almost every summer of his fifty-four years, and the wind was familiar enough on the Tobias point. His father, a New York lawyer of some renown and a keen bass fisherman, had built the place just before the turn of the century. It was a white frame cottage, alone on the long smooth arm of bone-pale, garnet-veined stone that reached from the islands of the Inlet out to the open water. His father died in 1931, his mother twelve years later—leaving John the money he eventually used to buy property a day's trip to the south, for a boys' summer camp he wanted to run. He still came to the Inlet though, to the old Tobias cottage—for whatever time he could manage in June, before camp, and afterwards, for two weeks at the beginning of September.

He was accustomed to being alone. He was used to the darkness. He was perfectly at ease with the creaking joists; the wind-worried shutters; the stiff swing of the pulley on the clothesline; the rising, falling, and rising-again of gusts in the bank of heaving pines behind the house. He had no superstitions. After his last Black Cat of the evening, and after he set the slender ribbon into the spine of the wafery pages of his bible, he raised himself on one elbow and, with a spurt of practised accuracy, blew out the flame of the coal-oil lamp. He hardly noticed the wind. He said a prayer. He slept.

He was a methodical man: a keeper of dates, a flyer of flags, a tier of knots, a primer of pumps, an identifier of birds, a layer of fires. He could see the patterns of things. He had carefully managed the cottage for his mother; now, just as carefully, he managed it for himself.

As a young man, his face had been lean and earnest. It was now cragged and deeply wrinkled. His eyes sagged. His voice was roughened by his smoking. He was a tall man, and his stooping gait, like his manner, was a little stiff. He gave the impression, certainly to many members of his congregation, that he was older than he was.

At the cottage, he paid proper attention to things. The painter on the rowboat was beginning to fray. The loons had young. The pitcher plants were out in the back pond. The wood sorrel, for some reason was not as plentiful as in other years. There were new traces of algae on the reefs. The frogs seemed quieter than he could ever remember them being. The rattlers were almost gone; the bass were going. A hinge on the outhouse door had lost a screw. The barometer had fallen.

That night, the barometer had fallen more suddenly than John Tobias had ever seen it fall. By the time he went to bed, which was always nine-thirty, it was down more than a full point from where it had stood at dinner.

So he was not surprised to be awakened in the middle of the night. He was, even in the drift of his dreams, expecting a storm. He opened his eyes. What surprised him was the sound.

It was a banging. It was a repeated, hollow thud that he could not place. He thought he knew every sound of the old house. He strained to find it, through the darkness, imagining his way down the faded runner on the stairs, through the sitting room with the stone fireplace where the unspent ends of logs sometimes shifted, to the frames where the window sashes rattled when the wind was from the east, to the wall where the Empirion clock steadily ticked. He searched the map of his memory for an unfastened latch, a forgotten pail, an uncleated coil of rope. He could always tell, lying in his bed, if he was hearing mice in the kitchen, or a raccoon on the back step, or a porcupine under the porch. He could tell if a shingle on the roof above his second-floor bedroom was working loose. He knew, by the binding of the boat's rope bumpers against the boathouse slip, when the wind was shifting. He could tell by the twisting brittleness of bark against pulpy wood if the branch on a nearby birch tree would soon break. Once, on a windless night, unable to sleep for the heat, he sat out on the back step to watch the stars and have a smoke, and had heard, beneath the junipers, the rustling scurry of a field mouse suddenly silenced when it intersected with the still, dry path of a snake.

But the banging was a noise he couldn't recall. He listened, and as he did he became aware, not of the wind so much as the tightening grip of it. There was no gusting, no easing off. The blow was steady and hard. It was as if the house were enclosed in a fist.

He was a man who knew exactly where his flashlight was. He reached to the drawer of the bedside table.

On the landing of the stairs he stood in his blue-and-white striped pyjamas. They were buttoned to his chin but high at his bony ankles and long, white feet. He prodded the beam of light through the shadows in front of him. It passed over the diminutive castles, sunsets, and baptistry doors of the penny postcards that his parents had received regularly. They had pinned them up one by one. By the time he was nine or ten, the north wall of the cottage was covered with the summer travels of their friends—friends who must have wondered as they addressed their greetings from Maine or Southampton, from Paris or London, from Florence or Rome, at the eccentricity of the respected lawyer, Adam Tobias, dragging his wife, poor Winona, and their little boy, John, to some godforsaken island somewhere up in Canada.

He searched his light into the empty depths of the fireplace and over the round, butter-coloured face of the clock. Two-thirty-seven. He checked the windows. He listened. And he ascertained by a ponderous but thorough process of elimination that the noise came from the front porch. He started down.

Actually, he thought, it was a very convincing rendition of the sound that was so often described in ghost stories. When he was a boy, there were always ghost stories when the Inlet cottagers had evening campfires out on the reefs, on calm, bug-swirling, moon-poised nights. Not so much any more, it seemed. But in those days there were campfires, and singalongs, and there were ghost stories, and the stories that were told often seemed to have this kind of relentless and ominous noise: the dead son knocking on the door; the shuffling approach of the murdered Indian; the pegleg of a drowned boatman being hoisted steadily up the lighthouse steps.

He was halfway across the room when it lit up. He saw the shadow of the rocker as if it had been burned into the wall. He saw the shelf of books: the spines of old mysteries, of guides to wildflowers and birds and stars. He saw the calendar. Then it went black. And a few seconds later, from out on the bay, came the thunder. But he had heard too many ghost stories at too many campfires and had subsequently passed too many untroubled and ghostless nights to be frightened by a gale. He proceeded without hesitation. He opened the door to the front porch.

He had to say he had never felt wind like it. It was more like a solid mass than anything. It was like a driven weight. And he was surprised by the rain. He was surprised by the stinging force of it on his face, and he wondered whether he had, by coincidence, passed through the house and opened the door to meet, with perfect timing, the very front of the storm.

The mystery of the banging was quickly solved. It was the round, hard-rubber lifesaver that his father had hung beside the front door more than half a century before. The wind had worked its way under it, was lifting it from the wall, then letting it drop. This in itself was extraordinary. It was a solid, heavy thing. It had been painted over with the same white paint as the house, a dozen, two dozen times. It had come from an ocean-going freighter owned by one of his father's clients. It had been hung with some bravado on the wall of a cottage in Ontario, a thousand miles from the nearest salt water. But it had always had a point: an acknowledgement of the serious, sea-like bluster of the R___s.

___ wind wrapped the sleeves and legs of his pyjamas ti___round him. The rain felt cold and sharp. The flashli___ tucked under his arm. He was trying to see whether the ___e-ring could be fixed back in place or whether it needed to be taken down to await more serious repair.

The flashlight slipped. It hit the porch. It went out, and rolled somewhere into the darkness beyond his feet. "Damn it all," he said. He turned and crouched, patting his hand like a blind man over the planking.

He was facing the Shelter Narrows when the lightning

screeched through the blackness. He was feeling in the darkness for the flashlight. He happened to be looking up. He said he had never seen such lightning.

He said it actually hurt, it was so bright. It shuddered before him, and although he caught sight of the flashlight and grabbed for it, his eyes stayed fixed on the sudden illumination of islands and rock and water and sky.

It was unusual. He saw not a stark monochrome of brightness and shadow as was often the case in an electrical storm, but a vivid flare of colour.

The water was a royal blue, the sky slightly paler. The rock, tawny as manila, was grizzled with lichen and wrinkled with black faults. The shafts of the pine trees were red. Their boughs were the variated green that he could never quite bring to mind when he was away from the Reaches, during the winter, but that was always so deep and old and familiar when he came back. It left him with the impression of the Inlet on a calm, hot afternoon at the very height of summer. He thought he saw the Inlet as it used to be—when he was a child, when he and the other Inlet children swam, and paddled, and sailed, and played capture the flag.

Then everything disappeared. The thunder was right on top of him.

He turned back to the life-ring. He raised his hand toward it. And there, the back of his neck bristled with something he could never have expected. He was suddenly terrified. He stopped. He considered what he had just seen.

He stood frozen. He thought it through. What had he glimpsed in the flash of that lightning? There had been water and rocks and trees and sky, certainly. But there was something else.

There had been a canoe. He had seen a red canoe. It had a single paddler, kneeling well forward. Its stern was a little high. It was heading out.

Had he imagined it? He turned the flashlight away from the house, back toward the water. The rain shot aslant through the beam. He could see nothing out in the darkness other than black, rolling motion and the high glint of whitecaps and, at the gleaming rocks in front of him, the burst of spray.

"What was he doing, out in a storm?" Caz asked.

"I'm not sure. Maybe just being an idiot."

They stopped at a small, barren island early in the afternoon for bread and cheese and trailmix and apples. They hauled the canoe up on the smooth rock. Bay held the canoe at its gunwales, halfway along its length. "Here," he said. "Like this." Caz shrugged.

Bay could remember when Caz had been all eyes. All laughter. Bay remembered a little boy playing with a plastic boat in the shallows of the little green cove at the back of the Larkin cottage. He could remember a rainy afternoon and Caz triumphantly placing down his last card in a game of crazy eights. He remembered the child psychologist: her Monet prints, the herbal tea, the thunderbolts in her smile: "There is no good age for a child to deal with divorce, Mr. Newling. But six can be very difficult."

Now, Caz was twelve. They had talked for a bit that morning. But mostly they had paddled as they had paddled the day before—on long sad courses of silence. These bewildered Bay. They were like unexplained traffic jams. They just came upon them. Suddenly, in the whole wide world there seemed to be nothing to say.

"So Caz, tell me. How's school these days?"

"OK."

"What's happening on the girl front?"

"The girl front?"

"Yeah. Any girls, you know, in your life?"

"Nope."

Bay never understood this impasse. On the drive up north, they had hit it as soon as they were on the highway. Bay thought he could remember something about being twelve years old. "Help" came on the radio, on the golden-oldies station he listened to in the car. He started to tell Caz what it had been like to be twelve "when the Beatles. . . ."

"I know," Caz said. "Remember. You rented all those *Anthology* videos."

"Oh," said Bay. "Right."

Patience, Bay told himself. Patience is the canoe's great lesson. Lark had taught them this at camp. Lark had told them: "Hours will go by. That is the thing with canoe trips: you pass through time slowly, the way time should be passed through. You go slowly enough to see things. To pay attention. To watch everything go by."

Bay would have liked to explain this to his son. He would have liked to be the one to teach him about patience. But he couldn't. He knew what he wanted to say. He just didn't quite know how to say it.

Perhaps this was because he wasn't particularly patient himself. Because, by the time they had finished their lunch, by the time he'd cleaned up, and packed, while Caz sat, looking out to the empty water. . . . By the time Bay lit a cigarette, he was growing testy. He wanted to get to the Skin in good time that afternoon.

"Damn it, Caz," he said. Bay was lashing the food pack back into the canoe, as per *The Outdoorsman's Guide*'s instructions. Caz was watching him, waiting to get going, doing nothing to help, and Bay noticed that the boy was wearing nothing over his orange T-shirt. *Cuchugachugachchch* went the Walkman. "Put your life jacket on, will you? How many times do I have to tell you?"

"I'm not six years old any more," said Caz.

"Fine," said Bay. "Suit yourself."

NINE

WHEN ANYONE asked him, Bay used
to say, "Oh, I began a fair ways back.
At camp, as I recall. My first cigarette
made me sick as a dog, but even then I had an inkling."

He used to say that it wasn't just the taste; it's in the loft-
ing weight of a cigarette's smoke. It's a glint that looks like
the last, tranquil band of light in a pewter sky. The real
smoker can foresee that the storms of coughing and nausea
will disappear quickly enough, and that, with time, each in-
halation will hold that silver light in place, passing its placid
glow from nerve ending to nerve ending, like tag, like the
serial impulses of accumulating memory: there will be girls
lying in the sun, the scratch of a wooden match, the smell of
coal oil, the curl of burning paper, the acridity of autumn
leaves, the rumble of a voice.

This is what Bay remembered. The director saying: "So
I'd like you to think about what nothing means." And this
was the day Bay most clearly recalled, from the fold of another summertime.

At first, nothing: nothing was what Bay heard when,
after paddling Kathleen Hagan back, he returned to the
Larkins' cottage. He had tied the canoe at the dock; he came

up the path. He had his cheerful, disgruntled excuse at the ready: he was going to say to Sarah: Oh, well, you know, Kathleen said she knew a shortcut that turned out not to be so short. I must have paddled her halfway to Moriah Island.

This would not have been questioned. Bay was always getting turned around in the maze of islands that summer. He was always saying—with Sarah, in the bow, and Caz, asleep on the bottom of the canoe: That's the point we came around earlier, there's the channel we crossed before lunch. He was hopeless with his directions. Bay was always saying they were here, when they were always somewhere else.

But no one was at the cottage by the time he returned. Bay guessed that Sarah and Caz were at the back of the island, picking blueberries for the blueberry treasure recipe Sarah had found in one of Felicity's old cookbooks. He guessed that they were filling up the battered kitchen pots. Or perhaps, they were swimming in the back channel. Or looking for frogs. Or watching for beavers, for herons, for the first of the monarch butterflies. Perhaps they were side by side, lying on their backs on the warm slopes of granite that had so astonished Sarah. "I could just go to sleep," she had said. "But how can it be so comfortable? It's *rock* for God's sake." Perhaps they were lying there, on the rock for God's sake, identifying the camels and whales and dump-trucks and buses that had sailed slowly overhead all that beautiful, perfect day.

Perhaps she was reading aloud to him, somewhere in a little windless patch of afternoon sun.

Bay came heavily up the path. The Larkin cottage was silent. On a sunny day its interior had a dark stillness—the wood, the old books, the woodstove. By the kitchen door, there was a sheet of shirt-cardboard with a pressed flower and a handwritten inscription: "Sundew, Cavan Bog, August, 1971."

It was as if it hadn't happened. Bay undressed quickly. He shoved his polo shirt, his multi-pocketed khaki shorts, his underwear into the laundry bag. And even before he washed away the scent of baby-oil, of herbal shampoo, of the youthful perfume he had only encountered at close quarters before on the scent-strips in the inside-front covers of his magazine, he had crossed several times over the border between his recollection of fact and his invention of fiction. He wrapped himself in a towel. He walked out to the veranda.

From underneath the front railing, he picked up the blue plastic soap dish. Elizabeth Larkin had encouraged Sarah and Bay—had, as a matter of fact, ordered them, in the nicest way—to soap-up when they got out of the water and to rinse themselves on land, twenty-five feet back from the shore, well up on the rise of the island, in order to utilize, as much as possible, the natural filter of rock and moss and pine needles and earth. This was a condition of their renting her place, so she had made clear—this attentive care.

Bay remembered the instructions. He remembered Elizabeth Larkin, in her living room, in Toronto, when he went to give her the deposit for the cottage. When he went to get her instructions. There was an oval mahogany table between his knees and the armchair on which Elizabeth was perched. She had a lively, intelligent face—lively within the constraints of Canadian gesture, Canadian emotion. It was, in some ways, an unsurprising face: the downturned eyes, the steel-grey hair, the narrow features, the strong teeth, the full lips. It was a face you used to always see on a street in Rosedale, in the congregation at St. Simon's. But it was also, so Bay learned that evening, a face lined with concern: for clear-cut forests; for the phosphate levels of the Great Lakes; for pesticides; for the idiocy of cars, the short-sightedness of governments, the tyranny of consumerism.

Elizabeth sipped a sherry. Her long hands and thin wrists moved through the air as she spoke. "I struggled against it, of course. But it was no good. Not enough people cared, you see, about a nice little place up north. It was beyond me—how they could squander such a treasure. How could they turn such a jewel into so cheap a trinket? But they did. And I decided not to go up anymore. The poor place stood empty. No one was ever there for years—except once. I must tell you the story. Once, thanks to John Tobias, Mother had her last visit a few years ago. More sherry?"

Elizabeth told Bay how the woodstove worked. "You can be surprisingly precise about temperature once you learn how to adjust the flues." She told him how to light the propane fridge and where, at the end of their time, to dump the john box. But chief among Elizabeth Larkin's instructions to Bay were the rules for bathing at the cottage. She told Bay about phosphates, about algae, about the disappearing bass and loons. She told Bay that she didn't want him to think her mad but that she wanted them to treat the water almost as if it were a holy thing. She told him that when they bathed, they had to soap up on land and have buckets ready, high up on the island's back, far from the shore, for their rinsing.

But on this particular occasion Bay was intent on getting his wash over quickly. Surely once would make no difference. Surely, it suddenly occurred to him—picturing voided holding tanks; picturing leaking septic systems; picturing the oil slicks of outboards, the belching exhaust of cruisers, the spilled gasoline of Jet Skis—it made no difference anyway.

He marched down to the point, undoing his towel as he approached the shore. Without pause, he dove in. He clambered awkwardly back, onto the rock. He lathered thickly up, and dove in again: a bellied-flat *ka-shoom* of parting water.

He was back on the veranda in no time. He felt refreshed and cleansed. He spread a towel on the chaise. He tapped a cigarette from the package on the little twig table. He knew before he lit it that it would be a good one. He picked up a box of wooden matches.

He thought of the story Elizabeth Larkin had told him. He inhaled deeply. He tried to imagine the morning. He thought: It must have been that time of the morning when it is difficult to tell whether the sky is growing lighter or if you only hoped it would.

He could just picture it.

John Tobias woke and went downstairs, and out the kitchen door of the old cottage. The screen slammed. He was still in his pyjamas. The air was cold and the stars were clear. It was an early September weekend.

When he came back in, he lit the propane stove. He put on the kettle. He climbed back up the stairs and dressed.

The sky was lighter by the time he undid the boat. He could see from the boathouse that the black islands were outlined against the eastern sky—brighter, but still not bright enough to obscure the swath of the stars.

The wind was calm. The boat was a beauty—a mahogany launch. A 1928 Minett-Shields. It had belonged to his parents.

He climbed stiffly down. He was seventy-five, after all.

The boat scarcely moved under his weight. He placed the small cooler he had packed under the green leather of the back seat. He was wearing a windbreaker, a shirt and tie, pressed flannels, and large black shoes that had no business being in a boat. He lit a cigarette.

He turned the key with his left hand, and pressed the starter button with his right. The engine coughed once, twice, then caught. A deep inboard rumble. He pressed up the toggle for the lights.

The engine thunked into gear, and its noise lowered slightly. The boat backed out the slip, away from the shadows of the extra life jackets, and the tackle box, and the coiled rope on the unpainted boathouse wall.

John Tobias was a practical man. He knew there was nothing to be gained by looking to the stern as he reversed. He knew he could best guide the boat out by keeping its bow aligned with the V of old fire hose at the front end of the slip.

The Minett-Shields slipped through the grey mist of its own exhaust. The wooden hull passed the tied-back boat-house doors. It went from the smell of wood and shellac and gasoline into the suddenly quieter chill and the slapping of the black, flat water.

He swung the launch around. He headed off.

He ran to the Inletter Lodge, as he always did, down the Shelter Narrows, straight down the Inlet, through the network of islands and between the shores of the dark, endless reaches of mainland. He could make out the shapes; knew the distances anyway. There—there were the shoals new-comers always struck. There was the little opening to the secret bay where people liked to swim. There was the point where Felicity Larkin used to bathe every morning.

He thought: Sometimes things just don't work out. These days, people don't think that's possible. But it is. He thought, as he passed Larkins', of the day, now so long ago, when he had stood on that point with Felicity. He always called her Fliss. They must have been barely twenty, he supposed. When the light seemed to fly off her auburn hair. When he felt the moment come when he would finally ask. When he would stop everything, and circle his arms around her, and say, "Fliss . . ."

When he would ask her to marry him. And instead, only an awkward silence that somehow he could not overcome. Only the hush of the wind in the pines. The lapping of water on the stone. And, she laughed. She said, "Oh, Toby. Don't stand there like a totem. Let's pick some berries." And the moment had passed. Had passed, as a matter of fact, for ever. Was it the next summer, or the summer after that, she came up to the Inlet with her beau? He thought: Some things don't work out.

His wake opened out behind him. He moved as slowly as if he were trawling. The trip took almost half an hour.

He tied up the boat at the Inletter dock and walked up the path toward the parking area behind the lodge's vegetable garden. His leather soles crunched on the gravel. The sky was now pewter. He could feel the autumn in the thinness of the morning. There was no sign of life yet at the lodge. The interior of his car smelled cold and faintly sour.

By the time he reached the highway, the sky was the blue that reaches over the trees just before the sun.

The drive south to the city took over three hours. He kept precisely to the speed limit. On the hour, he turned on the radio for the news and the weather. When the news was over, he turned the radio off. He smoked all the way. He couldn't find Black Cats anymore, so he smoked Camels. He stopped once for gas, and for a muffin and a glass of juice.

They had Felicity Larkin waiting by the front door. She was dressed as if for church. He had called the nursing home the week before, from the phone booth at the lodge, and had made arrangements. He made sure they heard his name: Tobias, Reverend Tobias. He had told them that he was going to take her out for the day—for lunch, and for a sit outside, and then for dinner. This was precisely true. He did not like to lie. He did not tell them what they did not need to know.

She had stared at him blankly in the reception area when the nurse had said, "Now look, Mrs. Larkin. Look who's here."

She sat beside him in the car. She looked straight ahead. He drove immediately back out of the city, heading north.

They stopped at the same restaurant and gas station. He had a grilled cheese sandwich. He ordered cream of mushroom soup for her. She had always liked cream of mushroom soup. She didn't move when the waitress put down the bowl and the little envelope of crackers. He moved over beside her and lifted the spoon to her mouth.

At the lodge, Beth, one of the two sisters who owned and ran the place, was coming from the garden with a basket of tomatoes when she saw Reverend Tobias with Mrs. Larkin. He had both hands under her elbow. The two of them were taking tiny, shuffling steps down the uneven path.

"It's all right," said Reverend Tobias. "I'm just taking Mrs. Larkin out to her cottage for the afternoon."

This was not an explanation that made much sense. Mrs. Larkin had not been to her cottage for years. Beth remembered the summer when she first heard the word: Alzheimer's.

Beth looked alarmed. Reverend Tobias repeated, "For the afternoon."

"Can I help?" asked Beth. She rushed forward on the gravel. "Mrs. Larkin," she said. Mrs. Larkin, intent on her own small black shoes, said nothing.

"No need, Beth. Thank you," said Reverend Tobias. "Things are proceeding nicely, thank you."

Beth later told her sister, "She's tiny now. It was like seeing a ghost."

He got her down to the dock, and eventually, with some difficulty, into the boat. She sat perfectly still, as she had in the car. He undid the bow line, then the stern.

He started the engine. He pushed off.

Approaching Larkins', you have to leave the channel and head east. You cut between the two shoals. They look like big brown whales under the water when the sun's out. If it's overcast, and if you're new to the Inlet and don't know what you're doing, you won't see them until they come through the bottom of your boat. But if you go between them, holding your course on the big pine, you can come in quite close to the point. To the point where Felicity always used to have her morning swims. It's deep there. You can head around the point, and down behind, on the leeward, into the little bay and Larkins' dock.

John Tobias had done this many times, bringing out her mail, her newspaper, a dozen eggs, a quart of milk in the last few years before she stopped coming up. Even then, at her age, if she wasn't out in the canoe, she'd be there, in her sun-hat, and her old shirt, and khaki shorts, and usually, in bare feet. She had thick white hair cut short and straight, and a wide, strong smile. Her skin was tanned and lined. "Heigh-ho," she used to say. "Thanks ever-so." Her voice had a warm, old-fashioned precision. "Well, Toby," she'd say as he puttered the boat toward the dock and she stood, waiting to take a rope and keep the hull from bumping. "I was just thinking about you."

The launch moved slowly toward the rickety grey back

dock. It bumped gently against the old tires. He cut the engine. He tied the bow and stern lines and hoisted out the cooler. The hard part was getting her out.

Slowly and carefully, he helped her up the path.

The cottage stayed locked. There was no need to open it. The chairs had been left under the porch, with the old canoe. He fetched them up and brushed off the cobwebs and pine needles with his handkerchief. They sat as they often had, in the old chairs on the veranda.

They sat there, in the sun. He lit a cigarette. They looked out to the far shore, and out to the open beyond. It was the best view in the Inlet. Everyone had always said so.

He brought out the sandwiches from the cooler. She had a few bites. She stared straight ahead. Her skin was like wax in the sunlight. He watched her; he was in no hurry. He listened to the water on the rock, to the eddies of wind, to the distant, steady slapping of somebody going somewhere in an outboard.

The breeze hushed through the white pines. The waves lolled at the shore.

He dozed. She sat, wide awake. He woke to the sound of voices; they came from across the water. He could tell they were raucous at their source—children swimming—but by the time the voices reached them, from perhaps half a mile, they were as thin as the sound of china being set for tea.

He had another cigarette.

It was after five o'clock when he said, "Well, Felicity." He put his hands to his bony knees. He stood. "That's the time, I think." He moved toward her.

That was when she spoke.

"Green," she said.

He stopped. He looked down at her. "Fliss?" She stared straight ahead.

In the old wicker chair, on the veranda of her summer cottage, Felicity Larkin smiled out to the point. The rocks were white. The pines were a deep green. They were bent by the west wind. She smiled directly at the view.

This was how she used to greet people: warmly, abundantly, with a graciousness shot straight and unwavering to the eyes. "Do come in," she used to say. "I am *so* pleased to see you."

John Tobias watched his old friend intently. He was amazed. Because she laughed

She used to laugh the way she spoke—with an accent of ornate precision, a swooping of exclamation. He'd forgotten the sound of it. It was like finding an old snapshot.

He held out a hand toward her, as if to hold her in place.

He was afraid to move. He felt as if some clumsiness on his part would break something.

She looked at him. "As green," she said. She fluttered her palm, stiffly, as if waving him back. "As green as green." She drew a quick little breath. "As greens can come." Then she turned again toward the water.

Half an hour later, they both stood. He replaced the chairs. They made their way down to the boat.

He expected the people at the nursing home to be upset when he got her back. It was much later than he had told them it would be. But nobody seemed concerned. The television was on in the lobby. It was almost midnight.

A young man at the desk looked up and said, "Oh there you are."

She stood there. She made no reply, just as she made no reply when the nurse came from one of the floors, and asked loudly and cheerily, "Did you have a nice day, Mrs. Larkin?" She stared at her feet. He noticed a pine needle caught on the folds of one of her stockings. She said nothing when he said goodbye.

The last pull in, the last sigh out. On the veranda, Bay butted out in his cigarette in the ashtray perched on the twig table, beside his paperback copy of *Pale Fire*.

Sarah and Bay had been reading together there earlier that day. He'd thought of a dream he'd had. He whispered something to her. She had smiled and said, "Bad timing, wouldn't you know." And later, before Caz and Kathleen returned, he had noticed that Sarah's book was closed on her lap and she was staring out at the view.

"What are you thinking about?" he had asked.

"Not what," she said. She paused. "Laird." And then, looking toward Bay, she continued: "Have you noticed that the rustle of the birch leaves has a more brittle sound than when we arrived. Already. Isn't that amazing? We've only been here, what? Two weeks. Two and a half. And already, the holiday is passing. At the beginning it had seemed so infinite. But now, already, we have to be stingy with it. Now, we have to parcel it out."

Now, alone on the veranda, with no one to disapprove, Bay decided to have another cigarette. He felt suddenly weary. This was all he was doing: lying on the rusty old chaise on the grey wooden veranda at the front of the Larkin cottage. He was having a smoke. It would not be a great one. He was thinking of nothing.

"Nothing." That was the word that entered his head. The sun was hot. He stretched. He thought: How quiet it is.

The people who had summered in the Inlet all their lives said they couldn't remember a better year for blueberries.

When Kathleen had arrived that day, coming round Larkins' point on a swerve of wake, a flash of white shirt, a sheen of blue bathing suit, a glint of the aluminium hull of her little outboard, Sarah had just found the old, hand-written recipe for blueberry treasure in one of Felicity Larkin's recipe books. *Inlet Favourites* was the title—typed on a manila label, stuck to the old black leather cover.

When she heard the motor, Sarah was standing in the kitchen, her black-framed glasses propped up on her head. She was reading: two cups blueberries, one-quarter cup brown sugar, one-half cup flour sifted, one teaspoon cinnamon, one-quarter cup butter. She was saying to Caz, "This looks good. This looks very good. I think we should try this."

For all of the importance Bay gave his notion of summer, and for all the details of summer stuff he jotted down on his notepads for his magazine story for Bunty Brownlea—the stone mantels, the rattan furniture, the cast-iron frying pans, the blanket boxes, the old cherry paddles on the log walls—Bay somehow missed the point. Somehow, he kept to himself, and somehow it was Sarah who made the connections that summer. She was the one who learned who was who in the Inlet. She was the one who discovered who had been coming the longest; by what complex descent of family—of cousins, of marriages, of poker hands, of quirks of last wills and testaments—a cottage had come through the eighty, the ninety, the one hundred summers to its current owners. She was the one who learned the names of the children, the places to picnic, the reefs to explore. She connected families to islands, islands to canoes and sailboats, canoes and sailboats to barking dogs. She was the one who met people, who fell most naturally into conversation, who put things together. Sarah got directions to the beaver lodge, the jumping rock, the osprey nest. She learned what the best ratio of sugar and water was for the hummingbird feeder.

Sarah was the one who came back from the lodge, through the drizzle, proud to have managed the canoe by herself. She came back with the forgotten quart of milk, the overlooked cheese, the dozen eggs. She came back, and told Bay of the girl she'd heard about. On the dock of the Inletter Lodge, she had introduced herself to a few other mothers—in for milk, for eggs, for cheese—and they had told her about the girl across the way who they knew had two afternoons a week free and who was looking for some extra work. "Oh, do yourself a favour," one of the ladies said to Sarah. She had a yellow rain jacket; her trousers were rolled; she wore no shoes. "Keep a few hours for just you and your husband. It'll make all the difference to your holiday."

Sarah was the one who picked up the history. Bay gathered descriptions of things, but Sarah gathered stories. She was the one who came back one day to tell Bay what she had heard a few of the women talking about on the lodge dock. Embellishing it, Bay had made the story his own. He imagined Sarah, on the dock, listening. He imagined the women saying:

"She didn't."

"She did."

"You're kidding."

Sarah was a little bewildered. "I don't get it."

"Well, she had her suspicions, you see."

"He didn't seem . . ."

"How to put it, politely?"

"Didn't seem to exhibit the same enthusiasm for his weekends at the cottage as he used to."

"So at the end of one weekend, when he was going back down to the city, she gave him the usual grocery list."

"All the things you can't get up here."

"Arugula. Chèvre. Avocado."

"The necessities."

"The bare necessities."

"But when he's down in the city, doing the shopping, he discovers one unusual item on the list."

"Her list says, 'Six black hens.'"

"So he looks everywhere."

"Can't you just hear him?"

"In his big deep voice."

"In his big, deep, Upper Canada-College, football-hero, stockbroker voice. 'Excuse me. I was wondering if you have any black hens.'"

"It must have been too priceless for words."

"Too, too funny."

"Of course, the people in the stores thought he was mad."

"Completely."

"And when he gets back up to the cottage, on Friday night, he says, 'What are these six black hens you wanted?'"

"And she says . . ."

"And she says . . ."

"No, let me. And she says, 'They're pall-bearers.'"

"'Pall-bearers?'" he says.

"She says, 'They're pall-bearers for that dead cock you bring back up here every weekend.'"

Sarah said, "Bay. You should have heard them laugh."

For the men were often away. They seemed, some summers, to be always away: down in the humid reality of the city every weekday, tending to real, muggy things. Like files.

Like lunches. The reality-bound, duty-weighted, faithless summer-suited men, leaving the women up north to deal with unreal things. Like children. Like sunsets. Like the skittering of water-spiders on calm water. Like baking blueberry treasure. Like teaching swimming. Like reading storybooks. Like mornings when the water was white as haze, when the light seemed as veiled as mist. This perfection. This green, high-boughed, breeze-gentled holiday.

Bay had angled the chaise into the sun. He looked out from the veranda—to sky, water, rock. He looked down to the point where, for seventy summers, Felicity Larkin had taken her morning swim.

fig. 1

HOW DO WE MANAGE to sustain our illusions—that we are kind, that we are generous, that we are honest, that things will work out? That we are attentive and loving? That we are not destroying? Not lying? Not polluting? That, under the circumstances, we are doing the best we can? That we are being faithful?

And even then—seeing all this—poor Bay could not see what was coming. He ignored the sad hollow in his stomach. He discounted his own prophetic fears. They shuddered around inside him, but were quelled—by reason, by probability, by his expectation that things would work out. He would, in the months ahead, be shocked, not so much by Sarah's rage, as by the endurance of her anger. It didn't diminish at all. It only grew—unreasonably, Bay couldn't help but feel. It seemed to feed on something—something that Bay thought they could leave behind them. "Here," she would say, flinging the half-dozen envelopes of their summer snapshots at him, "you keep your perfect holiday." For even then, that afternoon, alone on that cottage veranda, Bay refused to believe that he had come upon a serious moment. He would never identify the figure walking in the flames. He would never imagine that long after everything had changed—sun glinting on parked cars; forest-fires burning; Caz turning from an office window—someone Bay had never known would ask about his ordinary little story, would say, "Please tell me." Because I am here, after all. Because I am telling you this. Because Bay was too frightened to allow himself to see what had already happened.

(Egg, sperm.)

fig. 2

TEN

ELIZABETH LARKIN had told him that her mother, Felicity, had often sat in her wicker chair on the very spot where Bay was lying. Where Bay was calmly smoking. It had always been her favourite view. He thought: No wonder. Past the point, past the water, the wooded islands banked away. They overlapped in a retreat of perspective. They diminished in clarity and size. They dimmed from green to black to grey, out toward the open. To the horizon. To nothing.

"Nothing." Again, he composed the word in his mind. And then thought: No. Not nothing. It was quiet. But there were other sounds.

A bird was calling from somewhere out beyond the path to the outhouse. A fly buzzed around the screen of the front window. Beyond the rough, grey railing of the veranda, a hummingbird thrummed over the junipers. Across the water, someone was hammering: a dock, a deck.

This was one of the first things he had noticed about being there that summer: words came out of the blue. At the Larkin cottage, words arrived, disconnected from everything. The sentences to which they had been attached were still drifting, somewhere else, out of reach, like ghosts. At the Larkin cottage he had found himself thinking in bursts of recognition, like someone recovering from a stroke. Tree. Sky. Rock. Wind. Water. Stone. "What are you thinking about?" he had asked his wife. "Not what," she had answered. The words were conjured from nothing, in the same way people silently repeat the name of someone who has recently died.

And there it was: exhaled, drifting up through the golden air in front of him: the scratch of a wooden match, the smell of coal oil, the curl of burning paper, the acridity of autumn leaves, the rumble of a voice. He saw old Mrs. Larkin's view. Bright as could be: the blue crossing, the dark catastrophe of reefs, and beyond that—past the point, Bay knew, where the last friends will disappear; where memory will go; where children, waiting in hospital rooms, will awkwardly say goodbye to parents: the white tumult of clouds.

"Voices," he said to himself.

He pronounced the single word clearly in his mind. "Voices." And he could hear them coming, coming back from summers he had almost forgotten. He thought of the familiar clearings, the memorized paths, the overgrowth of forgetfulness.

Sarah and Caz were threading their way along paths as if they'd always known them. They came through the openings in the low pine branches, over the rock and the mapwork of lichen, between the junipers, past the rich brown of the dead-fall and the white shafts of birch.

"Dad," Caz was shouting. "Dad."

"Here I am."

"We have blueberries. Tons of blueberries."

It was Labour Day. It was the end of their summer holiday at the Larkin cottage, and they arrived back at their downtown house, after five hours of unbelievable traffic, to find the screens intact, the basement unflooded, the house unrobbed, the air still, the rooms quiet. The mail was scattered in the hallway.

Caz went up to his room. He said: to see how his action-figures were doing.

Sarah and Bay smiled at each other. They were relieved to be safely home. They were worn out by the drive.

"A drink?" Bay asked.

"God, yes."

And with bags still in the hallway, with Caz upstairs with Batman and Luke Skywalker and Superman, they sat down at the dining-room table to go through the bills, and the bank statements, and the new insurance terms, and the book-launch invitations, and the grand announcements that B. Nudding was almost certainly only a phone call away from one million dollars.

There were cancelled cheques, and flyers, and magazines, and water-meter readings, and new gas rates.

Bay hardly ever got real letters. Which was why he had been surprised by the turquoise ink; the perfect, rounded cursive; the cream-coloured stationery. It was from Elizabeth Larkin.

He read it. Then he read it aloud to Sarah.

"It seems to me that it is important for a family to spend summers at the cottage. In the end, that is what cottages are for. I am not yet ready to sell the place. I'm not sure I ever shall be. Perhaps this is only procrastination on my part, but it seems to me that your old camp connection with my brother does rather give things a pleasing continuity. And so, if you have enjoyed your time in the Inlet, and if renting again suits your future holiday plans, I would be happy to continue our arrangement for the summers to come."

"Isn't that nice," said Sarah. "That's really wonderful." She picked up her drink. She opened a letter that was addressed in a childish hand.

Sarah often got such letters. Children often wrote to the offices of Children's Press—inquiring about books, about authors, about how one went about becoming a writer—and Sarah took the trouble to reply. Sometimes, using her home address, she took the time to keep the correspondence going.

She was sipping her drink as she read it. It took only a few sentences before she realized her mistake. But she continued. She could feel her face tightening. She forgot to swallow; the gin and the tonic sat there, like a puddle in the bottom of her mouth. Slowly, she placed her glass down. She read a few more lines, then turned the letter over to the signature. She checked the envelope. She swallowed. She said, "I think this must be yours."

THE PRY

---

*The chief joy of a canoe trip is often over-looked. Why?
Because it is so simple a pleasure. After all, it is only
breakfast in the crisp early morning, breaking camp, the
long, steady meditations of paddle, the cold swigs of lake
water, the afternoon swim, the establishment of another
campsite. This ordinary ritual is, in the end, why we
head out with our packs and our paddles and our
compasses and charts. It cleanses the city's rushed clutter
from our souls. It returns a balance. It is what we reflect
on with such calm avidity at the end of the day. It is what we
so thankfully contemplate when we find ourselves sitting
beside the last glow of the campfire's embers, with our pipes
lit, listening to the northern quiet, looking up at the great
turning silence of the stars.*

fig. 2

– The Outdoorsman's Guide

THEY PASSED MORIAH ISLAND and approached the mouth of the Skin River at about four in the afternoon. The river opened into a small bay on a broad point of mainland. At the gap of the river's mouth the water was moving quickly.

Deep swirling eddies cut swiftly between the smooth line of rocks. It wasn't white-water, but the flow spilled out into the bay in swirls of yellow pollen, in traces of foam, in depths of loose, unravelling whirlpools.

Bay pointed the canoe to a narrow thinning in the reeds on the right shore. He said, "There. That must be the portage."

After three days on flat water, Bay felt the canoe's hull shift in the current. The stern swung unpredictably. This was a kind of giddiness. It occurred to him that the current made things feel the way a canoe feels when, for the first time, you settle yourself tentatively between the gunwales.

They crossed toward the river's mouth. The water slapped beneath the aluminium hull.

Caz's mood seemed suddenly to change. It may have been the rush of the water. He turned in the bow seat. He grinned.

"Come on, Dad. Screw the portage. We can take this." Caz pointed. He wanted to paddle *up* the little gap of fast water. He turned forward and bent into his stroke.

Well, Bay thought, this is something.

Caz was paddling hard. "Come on, Dad," he said.

Bay swept his paddle through the water. Once. Then with a deeper stroke, again. The bow swerved away from the easy reeds, away from the sensible portage.

Bay looked out over the scene from the stern of the canoe. He thought: A perfect summer's day. There are not, in the end, very many of them. The trees, their branches as fine and dark as cracks in old china. The green reflections of pine boughs, hanging from the blue waterline.

They stayed close to the right shore. The mainstream curled into itself there, and they found themselves riding a back-current that sped them forward. It pushed them with surprising quickness against the river's flow, and they both laughed at their clip.

They were, by then, both reaching forward with full strokes. Bay could feel his chest heaving. He was already panting for breath. He was already aware of a burning sensation in his arms.

They had expected the smack of the current against them. They had seen it coming. It bubbled down the middle of the gap, more tumultuous than it had appeared from a distance. The water was smooth not because it was too slow and gentle to be white, but because here the riverbed was too deep for the flow to break over itself.

Bay called out, "This isn't going to be so easy."

Caz shouted, "Here we go."

They stretched their strokes forward. They dug their paddles deep. And Bay noticed, for the first time, Caz's strength: the young back, the determined dip of narrow shoulders.

What they didn't expect was that their paddles would suddenly feel as if they had missed the water altogether. Because the current was slipping beneath them, because it was moving against their direction, their paddle blades were suddenly unopposed. It was as if the wood was passing through thin air. Caz almost flew over the gunwale.

It happened as if in slow motion: an error, an attempted correction, a bigger error. The canoe wobbled violently, once, twice, three times. It seemed not to occur in a single moment of time. It unfolded in fragments, and not just in memory. Even then. Even as it happened.

Caz just caught himself, but not before dropping his paddle overboard. They took on a deep sluice of water. They passed, broadside, into the main thrust of the river.

Caz was still laughing. So was Bay. He knew nothing could really go wrong. The river wasn't that fast; the water wasn't that cold; the rocks weren't that dangerous. He knew how carefully he had re-sealed the waterproof packs and lashed everything under the thwarts of the canoe. "A major pain," had been Caz's glum description of Bay's strict adherence to *The Outdoorsman's Guide*. Bay thought it funny that the stodgy old instructions should actually pay off.

So, no harm would be done. It would be an adventure. They would get wet, but they wouldn't lose anything.

Bay came through the flapping cream of his splashing, through the fish-green rushing round his ears. He came up sputtering, laughing. His sunglasses, saved by the rubber safety cord the outfitting salesman had convinced him to buy, had been pushed down around his neck. Diamonds of water-drops shimmered in his blinking. He laughed, just above the sun-dashed water, just below the blue wind in the green trees. The diamonds shimmered—a hardening of a wide vein of time into tiny glints of light.

Bay could not see his son. He shook his head. And the spray of light was gone.

———————

Kathleen sat in the stern, facing him. She had a lifejacket and a towel propped behind her back. She was wearing a man's white shirt and, under it, a shiny, blue bathing suit. Her feet were bare. She had them up on the thwart in front of her.

She had turned her head to the left, as if to show more clearly the elegance of her profile and the line of her throat. Her hair was dark. She encircled the thick fall of her pony-tail with her right hand. Her bracelets slipped to the un-done, loosely rolled french cuffs.

Catching the twirl of pale ribbon with her little finger, she slid it down. She turned back, smiling, and shook out the black skirts of sunlight. Her hair swung around her face in sheen and shadow, and then settled to her shoulders in some slight and practised disarray.

She said, "Isn't this beautiful?"

He said, "Yes it is."

"I could stay here forever."

He was close enough to smell the summer scents she wore. Gleam of baby lotion. Trace of perfume. Shampoo.

He leaned forward with each stroke. The canoe veered right. Then back, left.

After a time, he realized that it was better to look directly at her than to try to pretend that he was looking somewhere else. Her eyes were half-closed against the sun. Her lips shone with some protective gloss.

It was my mother who said, "Don't you wish the summer would never end?"

And my father who replied, "On days like this. Yes."

Bobbing in the current, at the mouth of the Skin River, Bay looked across the glistening jostle of the surface, and saw nothing. There was only vacant water, an empty sky, and the upturned hull of the aluminium canoe.

He splashed and turned. He floundered through the rocky shallows. He called for help—uselessly, for the last cottage they had passed was more than a mile back.

He stumbled over the slippery rocks. He held his paddle, like a torch, using the blade to cut down the glare of sunlight on water. He couldn't see anything. He turned, now with dread, now in panic. The fear seemed as if it would burst through his chest. And then, so he would say later that night, something inexplicable occurred. Something that was, so he would say, sitting up late in front of the campfire, miraculous. Possibly the Lord did speak. Perhaps the ram was caught in the bush. He couldn't dismiss such things anymore. As a child he had often wondered about the certainty of prophets—how did they find their way from the present to the future?—and now, in a way, he knew. Sort of. "An inkling," he said. For, as he turned, splashing, in the river, a strange calm settled over him. "Settled is accurate," he said. "It seemed to come down over me." A calm descended, and suddenly, inexplicably, he knew exactly where he would find his son. He stepped deliberately and quickly upstream. He could see the spot, and made for it, cupping a hand through the water as if swimming.

Caz was just below the surface. He was only an inch or two under. His face was upturned. His eyes were wide. His arms and his hair were outstretched, spreading away. His face streamed.

At first, no sense could be made of this. Then, Bay realized: like Bay, Caz had been washed over toward the shore. He must have tried to plant his feet on the rocks. (Bay remembered *The Outdoorsman's Guide*'s instructions: "when overturned in white-water, follow two cardinal rules; protect your head and keep your feet up.")

Caz's foot was caught. His running shoe was wedged under a pale stone. The current had pushed him over, backwards. He was stuck there, knees buckled, on his back. He was not strong enough to right himself against the rush of water.

Bay lifted Caz's head. Caz sputtered and coughed and gulped a breath.

Bay said, "Hang on."

He tried to move the rock with his foot without success. He had to let Caz's head go so that he would have both hands free to reach down.

He crouched below the surface, level with the stone. He found some purchase under his feet. He worked it as hard as he could.

He felt some give. He pushed. He held the weight away with one hand while working loose the ankle with the other. It came out with a sudden twist.

Caz rolled to his stomach. They both flopped toward the shore. They sat there, half-in, half-out of the water.

"Jesus," Bay said.

Caz was crying. Mostly because he'd been so frightened. But his ankle had been badly twisted. And now, sitting in the back eddies, looking at the drifts of red coming up from his foot, he said, "Dad. My toe's practically cut off."

An edge of rock had cut through the running shoe. It had cut through the second toe on his right foot. The gash was deep, but was, Bay decided, not as bad as it looked. It could wait a few minutes. It would have to.

There was the canoe to retrieve downstream. With the packs lashed in, with the first-aid kit sealed in with the tent and sleeping bags. The heavy, overturned canoe to be dragged over to the shore. To be hoisted and drained. The paddles, further along, caught on an outcrop of rock, to be swum for, and brought back. Brought back, against the current, with considerable difficulty. Brought back so that the canoe could be paddled back across the river to where Caz was waiting—foot up, a largely useless tourniquet of Bay's polo-shirt around his swollen ankle.

All this was undertaken by Bay with out-of-breath haste.

But undertaken, of course, with stalwart, comforting shouts back to the shore. "Hang in, Caz. I'll have that foot of yours fixed up in no time."

And actually—rather to Bay's surprise—in what seemed like no time, he did. He cleaned the cut and dabbed it gently with peroxide. He concluded that the ankle—tender, un-able to support much weight—was not broken. He joined the two flaps of the badly cut toe, and bound the gash up with gauze and adhesive and Polysporin. He wrapped the ankle with a tensor bandage.

Bay said, "There. Now I better get a campsite set up."

Caz sat and watched Bay pull the tent and the sleeping bags from the pack.

"Ta-dah," he said. "You will note. Bone dry."

"All right, all right," Caz said, trying to control his widen-ing smile.

And soon, the tent was pitched, the sleeping bags un-rolled, a scrappy pile of firewood collected, the fire made, the dinner of pasta and tomato sauce cooked. And soon: as the night closed in, as the stars turned above, as the crickets rose, and the coals settled, they laughed. They laughed, and they found, to their surprise really, that they were talking. They laughed, and Bay smoked. They laughed and he drank cognac from a yellow plastic teacup, and they sat in front of the campfire, and, turning the day in the flickering

light of its close-call, they stayed up to enjoy the unexpected rise of happiness and relief.

They talked until very late—until Bay said, "Caz, I'm
going to show you something."

He stood stiffly, and headed down, uncertainly, through
the darkness. A lit cigarette was pursed between his lips as he
hoisted the canoe, and moved it toward the black water.

Caz said, "I don't think this is such a good idea."

"I'm going to show you something," Bay said.

Caz asked him not to. He said it was too late.

But Bay pushed the hull out into the water. He placed
his paddle across the gunwale and, pushing off, hoisted his
weight in. He said, "Peter Larkin used to paddle at night.
When he was on a trip, coming here, they'd do the last leg
at night, so that they could see the sun coming up as they
approached. At the mouth of the Skin. He said it was like
the place was on fire."

Caz said, "Watch it, Dad."

"See," he said. "See. Let me show you. It's like this."

Bay was out for ten or fifteen minutes. Caz could hardly
make him out in the darkness. "It's a simple thing," Bay called
back toward the shore. "A simple thing, a canoe stroke. But
sometimes simple things aren't so simple."

And when Bay came back in, and after he pulled the aluminium hull clumsily back up on the rocks, he said, "Have
you noticed how when you get tired you start to feel the
cold more?"

———————

It must have been just before the first hint of dawn that
he died. His son was beside him in the tent. Through the

sleeping bag, he could feel the curve of the boy's back against his arm. He thought: it is as if I am asleep. He thought: I remember this. I've known this before. He couldn't quite make out where he was going. He didn't know how this would be resolved. But he could see that he was paddling her back.

There he was. It was hot, and the wind was still. There was no warning. It was the last thing he expected.

Kathleen wore a small pendant around her neck. She slid her right hand across the top of her chest, as if smoothing away the heat. She lifted the necklace over the back of her hand. The stone was a little round piece of cut-glass. It was plain and simple and cheap, the sort of trinket a very young girl would wear.

For several minutes neither of them spoke. He paddled slowly and steadily, and did not take his eyes off the little dangling piece of glass. He bobbed forward and back with his stroke.

She held it, just off her skin. After a time she laughed.

She said, "It's like I'm hypnotizing you. Only, instead of the pocket-watch moving back and forth, you are."

He smiled tightly.

It was like the pulse of the sun. It was like the drip and splash and drip of the paddle. She laughed again, more softly, and then she put on a stagey, European whisper. "You vill remember nuzzing."

And when she spoke again, he couldn't have said how much time had passed. He wasn't sure where they were. She said, "Land here. There's a secret place that's nice to swim."

He looked around. They were in a back channel, some-where out toward Tobias's, about halfway to the cottage where she was staying. He could see an opening to the left, between two rises of rock.

They were well away from the nearest cottage. A canoe could just get through to the pool beyond.

He turned back toward her. She moved her right hand and the cheap light sparkled. He could smell her perfume and suntan lotion. There were summers there: gin and tonic, the fresh brown and white of a new deck of cigarettes, the laziness of hot wooden docks, the sleepy lap of waves passing through cribs, the smell of gasoline, and the noise of waterski boats, and the pressure of a hand against the smooth, taut crotch of a bathing suit.

He could see the cities where the men spent their weeks. The houses with pulled blinds, and air-conditioners, and television sets; the places where lonely men passed time in a limbo of takeout food and untidy kitchens, waiting until Friday to leave work early. To beat the traffic. Oh, never to beat the traffic, no matter how early. To drive past the outskirts: the warehouses, the overpasses, the industrial parks, the horizon of apartment towers.

To head up north, with the car radio loud on the golden-oldies station: *All my loving, I will send to you. All my loving, darlin' I'll be true.* Up the highway, on and on. And finally, as the distance from the city becomes too great and the summer countdown begins to fade, to come down the long, gravel road. Those summer roads, finally, through the woods. Finally, to the water.

To where they see their wives waiting with white, open-necked shirts. Opened one button extra. Waiting with an extra touch of perfume on their wrists, on their throats. With their hair blonder, their skin browner than it had been the week before, with their blue-jeans tight and freshly laundered, and with their barefeet on the white vinyl of the boat seat. With the lake and the islands behind them. Cigarettes poised. Nails red. Waving, from the dock.

He could see all this. And then, through the blue heat, the slip of bangles, the open folds and the shadows of creased white cotton, his time was slipping out of him and into the unordered cold. The line that marked his waking was sharp and bright. He gasped at the pain of it. He opened his eyes in astonishment, closed them again tightly. It was as if he were going through a rip in the fabric of the darkness. He reached into emptiness. He was rising—through the fall of dew, the shadow of pines, the refrain of stars. He was as lonely as a little boy. He was forgetful of everything.

DAVID MACFARLANE was born in Hamilton in 1952. He is the author of an acclaimed family memoir of Newfoundland, *The Danger Tree,* which won the Canadian Authors' Association Award for Non-Fiction in 1992. He began his career as a writer and editor with *Weekend Magazine* and has since been published in *Saturday Night, Maclean's, Toronto Life* and *Books in Canada,* among others. The recipient of eleven National Magazine Awards and a Sovereign Award for Magazine Journalism, David Macfarlane is now a national columnist for *The Globe and Mail.* He lives in Toronto with his wife and two children. *Summer Gone* is his first novel.

The text of this book is set in Bembo.
Based on an early sixteenth century
typeface by the Venetian punchcutter
Francesco Griffo, this version of Bembo
was designed in 1929 by Stanley Morison.
It has since proven to be one of the most
popular types for the composition of books.